Books by Daryl Wood Gerber

Stand-alone Suspense
Girl on the Run
Day of Secrets

Cookbook Nook Mysteries
Final Sentence
Inherit the Word
Stirring the Plot
Fudging the Books
Grilling the Subject

Cheese Shop Mysteries (pen name Avery Aames)
The Long Quiche Goodbye
Lost and Fondue
Clobbered by Camembert
To Brie or not To Brie
Days of Wine and Roquefort
As Gouda As Dead
For Cheddar or Worse

Day of Secrets

by Daryl Wood Gerber

Day of Secrets

ISBN-13: 978-0-9973611-2-4
ISBN-10: 0-9973611-2-3

Cover and Interior Design by SheridanINK

www.darylwoodgerber.com

First Edition

Printed in the U.S.A

DEDICATION

To my nephew, Kevin, and your strength of character—despite the odds.

ACKNOWLEDGEMENTS

"You gain strength, courage, and confidence by every experience in which you really stop to look fear in the face."
~ Eleanor Roosevelt

Thank you to my husband, Chuck. You fill my thoughts constantly and you always will. I am so blessed that you loved me. I am so lucky that you believed in my work.

Thank you to the two women who have helped me, yet again, on another amazing journey. Sheridan Stancliff, you are an Internet and creative marvel. Kimberley Greene, you are a blessing to me.

To my family and friends, thank you for your support. Thank you to my first reader, Hannah Dennison, for your amazing input. Thank you to Kristen Weber for your feedback, as well. Thank you to Madeira James and your team for creating an amazing website.

Thank you to my BETA readers from the Cake and Dagger Club who inspired me to move forward with this project. Your enthusiasm has been infectious.

Thank you to my early reviewers for your positive responses.

Thank you to all my future readers for taking the journey with Chase Day as he finds the truth that hopefully will set him free. Thank you for sharing your enjoyment of this story with your family and friends. A book cannot come alive without readers! A book cannot thrive without positive word of mouth.

"Then imitate the action of the tiger:
Stiffen the sinews, summon up the blood."
~William Shakespeare
***Henry V*, Act 3, Scene 1**

CHAPTER 1

December, Present Day

I charged into the Outreach Hostel, my adrenaline jacked up from the hectic ride after the sit-in at the university. My cell phone buzzed in my pocket. It had to be Reggie, ready to chew me out. I shrugged out of my wet raincoat and scanned the foyer for her. She wasn't waiting with a sledgehammer. Lucky me. *The guys in the art therapy class need normalcy, Chase,* she had said on more than one occasion. Like I didn't know. Like I hadn't been the poster boy for post-traumatic stress disorder once upon a time, not that it was ever documented. *You're their art teacher, the adult.* Did she care that I wasn't a trained therapist? Not on a bet. Because art therapy had helped me, she believed that I, a history professor and former Navy lieutenant, was gifted enough to teach the veterans at the hostel how to conquer what ate them up inside. I do my darnedest every Saturday, but face it, I am adequate at best. No one at the de Young Museum is pining for my artwork.

My cell phone rang again. *Pleading*. I ignored it while racing down the hall to the art therapy room, catching my reflection in a window as I passed. Yes, I looked ragtag. Yes, I had bags under my eyes thanks to an all-nighter grading term papers. Yes, my forehead was pinched. But at least my hair was finger-combed and my tie was straight. Reggie would have to take me as I am. If I hadn't had yet another run-in with the dean of students this afternoon, maybe I would look decent. How was the guy always able to track me down as I was leaving campus? Did he have built-in sonar? What was it about my political views that irked him? Okay, sure, I was a left of his right, but c'mon.

I darted into the art therapy room and drew to a halt, shoulders squared, chin up. The space was a hollowed-out hull. No amenities; all white and sparse. Reggie claimed that in order to clear out the mind, the environment needed to be clutter-free. She hadn't earned a therapist's license, but long story short, she would give her life for veterans. A board spanned the wall on the far side of the room—the *teaching wall*. Sheets of white paper were pinned to the board. Easels were set with brushes, paints, and a tin can filled with water.

Eight veterans, wearing white smocks over various stages of dress, were sitting on chairs set in a semi-circle. If they didn't stay seated, Reggie Ramirez—Regina the Queen-a Latina to the vets—wouldn't let them paint.

A thickset guy who sneaked sweets from the hostel's kitchen spotted me and raised his hand. He eyed Reggie, who was leaning against the rear wall, cascades of brown curly hair pulled forward over her shoulders, muscular arms folded across her ample chest. She nodded. The guy proceeded. "Why are you late, Blue Eyes?"

"A day late and a dollar short," a longhaired veteran joked. "Get it? His last name is Day. He's a *day* late."

The other vets sniggered. I grinned. I had been working with them for nearly three years. They were on the mend, which did my heart proud.

"Ahem," Reggie said, her mouth twitching at the corners as she tried to maintain her stern demeanor. "Welcome, Chase. Let's get started." No mention of my tardiness. No ribbing about my thirty-six-year-old body looking worse for wear. She would get me alone later and trash me. Gee, I couldn't wait.

I hung my coat on a rack and set my briefcase on the floor. At the same time, my cell phone pinged. Whoever had been hounding me before had left a voicemail. Reggie gave me the evil eye. I ignored the call. "Where's Kimo?" I donned a smock. The scent of bleach clung to the fabric. "He left the campus before I did."

Reggie smirked. "Lost, no doubt."

"He doesn't get lost."

"I'm here, bro." Kimo Cho strode in and hung his umbrella on the rack. Then he set his briefcase on an empty chair and loosened his tie. He stood a little over six feet, same as me, but there the comparison ended. He was as brawny as a Hawaiian warrior god; I had a leaner athletic build. His hair was black; mine, a dusty brown. "A student consultation ran long."

"A likely story," Reggie said.

"Can it, beautiful. I'm here out of the goodness of my heart." *Translation*—my best friend had a thing for Reggie something fierce, and he had come to class to try, yet again, to woo her with his magnanimous spirit. Not every volunteer is altruistic. He took up the duty of handing out paintbrushes. "Hey, Chase, Christmas Eve dinner. You up for it? My pretty cousin will be there."

"No."

"Are you going to spend it alone again?"

"Let's talk later." Now wasn't the time. Never was better. Ever since I was five, when my mom died on Christmas, I'd hated everything about the holiday. People laughing in the malls. Carolers. TV specials. My nightmares were plagued with creepy animated reindeer and exploding ornaments. Art therapy—it helps.

"You've been date-less how long, Chase?" a vet asked.

"Long," Kimo said, answering for me while stretching out his arms to demonstrate. He knew me better than anyone. We went to high school and college together. We even joined the Navy via Naval Reserves Officer Training Corps, aka NROTC, at the same time. Neither of us considered the Navy a calling—we wanted to *see the world*—but our *lead or be led* attitudes took us far. Both of us went on to become officers. My stint in the Navy made me take war seriously. I needed to understand who and why. Subsequently, I became an expert in the field. Kimo liked what I had become, so after he was asked to leave the Navy—career would have been in his cards if he could've reigned in his temper—he went to grad school, became a history professor, and lo and behold, wound up at Weyford University, like me.

My cell phone pinged again. I picked up a paintbrush and dipped it in red paint. "Okay, fellas, let's get that junk inside our damaged skulls on the canvas today." I made a bold diagonal swoosh on the white paper taped to the teaching board.

The veteran students copied the move.

"Paint your heart," I said. "If it's family you're thinking about, put them on the paper. If you're feeling like you can't talk to someone, paint his mouth closed. Remember, as Napoleon Hill said, 'Man alone has the power to transform his thoughts into physical reality.'" During high school, at my grandmother's insistence, I had taken therapeutic art classes designed for orphaned kids. The therapist, like my grandmother, had loved spouting inspirational quotes. Hundreds of them were emblazoned in my brain. Do they help? Sometimes.

A frail veteran raised his hand. "My father doesn't recognize me, Chase. How do I paint that?"

"Make him blind," a buddy shouted.

I made another swipe on my canvas and thought of my own father. I had never met him. Would I recognize him if I ran into him? Did I care? I used to.

Kimo joined me and glanced over his shoulder to see if Reggie was gazing at his Grade A rear end. She wasn't; she had left the room. I mouthed: *Loser*. He smirked then said, "How are you doing since the run-in with the dean?"

"Don't get me started." Weyford, which wasn't far from Stanford University, used to pride itself on offering a cutting-edge education. The dean's policies were: *Restrict fun* and *Enforce regimen*.

"I heard he had a heart attack as he was dressing you down. I also heard you saved him by using good old mouth-to-mouth."

"Nasty rumors. No heart attack. No mouth-to-mouth. Just a spirited faceoff. Though if I'd had to revive him, I would have." At least I'd like to believe I would have.

"Ooh-rah." Kimo toured the room, freshening paint water and switching out paintbrushes.

When the art therapy class ended, and before Kimo left in search of Reggie, he and I made plans for the weekend. If he didn't score with her—and he wouldn't—we would hang out, drink beer, and play basketball or video games. In the past, both of us had roamed bars; both had engaged in mindless sex with faceless beauties. We didn't choose to any longer. When the time was right, we would find the women of our dreams. Maybe. I had demons; he was picky.

On the drive home, my cell phone rang again. I hadn't listened to the voicemail left earlier. I inspected the readout: *Blocked*. Not Reggie or Kimo or the dean of students. I answered anyway. "Hello."

"Choochie?" a woman whispered.

My lungs constricted. The air around me turned thick. She was dead. She had died in the fire. And yet I knew the distinctive rasp of my mother's voice as well as my own. She was the only person who had ever called me *Choochie*—her little choo choo train.

"Come to the trailer. Quick. I need—"

The connection clicked off.

I stabbed Redial. No answer.

CHAPTER 2

Rain pelted the windshield as I drove like a fiend to South Redwood City. Doubt invaded my thoughts and I found it hard to swallow when I steered left on Florence and saw rows of trailers, each yard littered with beaten-up bikes and trikes. Was this a trick? Had some woman—not my mother—called me? No. I had recognized her voice. She may have disappeared thirty-one years ago, but she hadn't died. Why hadn't she contacted me before? Why—

Each Christmas for the past twenty years, ever since getting my driver's license, I had cruised the area. Why did my mother want to meet me here? Did she think that meeting in a familiar place, no matter how the area had declined in value, would help soften the shock that she was alive?

I screeched to a halt in front of the doublewide. A *For Sale* sign stood in the dead grass. Across the street, a blow-up motorcycle-riding Santa whooshed to life, its arms flopping in the air. I didn't feel much more solid. I bolted from my aging Tacoma truck, my first purchase out of the Navy, and tore up the dirty-white gravel path. I drew up short at the top step. The screen door hung from its hinges. The front door stood open. I pushed it back.

Even in the gloom of dusk, I could see the trailer was bare. No furniture. No suitcases. I moved inside. Rainwater dripped off me onto the floor.

"Mom?"

I tramped to the kitchen. Grime coated the counters and the windows. The backyard was as I remembered—gravel, no grass, rusted chain link fence, bleak. Yet I remembered the grating sound of the swing and how I would kick my feet up and yell, *Push me, Mommy*.

Working my way back through the trailer, I yelled, "Mom, are you here?"

At the arch leading to the rear of the trailer, I saw smeared blood on the floor. I caught the odor of it. Fresh.

"Mom!" I screamed.

I heard breathing. Short gasps. Coming from the bedroom on the left. The room where I'd spent nights hidden beneath the covers hoping that my mother's rages or the various attacks by her boyfriends—on her or on me—would subside.

I sprinted down the hall.

A woman lay on the floor on her stomach, head twisted to the side, face away from me. Salty-gray hair clung to her scalp, but I knew it was my mother. I recognized the black and turquoise butterfly tattoo that decorated her left shoulder. She'd been shot. A bullet had gone right through the word *Dead* in her Grateful Dead tank top. Blood oozed from the wound.

I darted to her and crouched down. She was breathing. Barely. I grabbed her wrist to check for a pulse. Weak. She wore a hospital band on her arm, the white kind with her name, date of birth, the works. With one hand, I tried to stanch the blood. With the other, I stabbed 911 into my cell phone.

My mother roused. "Chase?" She flicked her finger urging me to come to her level. The butterfly twitched.

My mouth flooded with the taste of dirty pennies as I remembered a trek to the tattoo parlor and watching with horror as the guy pierced her with needles.

"You're wet," she whispered.

"It's raining."

"I'm so sorry for"—she coughed—"everything."

For lying about being dead for thirty-one years? Or for the anger, the overdoses, and the pain she caused me? I flashed on myself, age three, flying across the bedroom after she backhanded me. Age four, cleaning up a bout of vomit after she pulled a drug-induced all-nighter. Age five, Christmas morning, sitting on the step outside the trailer wondering where she was.

"It's okay," I mumbled, realizing I meant it. She was alive. Except now I was losing her all over again.

A gravelly-voiced woman came on the line. "What is your emergency?" Could she sound more detached?

"My mother. She's been shot." I gave the address.

Mom coughed again. Harder. Blood gurgled from her mouth. And then her eyes widened in terror. "Run!"

CHAPTER 3

An Asian man in black clothing charged me. Thick nose, a mess of a right ear, Japanese not Chinese. Teaching the courses I did, one of my jobs was knowing the difference. He raised his gun, a Glock 19C. Fear surged through me. I leaned left just as the guy fired. The bullet grazed my arm. I'd taken a bullet before. Officers didn't always get the cushy assignments. I winced and tried to ignore the pain as the first rule of ground fighting, drilled into me in the service, sped through my mind: *Take the guy down. Use your bodyweight.*

I glanced at my mother and felt a gnawing to help her, but the second rule of ground fighting was: *Keep your emotions in check.* If I didn't save my own neck, I sure as heck couldn't save hers.

Tucking my chin, I charged my attacker. He hit the bedroom floor with a thud. His Glock went flying and skidded into the wall. I punched the guy in the arm. He elbowed me in the jaw. Bolts of pain rattled my brain. I recoiled, giving him enough time to get free. What an idiot I was.

He scrambled for the gun. I leaped to my feet and ran after him. I kicked his thigh. He stumbled but spun around, gun in hand. I whacked his wrist; he released the Glock. I hit the floor and booted it like a hockey puck into the hall. Then I thrust my fingertips, two together, into my attacker's neck. The collar of his turtleneck sweater protected him. He reeled back and rammed the wall, but he didn't lose his footing.

I clawed, intent on scratching his eyes. He dodged left. I lashed out again, this time with an upper cut/knee strike combination. My knee missed his groin, but my fist connected with his previously broken nose. "Had enough?"

"Screw you." No accent. American? American-educated?

The wail of a siren pierced the air.

In the split second that my opponent glanced toward the sound, I raised a hand to chop his neck, but he caught my wrist and twisted my arm. He drove the thumb of his other hand into the hollow of my neck, right above my esophagus. He was wearing gloves, so the thrust wasn't as sharp as it could've been. Even so, I doubled forward gasping for air and cursing myself. Stupid mistake. I was out of practice.

The siren's blare swelled. Blue and red lights flared through the windows of the trailer. Help had arrived.

My opponent shoved me to the floor and darted past me. I was certain if he'd had the time, he would've gone for the kill and broken my neck. Rusty hinges screeched. He was exiting out the kitchen to the backyard.

I heard another door open. Not the front door. A bedroom door. The air shifted in the trailer. High heels clacked down the hall. I twisted my head to catch a glimpse of the woman. Too late. I heard the kitchen door open and slam shut. She had escaped.

I crawled back to my mother. She was still breathing. "Mom, I'm here." I lowered my face to hers. I applied more pressure to the wound.

"Your father," she said.

"Joe's dead." Twenty-five years ago my stepfather, who was a decent guy and did his best to be present in my life after my mom *died,* for a few years anyway, tried to break up a fight outside a grocery store. He ended up with a shiv in his gut.

"Not Joe. Your…real father."

My insides tensed. Was she ready to reveal his identity? Did she know who he was? Was that why she had ended her ruse and summoned me?

"He and ooh—" She winced and licked her lips. "My fault."

"What was your fault?" I jammed my teeth together. If I could have, I would've chewed right through them.

She moaned again. "Ooh." She worked her mouth as if trying hard to form a word. "I told her. I saw—" She hummed then coughed in jags.

"Hospital."

"Yes, I'm going to get you to a hospital."

"Save—"

"Mom, shh. Help is coming. We'll get you stable, and you'll tell me the rest."

She dug her ragged fingernails into my trousers. "Your father. Luther."

"His name's Luther?"

"He—" She paused.

"He what?"

"They—" She stopped again.

"They who?"

"I thought he—" She clawed the silver heart-shaped locket around her neck.

He...they. I shook my head. She wasn't making sense. She had to be hallucinating. Years of heroin had fried her brain, yet her eyes looked clear.

The trailer rocked. A man yelled, "Anybody here? Emergency medical team."

"Down the hall, to your left!" I scrambled to my feet to meet them. There were two men, both young, one taller than the other, both in raingear. I gestured for them to follow me. "This way. She's bleeding badly."

Their walkie-talkies crackled.

The shorter man said, "Your arm."

"Flesh wound."

"I should treat it. And your jaw."

"Forget about me." I would survive. I was a survivor. I rushed down the hall and pointed. "In there. She's been shot."

The EMTs set to work. The taller guy placed an oxygen mask over my mother's mouth; the shorter, and obviously more senior, shouted questions at me. "Name? Age? Medications?"

I answered with staccato replies. "Sybil Day. Fifty-five. No, fifty-six. Her birthday was in September. She's a junkie. Was...I don't know." Had she changed? Had she wanted to show me she could make a fresh start? Where had she been for thirty-one years? "Is she…" I couldn't say the words.

Neither EMT responded.

As they tried to perform a miracle, more sirens slashed the air.

"That'll be the police," the lead EMT said. "They'll have questions." He eyed my arm.

"I told you. I'll do it myself. Ex-Navy. I've patched up plenty of other people."

He pulled bandages and ointment from a kit, thrust them into my hands, and jabbed a finger at his partner. "Get the gurney."

My wounds throbbed; my gut was in knots. Had my mother come to tell me about my father? His name was Luther. Like the devil or a reformer?

I glanced at my mother and spied the locket. She wanted me to have it. Was there a picture of my father inside? "May I talk to her?" I said to the lead EMT.

"Sure."

I knelt down. "Mom, I'm here."

Her eyes fluttered and closed. She didn't speak.

The second EMT yelled from the front of the trailer. "A little help."

The lead guy hurried out of the room, and I thought *no time like the present*. I unlatched the necklace and dropped it into my shirt pocket.

Seconds later, the EMTs returned. They set my mother on the gurney and raced her through the trailer.

I glanced at the spot where she had lain. A photograph—a Polaroid—was on the floor. I fetched it. In the picture, my mother and I were sitting on the grassy steps of Frost Amphitheater, a venue at Stanford University, waiting for a Grateful Dead concert to begin. It was the night before she *died*. My mother's arm was linked around my neck, and her left hand was knuckling my shaggy hair. She used to cut my hair; I never went to a kids' barber. We didn't have the money. We had stolen into the concert with a blanket, two peanut butter sandwiches, and a can of cola. Had she brought the Polaroid to confirm who she was, in case I didn't believe her? I recalled a flaccid-faced guy in a tie-dyed shirt taking the picture. Was he my father? Would his face match the picture inside the locket?

Sirens bleated and went silent. Doors slammed. Footsteps crushed gravel. A man yelled, "Witness inside!"

The front door wheezed open. Footsteps tramped down the hall.

I dropped the photograph into the pocket holding the locket, balled the bandages and ointment in one hand, rose to my feet, and raised my arms overhead. I knew the drill.

CHAPTER 4

"Chase Day," I blurted as two Redwood City policemen in wet raincoats entered the bedroom. One was African American with a gleaming bald head. His partner was Caucasian with a buzz cut. Both aimed .357 Magnums at me. "My name's Chase Day. My mother. She was shot." Words raced out of me. "The EMTs took her. I'm unarmed. My mother—"

"Was shot. Got it," the African-American said. His nametag read: *Detective Philips.*

"I'm holding medical supplies," I continued. "The EMTs gave them to me. They took my mother."

"To RCH. Redwood City Hospital." Philips holstered his gun and approached. "Hold steady, Mr. Day." He patted me down and withdrew my wallet from my pants pocket. Buzz Cut remained near the door, gun still aimed. "You can put your hands down now, sir. Bruno, stow the gun."

Buzz Cut—Bruno—obeyed.

Philips's gaze went from my injured arm, to the floor where my mother had lain, and back to me. "What happened? Slowly. Deep breath."

"A guy shot my mother. He attacked me." My lungs felt tight, my voice dry.

"What guy?"

"Five-eleven. Asian. One-eighty. Built."

"Name?"

"No clue. Broken nose. Bashed in ear. Neither recent."

Philips started rifling through my wallet.

"The guy fired at me. Grazed my arm. Can I treat the wound?"

"Are you bleeding out?"

"I'm still steady on my feet, so no." I cursed myself. This was no time to be glib. "But it hurts like a son-of-a-bitch."

"Hold on." Philips reviewed my license and handed it to Bruno. I stood still. Bruno handed the license back to Philips, who passed it to me. "Okay. Tend to your arm. You said the victim is your mother?"

"Yes. Sybil Day." I pocketed my wallet then removed my jacket and shirt and inspected the wound. A nick. It wouldn't fester. I swabbed ointment on the wound, quickly tied gauze around it, shrugged on my shirt and jacket, and pocketed the supplies. "I thought she died thirty-one years ago."

"Died?"

"In a fire. Long story. About an hour ago, she called. I was teaching an art class."

"You're an art teacher?"

"No, history."

"Art history?"

"Actually, I'm a professor at Weyford. I teach New World Threats. The art class is for some veterans at a hostel."

Philips seemed unimpressed by my credentials. "Thirty-one years have passed since seeing your mother. How did you know this woman was her?"

"I knew her voice, and she had a tattoo on her shoulder. A butterfly. She was also wearing a hospital ID." I tapped my wrist. "I think she was just released."

"Was she sick?"

"I don't know." I sounded like a schmuck. I was being no help.

Philips twirled a hand to continue. "What did she want? Why did she call you?"

"She didn't say. She'd been shot. It was hard for her to talk."

"Dear old mom doesn't call you for umpteen years, and just like that, you come running?"

Philips's sarcasm wasn't lost on me. I would've reacted the same. I said, "She was a drug addict."

"Meaning you're an enabler."

I jolted. "No."

"Did she want cash?"

I believed I would have denied my mother money if she had asked for it, but after so many years, how could I be sure? At five years old, I couldn't deny her a thing. Whenever she asked me to give my measly allowance back, I did. Anything to please her, to keep her calm. I said, "I found her lying in the bedroom, a bullet hole to the chest."

Philips ogled my hand, the one patting my thigh, trying to beat the rhythm of life back into my body. "Are you nervous, Mr. Day?"

"No." I willed the drumming to stop.

"Do you think this was a drug deal gone wrong?"

No, I didn't think it was a drug deal. There were no drugs on my mother, none scattered on the floor. The Asian hadn't been carrying any kind of backpack. If money had exchanged hands, where was it? "Maybe," I mumbled. I've been wrong before.

"Are you a drug addict, Mr. Day?"

"No." I pressed my lips together. I had overindulged in booze during high school, mainly cheap beer, but I'd never touched drugs because the memories of my mother's binges were vile. What if she wasn't on drugs any longer? She said it was her fault. What was? She said a woman was involved. With what? Did it matter? My father's name was Luther. Luther *what*?

"Mr. Day." Philips clasped his hands together and blew into them for warmth. "Why should we believe you about the attack? Maybe you had a scrape with your mother. Maybe you killed her. Is that what happened?"

"No."

"There's no need to raise your voice, Mr. Day."

Had I? Of course, I had.

"My attacker was real. We fought." I inhaled and exhaled as years of high school run-ins with cops came zooming at me. Loud parties. Road races. General MacArthur said, *In war, you win or lose, live or die—and the difference is just an eyelash*. I had survived a downward spiral by an eyelash. No arrests. No convictions. I hadn't had a set-to with the law since joining the Navy, but I knew the typical cop response: *Suspect first, ask questions later.*

"Look, this guy rushed me..." I recounted the fight. I gave a brief description of him again.

"You said you teach art. Can you draw him?"

"I'm not that kind of artist."

"What kind of art do you do?'

"Therapeutic. Get emotions on the paper. Nothing I create will hang in the Louvre."

Philips frowned. "You scared off this attacker?"

Another troop of people entered the trailer. A technician carrying a kit appeared at the door. "Where to, Detective?"

Philips pointed at the floor. "One of you in here. The other—" He eyed me. "Where did you say the guy exited?"

"Through the kitchen door. There might be footprints in the yard. His Glock is in the hall."

Philips directed his subordinate to retrieve the gun. "Style?"

"19C, nine millimeter." I shifted feet. "Like I said, I was in the Navy. Lieutenant. I've trained with weapons."

"Did you touch the gun?"

"No." Luckily I hadn't. "The attacker was wearing gloves. I doubt you'll get prints. I think he had an accomplice. Female. I heard someone in heels run out after him."

Philips said to Bruno, "Detective, take Mr. Day out front while we search the trailer."

Bruno ushered me down the steps. The rain had subsided. A dark, foggy gloom hung in the air, mirroring what was taking residence in my soul.

"Let's start at the beginning," Bruno said, tripping over the S in start. It was a slight stutter, one he had probably worked hard to lose. He asked a series of questions with dogged determination.

I answered without attitude. No sense alienating the guy. Name: *Chase Day.* Age: *Thirty-six.* Married: *No, never have been.* For a variety of reasons that I didn't expand upon. Family: *Grandmother named Barbara Rita*

Day and a Labrador retriever named Buddy. Address: *A duplex, small yard, no upkeep*. It wasn't much. I didn't need much. I never had. After seeing the trailer in which I had spent my formative years, I knew why. *No, I didn't know my assailant*. How many times did I have to tell these guys that? I described the Asian for a third time.

While Bruno took notes, I watched in dull horror as Christmas lights flickered on, up and down the street. The whole scene felt wrong, decadent. I thought of my mother again. Had she made plans to meet the killer? Had she come armed? With the Glock? No, the Glock was too big a gun for her. She had small hands, delicate fingers. Had she hoped to get the jump on her assailant? Was I wrong? Had it been a drug deal gone wrong? I craved answers.

Cold from the damp sidewalk shot through my shoes, up my legs, and into my spine. I smacked my arms for warmth. Not nearly enough punishment. This was my fault. Granted, Reggie had rules, and she would have snapped off my head if I'd answered the call when my mother first contacted me, but if I had—*if I had*—maybe I would have arrived with time to spare. Maybe I could've taken down the man in the trailer and prevented him from killing my mother.

Bruno waved at me. He was saying something.

"Sorry, what?" I asked.

"License."

"Again? Detective Philips—"

"License."

I took out my wallet and handed him my ID. I remembered the locket and photograph and hoped he wouldn't ask me to empty all my pockets.

"You said you're a history teacher at Weyford." Bruno looked incredulous. "Big guy like you?" He smirked. Was he intentionally trying to rile me? That wasn't going to happen. I could keep my cool most of the time.

"Some of us have brains," I replied. With a mother who did heavy drugs during pregnancy, I was lucky to have been born alive, let alone born with my body parts intact.

Bruno scanned the back of my license. "History professor, huh? I don't get history."

"I didn't either until high school. My girlfriend debated with me all the time about the various wars we were in: Operation Desert Storm, Operation Deliberate Force. She hated anything violent. I argued our right to defend." After my stint in the Navy, after becoming aware that war could erupt at any time given the delicate balance of global finances and resources, I realized that I wanted to devote my life to understanding the complexity of war.

"The present. That's what matters," Bruno said. "What did you say your specialty was? New World Threats? What's that?"

"I analyze war."

"R-e-a-l-l-y." Bruno drew out the word as if I was trying to put one over on him. He read from front of the license: "Chase T. Day. What's the T stand for?"

"The."

"Huh?"

"The word *the*."

"Chase The Day? Get real."

"It's no lie." Man, had I gotten ribbed for that during grade school. For that and so much more. The outbursts. The fists through walls. The Navy kicked my hot temper to the wayside.

The door to the trailer squeaked open. Philips exited and walked toward us. His mouth was twisted down in a frown. When he joined us on the sidewalk, he said, "Mr. Day, I'm sorry to inform you…"

I knew what he was going to say. The moment my mother left on that gurney, I'd known she was dead. I choked as if I had swallowed a walnut whole.

"Mr. Day? You okay?"

No, I wasn't okay. My mother didn't simply die once, she died twice, and this time, I could have prevented it.

CHAPTER 5

Two hours later, Detective Philips said he believed it was a drug deal gone wrong and released me. I still didn't agree. I had never been the kind of person to accept the obvious. He didn't seem to care about my opinion. He handed me a business card and asked me to come to the precinct in the morning, after I collected myself, to provide a sketch.

Frustration ate at me as I plowed through southbound traffic on the 101 Freeway. The rain had regained its intensity. Wipers batted water off the truck's windshield in steady swipes. Headlights from a sedan behind me flared into my side and rearview mirrors. I glowered over my shoulder, as if glaring would make a difference. The car—a sedan; I couldn't identify the make—was tight on my tail. I cut right. So did the sedan. Was I being followed? I had felt like someone was tailing me earlier in the day, to the university first thing in the morning and, later, to the peace rally. The driver was square-headed and flat-topped. All I could see was a silhouette. No features. Was it Detective Bruno?

As I left the crime scene, I had caught Bruno and Philips eyeing me with outright suspicion. Did they suspect me of killing my mother? The Glock was unregistered. What other significant evidence would they find other than mine: my hair, my fingerprints. Had their request to provide them with a sketch in the morning been a ploy to make me feel safe and secure? Was I *numero uno* on their suspect list?

To double-check my shadow theory, I zigzagged left then right, as if changing my mind about switching lanes.

The driver copied me.

I dodged an Escalade and swerved left. This time my supposed tail didn't mimic the move. I saw the car's right-hand blinker go into action. Seconds later, the sedan exited down a ramp.

Relief swept over me. I thought of a quote my therapist had hanging over his desk: *The facts will set you free.* That was what I needed. Facts. About my mother from the time she abandoned me to the present. And I needed to know who had killed her and why. If the police weren't interested in learning the truth, I was.

I sped forward, my new goal gaining momentum now that I didn't have a tail, imaginary or real, to evade. For thirty-one years, I had believed my mother was dead. What kind of chicken-livered person did that to a kid?

Needing music, I cranked the stereo on, but even the Eagles' *Heartache Tonight,* transferred to a CD from the tape I had found in my mother's belongings the night she left, couldn't drown out the chatter running roughshod through my brain. Why had my mother brought the photograph? Maybe she wanted me to be certain of her identity. Maybe she wanted me to remember the guy who had taken the picture.

Moving my gaze from the road for a split second, I pulled the Polaroid from my pocket. My mother's mouth was open. I remembered the song she was singing, "Uncle John's Band." The lyrics were about danger at the door. She sang off-key on purpose. I laughed until my sides hurt.

Why did she abandon me the next day? Man, I had hated her for that. Despised her, loved her, missed her.

Had she staged her death by fire thirty-one years ago? If so, she must have been afraid of someone. Was it the woman she referred to as she lay dying? I felt like I was trying to piece together a puzzle with only a third of the pieces. Why did she mention my father? She said, *I saw—* Then she hummed. Had she been trying to say the word *him*? Had she seen him somewhere? Why tell me his name now? I tossed the Polaroid on top of the mess of art supplies on the passenger floor and snapped off the music.

At the same time, my cell phone buzzed. I recognized the number. It was the dean of students. He could wait. Everything could wait. Term papers, finals, the whole enchilada. I needed answers. Maybe my grandmother, Barbie, could provide them. She had lied to me. She said she had ID'd my mother in the morgue. Why did she lie? That wasn't like her. If I was a poster child for PTSD, my grandmother was the poster child for Alcoholics Anonymous. The moment mom died—*disappeared*—my grandmother had joined AA. She rebuilt her life. Why had she kept this secret for over thirty years? Did her sponsor know about her deceit? Why hadn't she come clean with me? Not at six- or seven-years-old, but when I was in high school or something? I could've handled the truth. Every tawdry bit of it.

My jaw tensed. Barbie had coddled me before; she would try to coddle me now. I wouldn't let her. I would force her to tell me everything, beginning to end, even if I had to rip the truth from her throat.

I exited the freeway and sped to her office in Los Altos. She didn't leave until after nine P.M. on Saturdays. I pulled next to the dented green Buick LeSabre in the travel agency's driveway, slammed the Tacoma into park, and sprinted into the one-level stucco building.

A set of loafers, the only shoes my grandmother wore other than tennis shoes, sat on the floor by the front door, toes to the wall, directly beneath the placard she loved: *Self-destruction is not good. Self-discovery is.* For years after my mother supposedly died, Barbie had drummed that mantra into me. I grasped the first half. My therapist—yeah, I still saw him once a month—was working on the second half. I could only imagine what I would paint at the next art therapy session.

"Barbie!" I yelled. She wouldn't answer to her full name, Barbara Rita, and not to any made up granny-type names either. Not to me. Not to anybody. I raced down the carpeted hall, bypassing Mexico and South American travel posters.

Barbie's assistants, a frizzy-haired woman and a razor-thin guy I'd dubbed the Zipper, leapt from the storage room to impede my path.

"What happened to your face?" the Zipper asked.

"Ran into a guy's elbow." I dodged them and barged into Barbie's office. It was cluttered with steel cabinets, file folders, and pictures frames filled with pictures of me. Only me.

Barbie stood at her metal desk. She was fiddling with the sleeve of her jogging outfit, telephone to her ear. Though she was pushing seventy-five, after going through AA and abiding by a daily regimen of exercise, she looked nearly as fit as her twenty-something assistants. She spun around and pressed the phone to her chest. "Your face. You're hurt."

"She was alive," I blurted. "Mom was alive. She's dead. For real this time."

My grandmother didn't react. She didn't blink.

"A man shot her," I went on. "He and I fought."

Both assistants moaned. They stood squished into the doorway.

Barbie strode across the room, asked them to leave, shut the door to give us privacy, and turned back. She swept a strand of bleached hair off her face. "From the beginning."

"Mom called and begged me to meet at our old trailer. She was alive when I got there, but she'd been shot. She mentioned my father."

"Joe's dead."

"Not him. My real father. Luther."

Barbie's face turned white. She looked ready to crumple to the floor.

I grabbed her, my fury replaced with concern. "Are you okay?"

"Yes," she whispered, but her lips were trembling, her eyes fluttering.

"Why didn't you tell me she was alive?"

Barbie wrenched away and fled from the room.

CHAPTER 6

I raced down the hall to catch up to her. Phones were ringing, but the assistants looked too stunned to answer. I followed my grandmother into the coffee room. It was crammed with a chipped laminate table, old metal chairs, a well-used coffee maker, and microwave oven.

"Barbie, talk to me."

Without looking at me, she crossed to the dishwasher, whipped open the door, and started unloading coffee cups. The porcelain clattered.

"Why did you lie?" I said.

"I didn't want you to hope." Her voice cracked. "I didn't want you to—"

"Enable her. I wouldn't have."

"You *did*. She called and you came running." Barbie shoved the cups into a cupboard and slammed the door. "She asked me to pretend she was dead. She wanted you to have a chance. It was the one selfless thing she ever did. I promised her I would."

"Who tells a kid his mother died in a fire? Who puts a kid through that kind of pain?"

My grandmother pressed her lips together.

"Did Joe know?" I asked.

"He didn't have a clue. He had been out of your mother's life for two years."

I ran my hand down my neck. All these years, I had gotten used to my mother being dead. I had told myself that I was okay on my own. I had convinced myself that I didn't give a hoot if I had parents. But I had cared. All kids did. I had needed my mother alive—sick or not sick, drug-addicted or clean. Would I have turned out differently? Would I be happier? Would I be married with six kids? I still hadn't given my heart to a woman. I hoped I could someday.

"Chase…"

Something snagged inside me. I assessed my grandmother's face, her bearing. She looked tense, like an animal ready to bolt. There was something she wasn't telling me. I pulled the locket from my pocket and popped the latch. I hadn't had the chance to look inside until now. As expected, I found a photograph of a man within. He wasn't the flaccid-faced guy who took the Polaroid at the amphitheater. He looked like I had at the age of twenty, raw cheekbones, haunted by inner demons. I thrust the locket at Barbie. "Is this my father?"

Barbie sucked in a tiny breath, confirming.

"You met him," I said.

"No. Never. Your mother described him. You…he…the same—"

"The same shaped face. The same eyes. Yeah, got that. Why do you think she mentioned him to me?"

"You know your mother has a tendency—"

"Had. She *had*, Barbie. She's dead. Murdered. A man shot her. The EMTs took her to the hospital, but she died."

My grandmother keened. She wrapped her arms around herself. "Where did you get that?"

"Mom brought it to the trailer. She also brought a picture from the concert we went to the night before she abandoned me."

Barbie continued to mewl.

I thought of something I'd noticed at the crime scene. "Mom was wearing a hospital ID bracelet. Do you know which hospital she was at?"

"Why?"

I dredged up those last moments with my mother. "For thirty-one years, she doesn't call. Why did she contact me? She could have stayed dead. She had a reason, an agenda. I've got to find out why she called me. The hospital is the place to start."

"You're sounding crazy."

Me? I was the one who was crazy? She was the one who had kept the truth from me. It took all my reserve not to grab her by the arms and shake her. "Which hospital was Mom at? I couldn't read the name."

She didn't answer.

"Barbie!" I yelled, my tone sharp, hostile.

"Keystone. She always went to Keystone. She couldn't afford more."

Keystone Hospital was a large facility in Redwood City. It had regular, full-paying patients, but it occasionally helped the indigent.

"She was so sick," Barbie went on. "Always on drugs. That's why she abandoned you." Tears ran down her cheeks. She covered her mouth with her hand.

"Tell me about my father."

Her hand slipped to her throat. "They met at a party she crashed."

"Where?"

"I don't know; I don't care. You were a result of one roll in the hay. Afterward, your father vanished."

"Vanished?"

"He abandoned your mother like a piece of trash. He left her pregnant with you."

"Are you saying I'm trash?"

"No, of course not. Don't put words…" She dropped her arms to her side; her shoulders slumped. "She was heartbroken."

After a one-night stand? The guy must have really made an impact on her. "Mom said something was her fault. Do you know what she meant?"

"No."

"Do you know his last name?"

"Whose?"

"My father's."

"Marcus or Marcussen." She swatted the air. "Chase, please. Let the police handle this."

"They're not interested."

"Why not?"

"They think she died from a drug deal gone wrong." I paused. "Of course, they could be playing me. They might suspect me."

"Of what?"

"Murder."

"A man of your integrity?"

"People with integrity kill."

Her eyes narrowed. "Did you?"

"Are you kidding me? How could you even think such a thing?"

Barbie pushed past me and hurried down the hall to her office.

I trailed her and stopped in the doorway.

"Do you know why your mother started taking drugs at the age of thirteen?" She cranked open a file drawer without glancing in my direction. "She claimed they made her feel beautiful. Alive. She was lying. I know the truth. When your grandfather left us, I dove into the bottle. Your mother started her downward spiral because he was a heel, and I was a lousy role model. It was my fault. She probably felt the same about leaving you. That's what she meant was her fault."

"I need to trace her last days. I need answers."

Barbie removed a slug of files, ignoring me.

"My mother is dead. For real. Do you understand? Someone shot her. Murdered her. She's my blood. It's on me to—"

"Your blood?" She whirled around. "I was the one that fed you. I put a roof over your head. I made sure you did your homework. I tucked you in at night. I went to soccer games and lacrosse games. I was at all your graduation ceremonies. I may have failed your mother, but I did not fail you. I picked up the pieces."

"Barbie—"

"Stop. Right. There." She smacked the files with the back of her hand. "You are always in a rush, young man. That's your greatest downfall."

"Not true."

"You joined the Navy without thinking of the consequences."

"It was the right decision."

"You got wounded."

After I made lieutenant and was assigned to a destroyer, something unexpected happened. While on shore leave, I was in a restaurant targeted by extremists. A bomb went off. Shards of glass shot into my neck. Though I could have stayed in the Navy—the injury was fully recoverable—I had served more than my required four years. That was when I left, entered Stanford as a graduate student, and earned my teaching degree. Though the physical scars were minimal, I rarely looked in the mirror without feeling the reverb of that explosion. Art therapy had helped me as a kid; it helped even more now.

"Take a moment and think about what you're doing," she ordered. "Think about what you might uncover."

"Like the truth? Like who my mother really was and who my father might be?"

"He was a thief in the night." Barbie hurled the files onto the floor. Papers flew out of them. She stared at the mess for a long moment before returning her gaze to me. "If you're so eager to dig into this, why not commission your war buddies to help."

I caught the snide tone. My *war buddies*, the guys who had survived and had come back from conflict with their bodies and minds wrecked. What Barbie hated even more than my joining the service was my donating time at the hostel. She worried that, by association, something would snap inside my brain, and I would become broken and useless. No matter how hard I tried, I couldn't convince her that I was healthy. I was moving forward. I wanted to drink up life, not shun it.

"Do you still have Mom's things?"

"I gave nearly everything she hoarded to the Salvation Army."

"Whatever you've got left, I want it. Maybe she put this Luther guy's telephone number in an address book. Maybe there are more pictures. More pieces to the puzzle."

Barbie crossed the floor and grabbed my shoulders. "Chase, stop this selfish—"

"No, you stop." I wrenched free. My heart pounded my ribcage. "I'm going to find out the truth about my mother, who killed her and why she contacted me, with or without your help."

My grandmother backed away and jammed her lips together. Long seconds ticked on the clock that sat on the top of the file cabinet. Finally she said, "You've got to plan your mother's funeral, do you hear me? It's the least you can do."

CHAPTER 7

When I left my grandmother's office, my stomach was in knots. Now I stood by the Keystone Hospital directory feeling nauseous. The stench of antiseptic solution made my skin crawl. Where had my mother stayed in this hospital? On what floor, for what treatment? Did someone follow her from there to the trailer? If only I knew why she had wanted to see me. I swatted my thigh.

Make a decision.

But I couldn't. Self-doubt was cutting into my thoughts. Maybe I was being selfish like Barbie said. Maybe I should be tending to my mother's funeral and letting the police do what they were paid to do. And yet…

Go. Now. Get answers.

I reread the directory. I wasn't stupid enough to expect a flashing sign saying: *Indigent Treated Here,* but I had hoped for something more explanatory than *Orthopedics* on the fourth floor, *Obstetrics* on the third.

Not willing to waste another moment deliberating, I boarded an elevator and stabbed number six: *Long-Term Care*. I would start at the top and work my way down. My stomach lurched as the ancient metal box left the ground floor and lumbered upward. An inane orchestral version of "Have Yourself A Merry Little Christmas" played in surround sound. The irony of the lyrics was not lost on me.

Agonizing seconds later, the elevator jolted to a stop and the doors creaked open. I stepped out. Nursing staff and doctors in rubber-soled shoes beat a path past me like soldiers marching to war, their faces implacable and their human sensors in check.

I cut right and stopped short.

Two female patients pushed chrome dollies with bags of liquids attached. I waited until they rounded a corner—neither looked in my direction—then I headed along a passageway crowded with wheelchairs, and I peered at room door nameplates and attending charts. Would my mother's name be listed on one? Had she checked out or fled the hospital?

After scouring every chart on the ward, I stood still and replayed those last moments with my mother. She had said the words *hospital* and *save*. At the time, I thought she had wanted me to make sure the EMTs took her to the hospital to save *her*. I hushed her to keep her calm and to preserve her energy. What if she was trying to tell me that she had seen my father at the hospital? Seconds later, she said the words: *your father. Luther*. If strung together, the sentence would have been: *Hospital…save your father, Luther*.

Adrenaline pumping, I rode the elevator down a floor to resume my search. I exited on the second floor, *Recovery*, and drew to a halt. The man I'd fought in the trailer was confronting a steely-eyed African-American nurse with psychedelic blue hair that matched her uniform. He must have spotted the ID tag on my mother's wrist, too. Had my mother wanted me to save my father from this man? Did the guy believe what I did, that my mother had seen my father at the hospital?

I squelched the urge to tackle him. What would that get me? Another fight and no answers. My grandmother had accused me of being hasty. She was wrong. Rash behavior had been drummed out of me years ago. As a new recruit, I dutifully obeyed orders; as a lieutenant, I gave them; and as a professor of New World Threats, I taught that battle plans, in order to be successful, were rehearsed and orchestrated in tedious detail.

Breath trapped in my chest, I ducked out of sight and counted down from ten. *Nine, eight, seven…*

By the count of zero, my breathing was calm. I sneaked a peek around the corner.

My mother's killer stood in profile. He asked the nurse something. She jutted her head right and left like an Egyptian dancer.

Again I considered attacking him, but instead, I pulled out my iPhone to call Detective Philips. He would be overwhelmed with gratitude for a tip, wouldn't he?

Yeah, and pigs fly.

I glanced at the signal strength. No bars. Danged if I shouldn't have stuck with Verizon.

Suddenly, the Asian gripped the nurse's shoulders. I tensed. There were no security guards around. I couldn't let him hurt her. Maybe I could fell him with a clip to the knees, keep him pinned to the ground, and demand to know the truth.

Before I needed to make a decision, the nurse batted the guy away and waved an angry finger in his face. "Now listen here, mister—"

"I want that roster," he hissed. "I want Luther Marcussen."

That answered my question. He was looking for my father.

The guy pulled a wad of cash from his pocket. "I'm offering five Ben Franklins."

The nurse flinched like he had accosted her. "Put that money away." She glanced at a security camera, as if worried that her superior might view the tape and believe she was open to a bribe.

Her response gave me an idea. I raised my iPhone and clicked on the camera icon. The nurse might not want her picture taken with a man waving cash, but I wouldn't be sending the photograph to a hospital honcho. I would send the snapshot to the police.

I clicked once, but the angle was bad. If I didn't capture all of the man's face, Detective Philips would laugh me out of the precinct. I crept around the corner and aimed.

At the same time, all hell broke loose. The Asian grabbed the nurse by both shoulders. He shook her.

She screamed.

Within seconds, a band of males and female staffers in blue uniforms emerged into the corridor.

"Hey, you," one of the females cried.

My mother's killer released the nurse and bolted for the stairwell.

I pocketed the iPhone and darted after him. In the stairwell, I could cold-cock him. No security cameras. Nothing caught on tape. I would call the police, have him arrested—

"Hey, fella. You in the blue jeans," a male in a blue uniform yelled.

I thumbed my chest.

"Yeah, you." The guy was taller and leaner than me. "Help me out."

In the melee, a couple of tube feeders had been knocked over.

I glanced at the stairwell door and back at the staffer. A security guard appeared over his shoulder.

In milliseconds, options rat-a-tatted in my head. If I ran after my target, the guard would pursue me, and I would lose not only the murderer but also the opportunity to gather vital information from the nursing staff.

I jammed my iPhone into my pocket, hopeful the photograph I had taken of the Asian man—bad angle notwithstanding—was worth something, and then I optioned for my spur-of-the-moment Plan B.

CHAPTER 8

While righting the feeders on the hospital ward, I asked the male nurse whether he had known my mother. That earned me a grunt. I tried another angle and asked whether he knew someone named Luther Marcussen. The guy didn't. I described my father, or how I imagined he looked thirty-seven years later. Was he tan? I wasn't. I used sunblock. Did he yo-yo with his weight? I didn't. Granted, every year I grew a little soft around finals week, but on the first of January, I rededicated myself to health.

The male nurse shook his head. I was stalemated.

As the chaos subsided and the contingent of nurses dispersed, I came up with Plan C, taken right out of Patton's primer: *Good tactics can save even the worst strategy.*

I stole to the nurse's station where the African-American nurse with the blue-streaked hair was sitting. She was filling out a report. A foot-wide cubicle divider stood between the two of us. I leaned forward on my elbows and sneaked a peek at her nameplate: *Darnell.* Her parents must have wanted a boy. She wore a miniscule diamond ring on the fourth finger of her right hand. Divorced or engaged?

"Um, hey, Darnell," I said.

She stopped typing and looked up. Her breath caught in her chest. "Your face."

Man, I'd forgotten about that. I didn't ache, but I was obviously not a sight for sore eyes. "Clumsy," I said and offered a lopsided grin. I couldn't come up with a savvier line. Back in high school, I was an athlete. I was cocky. I had the looks, the swagger. I was one of the guys that girls flocked to. And I worked hard at being Mr. Cool—anything to keep the mask over the hurt. After the Navy, following the explosion, I changed. I didn't want to be shallow and guarded. And I didn't want just any girl. I wanted a future with a partner who I could appreciate and who would appreciate me. Definitely not *Mr. Cool*.

"My mother was a patient here. Her name was Sybil Day. Did you know her?"

Darnell shook her head.

"Shaggy gray-black hair, butterfly tattoo." I flicked my fingers around my left shoulder.

"Oh, her. She called herself Stevie."

Nothing my mother did was going to surprise me again.

"Nice gal," Darnell said. "She loved her poetry."

"That's her."

"She's gone."

Yes, she is, I thought. *Forever.* "I think she saw my father in this hospital. He could've been a visitor. He might have been a patient. Maybe fifty-five or so. My mom's age." Twenty years older than me. I held out my mother's locket and popped the clasp. "This is him as a young man. Do you recognize him?"

Darnell glanced at the picture and back at me. "Sorry, no." She eyed the clock to the right of her desk and returned to her work.

"I don't have a current photograph, Darnell. I've never met him. His name is Luther."

"Luther?"

"Marcussen."

"Oh, no, no, no." Her tone shot up; her gaze blazed with indignation. "Just a minute ago there was a guy asking about him, and he tried to rough me up, so you can just—" She reached for the telephone. "I'm calling security."

"Wait." I lurched forward, blocked by the counter. I stopped shy of grabbing her wrist. "That guy who was here, the one that ran out."

"You saw him?"

"Yes. He—" How could I explain, in ten seconds or less, everything that had happened over the last few hours? Honesty was the wisest choice.

No mask. No lies. I held up my hands, palms forward. "You nailed it, Darnell. He's a bad guy. See this mess on my face?" I aimed a thumb at it. "He did this. He also killed my mother."

"Lord, she's dead?"

"He wants to kill my father." I wasn't sure if that was true, but the man had murdered my mother and had tried to off me. *Save. Hospital.* "I need to find my father, Darnell. I believe he was here. I believe my mother wanted me to protect him."

Of course, the question *why* cycled through my brain. Had he done something that made my mother's killer want payback? Barbie said my father was a thief in the night. Was she being literal? Had my father stolen something? From the woman my mother mentioned? Mom said she told the woman she'd seen him. No, she didn't say *him,* but she inferred it, and then *wham*! Mom was dead.

Darnell's eyes welled up. Before she could speak, an army tank of a nurse with flaming red hair marched around the desk. Darnell eyed the woman with fear, then blinked away tears and stared at her clipboard like it was the Bible. Her associate—her superior?—grabbed a file from an inbox, flipped it open, and jotted notes. I offered a silent plea to Darnell, but she couldn't be wooed. She set aside the clipboard, hit Enter on the keyboard of her computer, and began typing—nonsense or real stuff, I couldn't be sure. I didn't have a good angle to the computer screen.

My frustration escalated, but I wasn't ready to end my quest. I pretended to belong there. I scrolled through old emails on my iPhone. The clock above Darnell's desk ticked off 8:45 P.M. in sixty noisy seconds. Finally, the redheaded nurse slapped the folder closed, returned it to the inbox, and without a word to Darnell, strode away. Warm and fuzzy wasn't her style; I would make it mine.

I smiled and leaned forward on the counter. "Darnell, I can see you cared for my mother."

"No, I didn't. I don't like anybody here. That's not my job."

"She was hard not to like." A pang gripped my heart as I remembered a couple of times my mother had invited her friends to the trailer. When she was sober, she was the life of the party. She made people, including me, laugh. "Did she tell you jokes?"

Darnell opened a drawer and pulled out a date stamper. She slammed the drawer and adjusted the date on the stamp.

So much for my magnetic charm. I was rusty. I chose the direct approach. "Look, Darnell, is it possible that my father was a patient here? The guy before me, he asked to see a roster."

"I wouldn't let him."

"I know. Would you let me?"

"No."

"C'mon. Could I see patient file tabs? Something? Maybe my father was being released from the hospital the day my mother got here."

"I told you I don't recognize his name."

"Maybe he was using an alias. Maybe my mother saw him for a brief second. Ships in the night, you know."

Darnell opened the drawer, tossed the date stamp back inside, and closed the drawer. *Slam!*

I thumped the counter. "Please, Darnell, throw me a bone. My mom died." My voice was husky with emotion. Not put on. *Dead, gone, again.* "Wouldn't you want someone to help you if a jerk ended your mother's life?"

Darnell inhaled sharply. "A jerk did."

It was my turn to gasp. "Oh, man, I'm sorry. I—" An imaginary vacuum sucked the air out of my lungs. "How? When?"

"Sixteen years ago, but it feels like yesterday." Darnell bit out the words. "Mama owned a liquor store. Guy put a bullet in her stomach. She bled out. I do what I do because I made a vow never to let someone suffer like Mama did."

"Did they catch him?"

Her eyes grew moist. "No."

A beeper sounded. A light on a digital display to the right of the reception desk indicated that the patient in room twenty was calling for assistance.

Darnell glanced at the display and back at me.

"Please," I whispered.

After a long moment, she gave a hitch of her head at the *out* tray to her right. "If you have a mind to do some research, five men around your daddy's age left the hospital in the past few days. One of them never should've been here. Just saying." She rose from her chair, hurried down the hall, and disappeared into a room, leaving me alone...with exit patient files.

CHAPTER 9

In less than two minutes, I browsed the exit files and memorized the addresses logged onto the data sheets for men over fifty. I'm good with visuals; facts and figures are my specialty. Ask me something about the Crusades, the Irish-Bruce Wars, or the War of the Roses, and I can give you intimate details. I wished I could thank Darnell, but I wasn't about to stick around. I fled down the stairwell rehashing what I'd learned. Darnell hadn't been lying. None of the patients were named Luther. None had the surname Marcussen. But for each, I had obtained a home address, the name of the person who had signed him out, and a telephone number. It was a start.

I sprinted toward the hospital's front doors, eager to find a hint of a cell phone signal so I could call each patient. I drew up short when I spied a woman in sweater and jeans sitting on a plastic orange chair, a raincoat and knit purse bunched beside her. My heart snagged in my chest. I was seeing things. It couldn't be. And yet it was her. Holland Tate. My high school girlfriend. How many years had it been? Sixteen? Seventeen? Ebony hair, the tilt of her nose, the slope of her forehead. I wasn't wrong. How could I be? She was the girl I had hungered for, day in and day out. Even now, despite the tense circumstances, I felt a longing for her—okay, a *lust*. Some of our friends from high school said she had become an actress while others claimed she had become a narc or a bounty hunter. The latter wasn't likely. Holland never had the stomach for violence, given her family history. She leaned forward and braced her chin in her hand. She was crying.

Don't stop, I told myself. *Don't get involved. She's a blast from the past. Her issue isn't your issue.* So what if I wanted marriage, a family, and stability in my emotional life. This was not the time nor the place to rekindle a relationship.

I swallowed hard. Surely there was someone else to take care of her. What was the old saying? *You can't go home. Move on.* I hesitated. Was that what people had done whenever they encountered my mother? Had they avoided her and continued on their merry ways?

As if sensing me, Holland looked up. Her eyes were swollen from tears. A pang cut through me. My rational brain declared war on my irrational one. *You have work to do. Find your father. Save him…if he needs saving*. But my leaden feet wouldn't budge. Holland looked so vulnerable. I wanted to grab her, console her, make love to her.

"Holland?" I moved closer and thumbed my chest. "It's Chase. Day."

She tilted her head. "Chase? Wow, Chase." She reached for me.

How could I resist? I sat in the chair next to hers. Fresh tears pooled in her eyes.

"Are you okay?" I said. "What happened?"

"I…my mother…she died tonight. Heart attack."

I sank toward her and gripped her hand, struck by the fact that we were linked by the same yet different tragedy.

"She"—Holland raked her teeth over her lower lip, the motion helpless and at the same time sensual—"came back into my life. Recently."

Twenty-two years ago, when Holland was fourteen, her mother, unable to suffer any more abuse from Holland's father, walked out on her family. She moved to Texas and opened a diner. Holland and her three brothers were devastated. The shock of her mother's abrupt exit caused Holland's father to reverse his course. He stopped drinking. He enrolled in anger management classes. He found Jesus. Holland's mother would send a card every year on Holland's birthday. Holland would return the card, unopened.

"How was the reunion?" I asked, not knowing what else to say.

"Better than expected. We…liked each other." Holland sighed. "I was taking a moment to regroup before I drove home." She removed her hand from mine and, using a pinky finger, wiped beneath both eyes.

No wedding ring. I wanted to kick myself for noticing.

"Why are you here?" she asked.

"My—" Should I tell her the entire saga? I didn't have time. I had to go. *Stand up. Move, you idiot.*

"Your what?"

"Nothing."

A bittersweet smile tugged at the corners of her mouth, bittersweet yet full of potential. "You remember my mother, don't you?" she said. "The *no compromise* queen, and just like that"—she snapped—"life ends."

"Life's all about not compromising, isn't it?" I said. My mother and her mother. Their generation had been the first real *me* generation. Subsequent generations hadn't advanced much.

"Yeah."

"Holland, I'm sorry. I've got to go." I gazed into her eyes. She would survive without me. She looked tired and grief-stricken, but solid. "Maybe if you give me your number, I could call you sometime. For coffee."

Her eyes narrowed.

"I've reformed," I said. "No more bad boy. No more outbursts. I'm reliable. I did my time in the Navy. I became an officer."

"So I heard."

"I'm a professor now. I teach history at Weyford." At one time Holland had dreamed of going to college. Had she? Losing touch sucked. "I've got end-of-semester papers to grade so I've got to go." The lie caught in my throat, but I couldn't tell her I needed to track down my mother's killer and find my father. Holland didn't need to be burdened with all of that. I would return to my normal life soon enough, right?

She tilted her head. "I'll give you my number if you finish your sentence."

"Which one?"

"A second ago, you said, 'My' and you stopped. You said it was nothing. Your *what*? What happened? Why are you here?"

My face warmed. Like in the past, Holland was able to read me. I'd never met anyone since her who could. "My mother died today, too. She was murdered."

"Oh, lord." Holland clutched my hand like a vice. "What happened?" The passion in her voice nailed me. She wasn't simply curious. She wanted to comfort me, as if hearing about my pain would make hers easier to bear.

In a flash, I replayed my day: finding my mother, fighting the guy in the trailer, my mother's cryptic last words. "I came to the hospital to see if I could find out who killed her and why, but while I was here, I came to realize—at least I think I'm getting the right message—that my mother wanted me to save my father."

"Save him from what?"

"I don't know. I think she saw him here."

"Was he a patient?"

"I don't know. I didn't find him."

"You have to."

"I know." Maybe after talking to him, I could sort out my mother's life.

Holland slipped her hand from mine then wrapped her arms around herself and started rubbing her biceps so hard I worried that she would leave bruises.

"I heard you might have become an actress in Los Angeles."

"I was. Sort of. My career didn't, you know, soar, so I've come home to rebuild my life. I work a couple of"—she hesitated—"odd jobs to pay the rent."

"Bounty hunter? Narc?"

"Funny guy." She offered a wry smile. "Nothing that glamorous. Waitress. Dog walker. I'm in a local play right now. No pay but nice people. It's a period piece at a small theater in Los Altos."

"The Hole?"

"You know it?"

I shrugged. "My grandmother thinks I need culture and drags me to shows."

"How is Barbie?"

"Wiry. Fierce." Pissed at me, but I didn't add that.

"My mother wanted to see me act, but she never did." Holland's tone was undercut with sadness.

Out of the corner of my eye, I spotted a nurse with an angry shock of red hair exiting the elevator—the army tank. A security guard exited behind her; holster, gun, attitude. I tensed. Were they looking for me? Did the nurse know I had burrowed through hospital files? If they caught me, would they alert Detective Philips? Would he consider me an even stronger suspect in my mother's murder?

The nurse turned right, away from us. The guard followed.

I hopped to my feet. "I've got to go, Holland. No lie. I'm sorry for your loss." I headed for the exit.

Holland hoisted her purse, nabbed her raincoat, and pursued me. "Are you afraid of that nurse?" She punched my arm. "You are. You lied to me. You haven't changed a bit. You're in trouble, aren't you?"

I didn't slow.

"Walk me to my car," she went on. "It's the least you can do. The nurse and the bruiser will pay less attention to a couple." She grabbed my elbow. "Please. I don't want to be alone."

I held the exit door open. Holland passed through first. The moment I stepped outside, a feeling—bad vibes; a sense of foreboding?—coursed through me. Was someone watching me? I glanced around. Moonlight pierced the remnants of rainclouds. Straight ahead, people, probably thankful for a respite from the stormy weather, strolled near the water fountain in the center of the park. Doctors and nurses sat on benches eating meals from coolers or paper sacks. Nothing looked ominous.

And then I saw someone tall. A man. He disappeared around the outside corner of the building to the left. Was he a cop? He wasn't as tall as Philips nor as bulky as Bruno. Was he one of their minions hoping I would slip up and prove I had killed my mother? Or was it my mother's killer? Had he figured out I was at the hospital and come back to finish me off once and for all?

"Go back inside," I whispered to Holland.

"Why?"

"No time to explain." I released her and gave her a nudge, and then jogged toward the parking garage on the other side of the park. To my surprise, Holland caught up with me.

"What's going on?" she demanded.

I needed to establish distance. If I had learned anything in the Navy, it was to prevent civilian casualties. But if I left her behind, I might be putting her in harm's way. The guy tailing me—if there was a guy tailing me—might nab her to use against me.

"Chase?"

"I think I'm being followed."

"I don't see anyone." Holland's voice prickled with panic. "Are you sure?"

"No. Good old paranoia might be rearing its ugly head." Except my gut was tight. One of my naval superiors said I had a survival instinct, finely honed before the age of five, thanks to my mother and her freakish lifestyle.

A squirrel darted from a stand of bushes. Holland shrieked and rammed into me. The scent of pineapple and coconut flooded my senses. Memories of the two of us, lying on the warm sand at Half Moon Bay, swept over me. It was our first kiss. We were sixteen. In love. Before I ruined everything.

I pushed apart. "Where's your car?"

"Two blocks away. The garage was full."

"I'll give you a lift." I steered her toward my Toyota. "My truck's not pretty, but she's loyal. The only thing she needs is WD-40." I opened the passenger door; it groaned. I snatched the Polaroid I'd tossed onto the floor and shoved it into my shirt pocket. Then I allowed Holland to climb in.

"WD-40"—she tucked her purse onto her lap and toed the mess of art supplies on the floor of the passenger side out of her way—"and perhaps a good cleaning."

"Seatbelt." I slammed the door. I rounded the rear of the truck while scanning the garage and the nearby staircase. No movement. I crouched down to peer beneath vehicles. Zip. Had I been mistaken about a tail? I hurried to the driver's door and flung it open. It groaned, too, and I cursed softly. Why hadn't I invested in a nicer vehicle? Until now I hadn't found a reason to get rid of my aging friend. A ride was a ride. Sure, I could have afforded a Lexus, a vintage Mustang, something better, but I had denied myself. A sort of punishment, if you will. I'd promised myself I would purchase a better vehicle when I found my better half.

I drove out of the parking garage. "Which way?"

"Turn right on El Camino."

Once I was on the street, I glanced in the rearview mirror. I didn't spot a tail and breathed easier. The main strip glittered with so much cheap Christmas décor, my eyes hurt. I didn't like Redwood City. Back in 1851, lumber companies had used the deep-water channel that ran inland from Redwood City to San Francisco Bay to make shipments of logs. One would think that kind of trade would leave a city with character, but Redwood City, in my humble opinion, had none.

"That's my car." Holland pointed. "Three cars down."

While slowing, I spotted a gunmetal gray Ford Explorer in the side view mirror. Keeping pace with me. I couldn't make out the driver. Only a silhouette. Broad shoulders, thick neck. Nothing like the tall guy I'd seen running from the hospital. Were they both cops, tag teaming one another?

Holland said, "Chase, stop. You passed my car."

"Can't. We've definitely got a tail. An Explorer."

She swiveled in her seat. "I see it."

"I'll bring you back to your car in a sec, but first I've got to circle around. Okay?"

"Why is someone following you?"

"He must think I've figured out where my father is. The laugh is on him."

At Whipple Road, I veered left toward the freeway. The Explorer copied me. In a quick maneuver, I zigzagged around a red Corvette and merged onto the 101 Freeway. The Explorer did the same. Not faster than me, not slower.

My pulsed jagged. I had to keep cool. I was the lead car. I influenced any future incident.

"I thought we were going around the block," Holland said, sounding panicked. "Where are you heading?"

I glanced at her, hating myself for allowing her into my drama. I was ready to apologize, but when I caught sight of her eyes, I balked. She didn't look scared. In fact, she seemed remarkably calm. Suspicion reared its vile head. Was the immediacy of her mother's death giving her the courage to face fear head-on, or was she more than she appeared? Was she really a narc, like people said? Was she used to being under pressure? Being with her was giving me whiplash. One minute she was a heartrending jangle of nerves; the next, she was sexy and strong.

"Seatbelt tight?" I asked.

"Why?"

"I'm going to step on the accelerator. Are you okay with that?"

Back in my teens, idiot that I was, I couldn't fight certain urges. One time, Holland had asked me—no, begged me—not to drag race anymore. She knew a kid, younger than us, who'd died. I didn't know him, so I didn't listen. When I joined my buddies for a race that Saturday night, Holland went out and got high. An hour later, she hooked up with the quarterback. Rumors circulated; I heard about it. She tried to lie her way out of it; she said nothing happened. I lied, too. I said it didn't matter. But it did. We were through. I went to college and directly into the Navy. When I returned to civilian life, she had moved. No forwarding address. I put the past behind, finished up grad school, and dedicated myself to teaching, which had been a much more satisfactory mistress. Until now.

"Do it," Holland said.

Gritting my teeth so tightly that I thought they might pop, I swerved left, gunned the gas, and tore ahead. The driver of a Porsche in the fast lane bleated his horn in protest. I deviated right, darted into the narrow space between a Jeep and a Miata, waited a nanosecond, then pitched in front of a cargo van. I snaked between a banged-up Volvo and a truck towing a boat and charged down the next exit ramp.

Near the end of the ramp, I risked a look over my shoulder. The Explorer didn't manage the exit maneuver. It barreled ahead on the freeway. Someone rolled down the passenger window. Something glinted. A gun?

"Duck," I yelled to Holland. She did.

No shot rang out. I looked again. Maybe the gleam had come from binoculars or a camera lens. Why would my pursuer take a photo? Did he want to know who Holland was? Did having her in the car with me double the risk factor?

I careened around a black Hyundai, swerved onto the exit ramp's shoulder, and hit the bottom of the ramp at full-speed. The truck bucked like a stallion. I veered right onto a parallel road.

"Pedestrian!" Holland shot her hands to the ceiling to brace herself.

I swerved to avoid a tattered man pushing a grocery cart.

Out of nowhere, a whirl of red lights flared in my rearview. Not the tail. A squad car. I didn't want to pull over; I didn't know whom I could trust. A patrolman could be the enemy. On the other hand, the guys in the squad car could simply be doing their job. I could talk myself out of any ticket. I hadn't received one in over ten years. I slowed and moved to the side, showing good intent. The police car sped past me with its siren blasting. I breathed easier. I wasn't its target. The area crawled with dope dealers.

I resumed speed. "Are you okay?"

"Nothing like a car chase to clear the head." Her lips were parted; her chest, heaving; her eyes, brilliant.

"Who are you?" I asked. She was so different from the girl I used to know. "What have you done with the wigged-out girl who hated when I drag raced?"

"What? C'mon." Nervous laughter spilled out of her. "Me?"

"Truth. You used to brace yourself against the glove compartment and scream at me to be careful."

She winked. "Didn't I mention that I've become an adrenaline junkie? I've got to tell you that was the most fun I've had since I jumped out of an airplane with my mother."

"You did what?"

"She came back to town eager to make up to me. We jumped in tandem with instructors." Her voice caught. "It was her last hurrah."

CHAPTER 10

I offered to drive Holland back to her car, but she resisted. After a long moment, she asked to come home with me. Not because she was afraid, and not because she was coming on to me—she wasn't. She said she didn't want to be alone. I could give her a lift to her car in the morning. I didn't argue.

When we entered, it was close to midnight. To my surprise, a box of my mother's things with a cryptic note from Barbie: *Like you asked* was sitting on the dining table beside my laptop and the term papers that needed attention.

Buddy, my four-year-old chocolate Labrador, woke from a deep slumber. Realizing we had company, he sprinted toward Holland. The brute had manners, but he rarely saw a woman other than my grandmother inside the place. He leaped up and placed his paws on Holland's chest.

"Down, Buddy," I yelled. He obeyed.

Holland knelt to scrub his ears. "Aw, hello, Buddy." She eyed me. "You always wanted a dog."

I'd always wanted a family, too.

Holland stood and surveyed the place. "Nice. You're tidier than you used to be."

The place was as white and sparse as the hostel—the Navy had changed me in that regard. All I owned was a sofa, an end table, an HD-TV, a dining table with two chairs, a set of bookshelves stuffed to the gills with thrillers and books about war, a couple pieces of office equipment, bedroom furniture, and some artwork.

"All yours?" she asked.

I nodded. "It's a duplex. I have a tenant upstairs." At least I had invested in something worthwhile since I'd started earning a professor's salary.

"What's in the box?"

"Some of my mom's things." I itched to peek inside but curbed the impulse. I tossed the Polaroid and my mother's locket beside it. Later. "Thirsty?"

Holland shook her head and yawned. "I need to sleep."

Though I was crazy with lust for her—the urge hadn't subsided a bit—I didn't make a move. It would have been wrong. Her mother dead; my mother dead. Both of us vulnerable. I let her have the bed; I took the couch.

Sleep eluded me. A few hours later, around four A.M., I gave up. I went to the dining table, woke up my laptop computer, and searched the Internet for LUTHER MARCUSSEN. The name didn't drum up any hits. I added a middle initial, starting with A. When I added the initial M, I landed upon a man named LUTHER M. MARCUSSEN. The photograph of Luther—a mug shot—matched the picture in my mother's locket. The article was dated thirty-seven years ago. At nineteen, Luther was arrested for vandalism and petty theft. He robbed the high school he formerly attended, making off with forty-five dollars and change, and he spray-painted the boys' gym. According to the article, Luther had no living family. At the age of eight, he had been assigned to a foster family and then another and another. The bland-looking foster parents who had housed Luther when he got a record claimed no responsibility; Luther had been uncontrollable from the moment they had taken him into their home. They wished to wash their hands of him. I was pretty sure Luther had granted that wish. Additional Internet searches provided no more information on Luther M. Marcussen. It was like he was a ghost.

I leaned back in the chair and thought of my last conversation with Barbie. She knew more than what she'd told me. I was sure of it. I would have to reconnect and convince her that I was ready to make plans for my mother's funeral, and then grill her.

Next, I worked up my courage and opened the box she'd left me of my mother's things. Barely anything was in it: an aging copy of *The Three Musketeers* held together with rubber bands, a lock of my baby hair taped to a weathered slip of paper, and a number of syrupy poems written in my mother's tilted scrawl. One poem was pinned to a blue garter: *Something stolen, something blue, sing tra la, away with you*. Not much of a poem. They never were. Why had she kept it? Why had Barbie? There was nothing else in the box. No datebook, no address book. Worthless.

I pushed the box aside, jotted down the list that I had memorized of the five patients around my father's age who had exited the hospital, and then returned to my laptop computer and searched the Internet looking for information on each of them. None was named Marcussen, but that didn't stop me.

On a social networking site, I found a picture of the first in the list alphabetically, Barnes. His arm was slung around a golden retriever. According to his profile, Barnes lived near the city. He looked nothing like the picture in my mother's locket. No strong cheekbones. No aristocratic nose.

I drew a line through Barnes's name and moved on to Hooperman. He was a little closer to my father in looks, but his age seemed off. He appeared too young.

Despite the late hour—I can be a louse at times—I called the guy's house and pretended to be someone from hospital administration. We were missing a final statistic, I said. Hooperman's son, who sounded as mad as a bear awakened from hibernation, was not accommodating. He ranted about the hospital's ethics and how the hospital had released his father too soon. His father needed hourly care. The guy was going to sue the hospital's sorry butt. During the rant I managed to learn his father's age: forty-eight. Not old enough to be my father. When he hung up on me, I was grateful.

I stood and stretched. As I did, doubt crept into my psyche. What if my mother had been hallucinating about seeing my father? What if the search for him was futile? Would finding him help me solve her murder?

A car backfired outside. I startled. Buddy reacted, too. I reached down and rubbed his ears. "It's cool, pal." He whimpered. Usually he was a solid sleeper. My unrest had become his.

Nerves frayed and brain fried, I crossed to the window. I peered through the crack in the drapes and stiffened. A dark sedan was parked on the opposite side of the street. Someone sat in the driver's seat, window closed, tinted glass and dim light making it impossible to see inside. Was the guy watching my house? Was it my mother's killer? If so, why not charge inside? Maybe the driver was a cop that Detective Philips had ordered to keep an eye on me.

I fetched a pair of binoculars and gazed into the gloom. The sedan's driver appeared to be asleep. I revised my thinking. Maybe the guy was a nobody, a neighbor's lover arriving for an early morning tryst after the hubby went to work.

To the right, I caught sight of an SUV approaching, slowly, as if scoping out the territory. Granted, its dimmed lights could be an oversight—not all headlights turned on automatically—but worry sparked inside me. I couldn't tell the make of the car. Suddenly, it stopped short, quickly made a U-turn, and retreated the way it came.

Suspicion reared up inside me. Did the SUV driver not want the sedan driver to see him? The more I stared at the retreating SUV, the more it resembled the Explorer that had pursued Holland and me on the freeway. Who was driving? Why had seeing the sedan spooked him? Was I imagining that?

The car disappeared around the corner.

Minutes later, when the SUV didn't reemerge, I forced myself to calm down. If I wasn't careful, I might fabricate hundreds of scenarios for every car, pedestrian, and rodent that passed by.

Too wound up to research the remaining three exit patients and do the search justice, I fetched a gilded cigar box of mementoes from the bookshelf. The items within were random treasures I had collected from beneath my mother's bed the day I was told she died. I remember sitting on the tattered couch, doing my best to understand what my grandmother was saying: *Fire. Gone. Forever*. Like a wild animal, I had scrounged beneath my mother's bed. I chafed my bare knees on the shag carpet. I heaved my breakfast of champions thanks to the rancid smell of cigarettes that clung to the roots of the carpet. I would never forget the guilt that had churned in my gut as I hid the cigar box under my denim jacket and raced out of the trailer.

I pushed aside the term papers and the carton of my mother's things that Barbie had left me, and I removed the contents of the cigar box: a set of Matchbox cars, a frayed copy of *When We Were Young* by A.A. Milne, an eight-track tape of Linda Ronstadt songs, a trashy romance novel with a bare-chested guy on the cover, and an unused syringe.

Running my finger along the edge of the box, I could still feel the shame I had felt when I left my grandmother earlier. She was right. I should be planning my mother's funeral and burying these items with her. *Rest in peace and all that crap.*

But I couldn't. My mother had come out of anonymity to see me. Why? To save my father? How did she know he was in danger, if indeed he was in danger? Who was he to her? What was the real story?

A snort burst from my nose. My mother had been back in my life for less than a day, and yet she had snared me again in her drama.

Buddy, who had left the comfort of my feet to lap some water, returned and sniveled. I nuzzled his chin, marveling that he knew whenever something was bothering his *human*. In four years, he had never missed a signal.

"Hey, your mouth isn't wet," I said, realizing he wasn't concerned with my pain; he was thirsty. I rose to refill his water bowl. Before entering the kitchen, I aligned the frames of artwork that I'd hung on the walls to remind me of my journey: the day the extremists' bomb went off, the day Reggie's brother bought the farm, the day my mother died the first time. Given my current emotional state, I considered pulling out my paints and slapping new rage onto a canvas but decided against it. I didn't have time. I had to get answers.

In the kitchen, I refreshed Buddy's bowl of water then made a pot of coffee. Brewing didn't take long. The first cup tasted bitter, old before its time. I drank it anyway, set the cup in the stainless sink, and rinsed it out.

With a raw feeling roiling in my stomach, I returned to the dining room and eyed the mementoes. I lifted the Polaroid of my mother and me singing at the concert. *Why, Mom…Sybil…Stevie*? Even in her last days, she had chosen secrecy. *Why contact me*?

Tears pressed the corners of my eyes. I flicked the photograph away like it was a two of clubs. The snapshot spiraled in the air and flipped photo-side down on the table. I noticed something handwritten on the back. A date. *Oct. '80.* Nothing original.

I tossed the photo into the carton and eyed the rubber band-bound *The Three Musketeers*. It seemed like an odd book for my mother to keep, given her inclination to read romance novels. I pulled it out and removed the rubber bands. The front and back cover fell off in my hands. I noticed more photographs, slotted between pages. One was of my mother and what I presumed was my father standing with two other people, a trim, pretty blonde and a goggle-eyed guy with raggedy brown hair. They all looked to be about twenty years old. Where had the photo been taken? I flipped the photo over. A date was written on it: *May.* Thirty-seven years ago. Was it the day my mother and father met?

Wondering whether my mother's pictorial history might give me a hint as to why she had come back into my life, I lowered myself into the chair, and with the dedication I had given to my graduate thesis, I withdrew the rest of the photos—three in all. I reviewed the backsides of each: dates, no names. I stared at the other guy in the photos. He looked familiar, but he wasn't the man who had taken the photograph of my mother and me at the Amphitheater. Too young, too thickset. Who were these people?

I drummed my fingers on the tabletop.

Buddy placed his head on my feet.

I whispered, "It's okay, fella." It wasn't. I was lying. He knew it; I knew it.

I shuffled through the photos again. In one, the foursome posed beside a pair of elegant columns. Were they at a party at a mansion? How would my mother have gotten into such a swank place? Not that she couldn't class it up if she wanted to, but she rarely wanted to. She preferred T-shirts, tattered jeans, and sandals.

Was the other woman the one that my mother mentioned at the trailer? Mom said, *I told her I saw…*

Saw what? Saw him? My father? *No, you're reaching.*

If I could identify the architecture in the photo, maybe I could track down the location and find out what the event was or who the woman was. Maybe I—

The floor creaked followed by a whoosh of air.

CHAPTER 11

I leaped to my feet and grabbed the baseball bat I kept in the corner of the dining room. I reeled back.

"Whoa!" Holland froze in the doorway leading to my bedroom, arms raised for protection.

I lowered the baseball bat and gaped. I had kept myself in check last night. But now? All my good intentions evaporated. She was wearing one of my button-down shirts and looked so sexy I ached. Long legs, long neck, flushed face, tousled hair. She hadn't changed much since high school. A few more wrinkles. I had double the lines she had.

Buddy growled.

"Back off, you dumb mutt. She's a friend." I reminded myself to back off, too. Holland and I had a messed-up history. I didn't need that in my life right now.

"What's with the bat?" Holland finger-combed her hair as she moved toward me.

"I'm just jumpy." I set the weapon aside, embarrassed for mistaking her for an intruder.

Holland eyed the heap of papers and items on the dining table. Instinctively, I hurried to them and tucked the list of exit patients' names beneath the cigar box. Real slick.

Holland didn't seem to notice my move. She swiveled and eyed the artwork on the walls near the kitchen. "A little angry, pal?"

In addition to my quasi-masterpieces, there were five other paintings. Most were raw and bleak. For some insane reason, I wanted to toss them in the garbage. I wanted Holland to think the best of me. I didn't want her to think I was crazy. "I teach art therapy to veterans at a hostel. They're not all mine."

"That implies some are. Let me guess which ones." She pointed to a painting that was primarily blue. "This one. It's about a ship overcome by ocean swales. It mirrors your inner demons."

"Good guess, but no." She might have known me well in high school, but she didn't know anything about me now. Yes, I had inner demons, but I never painted anything blue. Too cool. I preferred red and black. Heat and anger.

She swiveled and read from a bumper sticker that I had pasted above the doorway leading to the street. '"Make art, not war.' Clever."

Reggie, not my therapist, had given me the sticker as a reminder to defuse before leaving the privacy of my home. *Reggie*. What would she say about me bringing a girl home? Not just any girl. *Holland*. Reggie had never liked Holland in high school. Per Reggie, Holland had *issues*. Like everybody else, including Reggie and me, didn't?

"Fess up," Holland continued. "Which are yours?" She made a sweeping gesture with her left hand.

My gut clenched. A diamond ring glittered on her fourth finger. She hadn't been wearing the ring at the hospital last night. "You're married," I blurted.

Holland glimpsed the ring; her face flushed. "No, it's—" She ran her index over the gem. "It's my mother's. I'd tucked it in my pocket."

Man, I felt like a jerk. What should it matter to me whether she was married or not, and yet I felt like we weren't being truthful with each other. I hadn't told her what was really going on with me. I was pretty sure she was holding something back, too.

Holland moved closer. "Your jaw looks better." Her voice was husky. "Sort of yellowy-purple. Does it hurt?"

"Not much." Actually, it ached like heck. So did the rest of my head. But I could bear it. In high school, I used to joke that the word *tough*, not *the*, was my middle name.

She picked up the Milne book and fingered the cover, the move so intimate and intrusive that I had to work hard to keep from snatching it away. It wouldn't disintegrate, and what if it did? My memories wouldn't vanish along with it. Memories were in the mind; they weren't tangibles.

As if sensing my discomfort, Holland laid down the book. Then she slid up behind me. I didn't budge. She began to knead my shoulders. "You're tense."

To say the least. Desire was ripping through me at warp speed. "Don't." I spun around and grabbed her wrists.

She wrested free. Her eyes were pinpoints of fear. "Don't, yourself."

"Sorry. I didn't mean to frighten you." I extended my arms and backed up a step. "It's…yes, I'm tense. Seeing you again. I'm only human. If we'd met under different circumstances, I'd—"

She moved in and clasped my face with her hands. Boldly she planted her lips on my mouth. We kissed, her tongue searching mine. Heat seared my insides. My heart wrenched with desire.

After a long moment, Holland pulled away. She licked her teeth and exhaled. "I'm sorry." Her cheeks were flushed. "I'm not usually like this. Not any more. I don't come on strong, but"—she wrapped her arms around her body—"you…me…" She hitched a shoulder.

"It's okay. We've got history. I get it."

The heater in the duplex kicked on with a vengeance. Holland shuddered. She moved a safe distance from me and returned her attention to the items on the table. She drew a photograph toward her by the corner. "Who are these people?" She picked up a photo.

In a flash, I felt as protective of the photographs as I did of the Milne book. I seized the photo. "I don't know."

Holland stiffened.

So did I. Why wasn't I spilling everything to her? The truth? Because I didn't trust her. She wasn't the girl I used to know. She had changed.

An uneasy moment passed between us, then Holland nudged the eight-track tape and sang a cappella, à la Linda Ronstadt, "When wi-i-i-ll I be loved?" She offered a cocked-eyed smile. "Whatever you do, don't offer a critique."

"I wouldn't dare." I remembered when she played the second lead, Rizzo, in a high school production of *Grease*. She won the part because she could act, not because she could carry a tune. Some of the guys had laughed at her. I punched out one of the jerks behind the boys' bathroom.

Holland laughed. The tension between us melted away.

"Hungry?" I asked. "I don't have much in the fridge. I eat meals on campus, but I make a mean grilled cheese."

"I could eat." She followed me to the kitchen. "You've done well for yourself. Me? I lead a threadbare existence. I've got a lot of debts with Dad's hospital bills."

"Don't you mean your mother's?"

"Hers, too, now. Dad's been dead a few years."

"Sorry."

"Life's a bitch."

I entered the kitchen and pulled a loaf of bread and a packet of American cheese from the refrigerator. "Well, even living a threadbare existence," I said, "you dress like a class act."

"Actresses are like magicians. All smoke and mirrors. Feed me."

When I finished cooking the sandwiches, I returned to the dining room. Holland and I ate in quiet, the only sound the water dripping from the faucet in the kitchen.

"By the way, you're a darned good driver"—Holland set aside half of her sandwich and wiped her mouth with a napkin—"for a history professor. Once a drag racer, always a drag racer." She arched an eyebrow. "What happened to your dreams of becoming a professional snowboarder, polar explorer, or punk rocker?"

"Drummed out in the Navy."

"Did you meet a lot of girls on the high seas?"

"There was only one for me. Ever. You set the standard."

She blushed.

I polished off my sandwich. "I thought you would have gotten married and had three kids. I hoped when we met again that you'd be as fat as a cow."

"Life isn't always fair, is it?" She laughed, the sound rippling out of her like wind chimes on a breezy day.

I laughed along with her, and for the first time in a long time, I felt comfortable in my own skin.

"What're these?" Holland lifted one of the term reports I had pushed aside. I didn't mind that she touched them. They weren't as personal as my mother's things. She read, "*Number one*: In less than two hundred and fifty words, explain the position of the US Government during the Cuban Missile Crisis. *Number two*: Present three facts that would exonerate President George W. Bush from being deemed a liar." She peered over the upper rim of the paper. "I'm sensing a definite leaning to the left on your part."

"The dean of students would agree with you."

She twirled a finger in my direction. "By that look on your face, I'm presuming you're in trouble with the powers that be."

"Let's just say that he considers me a muckraker and has given me one last chance to toe the line or else."

"Or else what?"

"I'll be on indefinite leave."

"Why is he after you?"

Better question: why was someone as uptight as him in charge of a liberal college?

I sighed. "I happen to encourage my students to attend peace rallies and chant, 'War sucks.'"

She eyed the paper again. "Get a lot of moans and groans for this one? '*Number three:* Name an advantage American forces had over the British in the Revolutionary War.'"

"The art of historical thinking doesn't come naturally to students nowadays," I argued. "If I ask them to contextualize the information, it helps them understand the reason behind the decision. Did you know that only twenty-two percent of graduating high school seniors know that our US troops were up against Chinese forces in the Korean Wars?"

"Big deal."

"If I recall, you used to love history."

"Still do. I've got a lot of it myself."

"Did you wind up going to college?"

"Much to my father's chagrin, I went for a year then skipped out to become a star. Want to see my website?" She rose from the chair and scoured the area. "Where did I leave my purse?"

"Over there." I crossed to the sofa and picked up her knitted satchel. By the wrong end. The contents spilled onto the cushions. "Shoot, sorry."

Holland raced to scoop up the fallen items. I tried to help by grabbing her cell phone. As I did, the phone pinged. She was receiving a text. She snatched the phone from my hand. "Don't."

"Don't what? Read the text?"

She forced a smile.

"Is it a message from a boyfriend? Your husband?"

"I told you, I'm not…Are you jealous?" There was a tinge of teasing, not annoyance, in her tone. "It's from my director." She dumped the phone into her purse, her actions as clumsily covert as mine had been earlier with the list of exit patients' names.

The niggling of mistrust that I felt returned.

"Don't look at me like that," she said.

"Like what?"

Her mouth curled up on one side. "You're so suspicious you should work for the government."

I smirked. Two could play this game. "Maybe I do."

Holland jutted a hip. The shirt rose up her thigh.

I swallowed hard. "Texting someone at dawn is a little, you know, in your face."

"That's him. Controlling. All directors are." She slung the strap of the satchel over her shoulder and glanced at the items on the table again. "What's this?" She drew the exit patients' list from beneath the cigar box, revealing that she had, indeed, seen my less-than-slick move.

I seized the paper and pocketed it.

Holland held up her hands in a gesture of peace. "My bad. First, I go ballistic on you, and then I invade your space. Everybody's got secrets. I get it. It's cool."

"Show me your website."

She glanced at her watch. "Another time. I should go."

"I'll grab my keys."

"No need. I called a cab."

When had she done so? She must have used the landline in the bedroom. Had she expected us to argue?

She hurried to the window and peeked out. "It's here. I'd better get dressed."

The fact that she was in a rush to leave stung, but at least that explained why a strange car had been trolling at less than five miles-per-hour through the neighborhood. Or did it?

"Thanks for everything," she said.

Her icy tone caught me off guard. I felt like I was trapped in the middle of a hurricane. The eye was calm, but wind was blustering around me. What had just happened? What had I done wrong?

I exhaled. "Are you mad at me?"

"No, of course not." But her eyes told me otherwise. Was she still upset that I went for her purse? Or was she upset that I'd tried to read the text or that I'd grabbed my things back like a child who wouldn't share his toys? "I've simply got to get going. I need to tend to my mother's funeral plans, not to mention that I have a full afternoon of rehearsal." She aimed a finger at me. "Don't tell me. I know. The two don't jibe."

Her words jolted me back to my own dilemma. I had obligations as complex as hers.

Holland strode to the bedroom. She paused at the doorway, her back to me, and brushed the jamb with her hand. Her back muscles shuddered as if she wanted to turn around and say something more. But she didn't.

CHAPTER 12

I was out of sorts after Holland left. I knew I should go to the police station, as promised, but I couldn't bring myself to do so. What if Detective Philips wouldn't allow me to leave? What if, right this very minute, he and his crew were amassing a case against me, including my fingerprints, my DNA, and the history of my bitter youth, which included a few encounters with the police? What if my affection for liberal sit-ins figured into the equation? I needed all the data I could drum up to prove my innocence, not to mention that I wasn't quite ready to tell Philips about the search for my father. Withholding evidence wouldn't earn me points in the trust department.

Instead, to the best of my ability, I drew a sketch of the man who killed my mother. The least I could do was send a fax to Detective Philips.

Yes, I have a fax machine. All of the professors at Weyford are required to utilize the most ancient of transmission devices. I set the drawing on my four-in-one-copier. I withdrew Philips's business card, typed in the precinct number, and then pressed Send. The fax didn't transmit. I checked connections. Everything looked right. The problem wasn't at my end. I tried again. Still no go. I folded the sketch and set it next to my car keys. I would hand it over in person after—*if*—I located my father. *Tick tock*.

Before leaving the duplex, I took a quick shower. Letting the water cascade over me, I rehashed the last few minutes with Holland. I wished I'd asked for her telephone number.

After drying off and slipping into a pair of chinos and a crisp white shirt—not quite as upscale as my professorial attire but presentable—I glanced at the list of exit patients' names. I'd cross off Barnes and Hooperman.

Levine was third.

The hour now being reasonable, I called him and tried a different tactic—the truth. I mentioned my mother was in the hospital at the same time he was. I didn't say she died. I told him she remembered seeing a man named Luther Marcussen. It was important I get in touch with him. Levine, who sounded raspy, admitted to knowing my mother—*Stevie,* he called her. However, he refused to talk to me further on the phone and invited me over for coffee. Recalling the guy's diagnosis—he was in bad shape; he'd suffered a heart attack—I agreed. If he was a marksman and wanted to shoot me, I could be in trouble, but I could probably take him in an arm-wrestle.

A half hour later, I pulled up to Levine's home, which was a sun-bathed ranch house with a newly shingled roof and yellow pansies planted in the yard. No Christmas décor. Levine was typically a Jewish name. If this was my father, did he know there were people after him?

I parked by the curb and forced myself to breathe slowly. One answer at a time.

A bluestone path led to the porch. I climbed the single stair and paused. Symphonic music was playing inside. Someone was humming along. I rang the doorbell. When it didn't chime, I rapped on the door. Within seconds, I heard footsteps on hardwood floors. The person inside halted; an eyeball filled the peephole of the door.

"Day?" the man on the other side of the door asked.

"Yes, sir."

Levine opened the door. He was a large man with dark hair and a prominent nose, and he wore thick tortoise shell glasses. Not my father by a long shot, unless he'd had facial surgery. He still had a hospital ID bracelet on his wrist. He welcomed me and guided me into his kitchen, walking like a man who had been advised to keep moving even if it hurt to do so.

"Sit down, son," Levine said. "Hungry?"

"No, sir."

"I am. Do you mind?" He didn't wait for a reply. He made laborious trips between his Subzero refrigerator and the counter while he told me about himself—widowed, retired psychologist, with three kids all living in

California. He prepared a sandwich of liver pate, tomatoes, and onions on rye, and set the sandwich on a white plate. Afterward, he crossed to a coffee pot. He poured himself a cup and held up the pot as an offering.

The thought of putting acid into my edgy stomach made me wince. "No, thanks."

"Good choice," Levine said. "I make lousy coffee. The wife, she could make great coffee. You married?"

"No, sir."

"Milk, soda, water?"

I shook my head. I wanted answers and then a stiff drink and twenty-four hours of uninterrupted sleep. "Sir—"

"Sit, please." Levine settled into a chair at the table and eyed the chair opposite him.

I obeyed and worked hard to keep my foot from drilling the floor. *Cut to the heart. Get answers. Get out. Tick tock.* "You said you knew my mother."

Levine took a bite of his sandwich, wiped his mouth with a napkin, and pushed the plate away. All very civil and too danged slow. He wanted company. I had been elected. Swell. "Your mother was a lovely woman. I saw her every day. She would come into my room and read to me."

One positive memory I kept of my mother, beside her love of music, was her appreciation of books. At least once a week, until the day she abandoned me, she had read to me. I could still remember the way she would change her voice to match the character.

"You like to read, son?"

"I do. Harlan Coben, Lee Child."

"I like that character in Dan Silva's books, Gabriel Allon."

"So do I." Allon is an undercover spy who is also an art restorer. I wondered what it would be like to live that kind of life.

Levine took another bite of his sandwich and swallowed. "Your mother read to me to beat the withdrawal."

"She was in withdrawal?"

"Four months and counting. She was in the hospital for a staph infection. Not pretty. Others on the floor shooed her away. She was a chatterbox. I could tell she needed to keep busy." He tapped the corner of his eye.

My heart wrenched as some desperate part of me wanted to believe, in the end, my mother had turned her life around, but if that were the case, why hadn't she contacted me sooner? Had she tried to beat addiction and failed repeatedly, year after year?

"She often spoke about a book," Levine went on.

"What book?"

"I don't know, but it seemed very important to her. It seemed that if she found this book, she believed she'd be safe."

"From…"

"Not sure." He paused then looked off in the distance. "'A book we took, by hook or crook.'"

"What's that?"

"A little poem she recited whenever she spoke of the book. Drugs can warp reality." Was his comment based on experience? A psychologist probably had a lot of drug-addicted patients. Levine reached for a pack of cigarettes then seemed to think better of the idea and shoved the pack aside; it fell to the floor. I reached for it. "Leave it. So tell me, why are you here? Not simply to chat with an old codger, I suppose."

I opened the locket and showed him the picture of my father. "Did you meet this man at the hospital?"

"No. Who is he?"

"My father."

"Ah, your mother mentioned him. She called him the Skipper. Was he a sailor?"

"I don't know."

"I only say that because of the *Gilligan's Island* reference. Skipper. You ever see *Gilligan's Island*?"

I hadn't watched any comedies growing up, not even reruns of classics. I had played a ton of video games. Still did, on occasion. "I was wondering if my mother might have run into him at the hospital."

"Hmm." Levine rested his elbows on the table and folded his hands.

"One time, when I was walking the hall, I saw your mother hovering over the bed of a pasty-looking guy. I think he was in a coma or something. Your mother was whispering in his ear." He pointed at the locket. "It might have been him."

My pulse kicked up a notch. "Did you get a name or see the placard on his door?"

"No." Levine frowned. "I'm sorry, but I think he died."

Something knotted in the pit of my stomach. Was my search at an end? We talked for a few more minutes, but I learned nothing more.

Not until I was speeding along the highway, did I reflect on what Levine had said about my mother obsessing over a book. Why would a book make her safe? *A book we took, by hook or crook*. What the heck did that mean? Then I recalled the bad poetry she had pinned to the garter: *Something stolen; something blue*. That wasn't the typical phrase. It went: *Something* borrowed*; something blue*. Was the book she had told Levine about stolen? Was she trying to tell him that she and someone else—my father or the woman she feared—stole a book? What kind of book? *Something stolen; something blue*. Was the book blue? What could possibly be in the book that could keep her safe? A NOC list? A secret code? I could conjure up conspiracy theories with the best of them. Was the book a rare volume that could draw a hefty price? Or was it another type of blue book, say a Kelly Blue Book, signifying a car?

CHAPTER 13

If my father died, as Levine believed, I could stop searching, but in my gut, I felt the good doctor was mistaken. My father was alive. My mother had seen him. Why else would she have called me? I contacted the fourth exit patient, a man named Nolte. When I contacted him by phone, he sounded the right age. Buying my explanation that I was looking for a college classmate of my father's, Nolte invited me over.

He turned out to be a crusty coot with a foul mouth, a penchant for recreating war scenes with toy soldiers, and a limited memory. When he asked who I was, I explained again while peering into his eyes for some sign of recognition. We looked nothing alike. His eyes were brown, mine were blue. He had gray thinning hair and looked about five-foot-six. I imagined my father was taller, stronger. Didn't all little orphan boys imagine their fathers were heroes? When I finally asked Nolte about my mother, he cursed and said he didn't know who Sybil Day was and didn't know any guy named Luther Marcussen, either. He ordered me to leave. I couldn't flee fast enough.

Before I tracked down the fifth and final exit patient, Dalton, I needed to see Kimo. I wanted a sounding board. I craved perspective. About my mother, my father, and Holland.

Chest tight, breathing strained, I strode into the fitness center at Weyford University. It didn't smell of sweat and testosterone. It reeked of sanitizer wipes, a smell I despised. One of the guys I had served with had been addicted to the things. I wasn't sure where the sailor got his stash of wipes, but he was definitely OCD.

Trying to block the odor from my nostrils, I headed toward the rear of the facility. Dozens of lunch-hour exercise fiends flexed near the bank of mirrors at the rear. Kimo, bigger than all of them, was bench-pressing.

"Well, well." He set his barbell in its bracket, sat up, and wiped down his thick neck with a towel. "Look what the cat dragged in. You look like crap."

"Kimo—"

"Reggie's mad at you. Is your cell phone turned off? She called me at midnight. I was hoping she might have been ringing me for a booty call. She wasn't." He winked. "Hope springs eternal."

"Kimo—"

"Hold it. Me, first. Reggie was upset because you left without setting up a holiday schedule for the guys. I told her I'd track you down today, and here you are."

"My mother," I blurted out before he could continue. "She's dead."

"I know."

"No, you don't understand. She was alive. After I left the hostel, she called me."

Kimo's jaw fell open. "Are you kidding me?"

"She asked me to meet her at the trailer where I grew up. When I got there, I found her on the floor. Dying. Some guy—a dude with a bad ear—shot her. He and I—" I gestured to take the conversation outside.

Kimo slung his towel over a bar, grabbed his warm-up jacket, and led the way. We crossed a grassy expanse known as The Green where students were throwing Frisbees or eating lunch or lying on towels and drinking in what little December sun leaked through the clouds, and I filled him in on the past twenty-four hours.

"That sucks, bro. To find her and lose her all over again. On the other side, you've got a father."

"He might be dead." I told him what Levine said.

"Oh, man, when God closes a door, he opens an elevator shaft. Bummer."

Bummer didn't half cover it.

We neared Chess Square where a group of professors and students sat hunched at wooden tables equipped with chessboards and timers.

Kimo halted. "That's not everything, is it?" I could never put one over on him. Twice a week, we strolled the campus. Sometimes we discussed the weirdness of war that pinballed inside our heads. Sometimes we simply hung out. "You didn't track me down just to tell me about your mom and pop."

"I saw Holland."

"Tate?"

"At the hospital. Her mother died, too."

Kimo cut the air with the edge of his hand. "You've got to promise me you'll steer clear. She's bad news. She screwed you over in high school. She—"

"Hey, Professor Day. Have a minute?" A bevy of young women in tight jeans and tank tops sauntered toward us. The weather never dictated their fashion sense. The one that called my name, a pretty girl who was full of vibrant youth, said, "I'm totally not getting what you want in our essays. I mean, how are we supposed to compare the differences between the onset of World War I and World War II?" She adjusted the stack of books she was carrying. "I set up a student-teacher conference for tomorrow. Hope that's okay."

"C'mon." A friend of hers pulled on the girl's arm.

"Give me a sec," she hissed and turned back to me. Big smile. "Hey, we're heading to the mausoleum for the Kwanzaa party. Want to join us? You don't have to be from Africa to party." The mausoleum, located at the entry to the university, housed the remains of Weyford's founding father. She twirled a hand. "Let the revelry begin."

I shook my head.

"You're missing out."

As her friend pulled her away, I spotted a dark car idling on the road at the far end of The Green. It wasn't a sedan; it reminded me of the SUV that had trolled the neighborhood. Something reflective, like the glass of a binocular lens, flared from the driver's side. I shielded my eyes from the sun and peered hard at the car. The sun's blaze made it impossible for me to make out the SUV's driver.

"Back to Holland," Kimo said.

I was certain the driver was watching me and not the co-eds.

"Bro, are you listening to me?"

The SUV started moving. Warning signals went off in my brain.

I spun to face Kimo. "I can't talk right now."

"You came to me—"

"I've got to go." I had to get to exit patient five. *And if that's a dead end*? a voice rang out in my mind. I would deal with it then. Not now. "Can you cover my conferences tomorrow?"

"If you slip up, the dean will have your head." Kimo pointed. "Speak of the devil."

"Day." Dean Hyde chugged toward us. What was he doing on campus on a Sunday? "A word." The front edges of the pintsized man's blazer flapped in the wind. So did his toupee. He reminded me of the mayor of Munchkin land. All he needed was a band of Lollipop Kid hooligans.

I steered Kimo toward the gym.

"Bro, you do not want to piss him off," Kimo warned.

I glanced over my shoulder. The SUV was moving forward. Straight at us. I made out the model, a Chevy Tahoe.

Kimo followed my gaze. "Is someone after you?"

"Not sure."

"Who's driving?"

"Either the guy who killed my mom or the cops."

"Or you're paranoid."

"Kurt Cobain said, 'Just because you're paranoid doesn't mean they're not after you.'"

"Professor Day, stop!" the dean yelled. "We need to have a serious chat."

The SUV spun out on some grass. Tires squealed. Students screamed. The dean whirled to face the oncoming car. It barreled past him. Right at me. I sprinted ahead.

Keeping pace, Kimo said, "How can I help?"

"Pacify the dean for me."

"Done. Anything else?"

I rummaged in my pocket and pulled out the drawing of my mother's killer that I had made earlier. I shoved it at Kimo. "Take this to the police. They wanted me to sit down with their sketch artist."

"I'll do you one better. I'll take it to Lancelot first." Lancelot, a high school buddy, was a video game creator. "He's into that animation stuff, you know, filming humans and making them into cartoons. I'll bet he can ID this guy using some special program."

"You're on."

"Remember, you're not invincible."

Near the tall hedge bordering the gym, I said, "Go left." I darted right.

"You suck as a friend," Kimo yelled.

"I know."

Over my shoulder, I saw the Chevy Tahoe lurch forward. Chess players scrambled to clear. Tables toppled. I cut through a break in the hedge, tore to the parking lot, and bleeped to unlock my truck. I grabbed the handle; the door stuck. I cursed my lifelong inattention to vehicle maintenance and bashed the door with my shoulder. The latch gave. I jumped inside, ground the key into the ignition, and gunned the car in reverse.

Just as the SUV broke through the bramble, I cranked the gear into forward.

CHAPTER 14

I tore away from the university and headed south through a tidy neighborhood. Later in the day, the street would be filled with children. I prayed no kid was home sick and about to charge in front of me. I wouldn't be able to stop.

Veering right at Portola Road, I sped ahead. A mile further at the Y, I bore left onto La Honda Road out of habit—*out of habit* because after Barbie got clean and sober, she would take me hiking in Wunderlich County Park. On one ambitious outing, she and I hiked to the edge of Skyline Boulevard, a ten-mile round trip. Barbie shot three rolls of film that day. The memory of her photography blitz propelled me back to the Polaroids that my mother had kept. How did those people know each other? When had they met? Why had my mother kept the photos hidden in *The Three Musketeers*? What was the book my father had stolen, if, indeed, he had stolen anything? Was he in danger because he had done so?

Save your father.

A flash of chrome in the rearview mirror jolted me back to the present. The Chevy Tahoe was on my tail and drawing near.

My adrenaline spiked; I pressed on the accelerator, but only for a short span. Seconds later, the road became a series of winding switchback turns. Steep wooded terrain bordered each side. Until I reached the rustic town of Skylonda, there were only a few neighborhood streets that cut in. Each had a sharp entrance. Each was a cul-de-sac.

I glanced in the rearview mirror. Who was this guy? Why was he following me?

I took the first S-turn tight, slowing at first then accelerating at the apex. The Chevy Tahoe did the same. I headed into the next turn faster, hoping I wouldn't fishtail, or worse, fly over the ridge. The SUV mimicked my moves. For a number of turns, we attacked the terrain in synchronized rhythm. At the sixth switchback, I got the feeling the Chevy's driver wasn't out to hurt me, only follow me. Was he a cop, hoping to bring me in? If so, why dog me?

The guy attempted to pass me on the left, a supremely stupid maneuver. Why in the heck would he risk life and limb? Amateur. He pulled alongside, and I caught a flash of him. Late teens, early twenties. Sunglasses, baseball cap, red curly sideburns. Hefty, almost toadlike. Not the guy that had tailed Holland and me last night. Not a cop.

The kid hitched his head as if signaling me to pull over. Not a chance.

A horn blared.

A Ford Super Duty 450, twice the size of my truck, was bearing down, nose first, on the Chevy Tahoe. The kid braked hard and slipped behind me. The truck sped past, and a mammoth gust of wind belted my truck. I fought against the gale.

Seconds later, the kid pulled alongside again.

At the same time, a car with a camper appeared. The kid didn't have time to back off and didn't have time to beat out the car with camper to the front of my truck. I cursed. Preparing for a collision, I tightened my hold on the steering wheel.

The Chevy Tahoe slewed right and slammed into my truck. I tried to hug the road but couldn't. My right tires skidded across hardscrabble rock. I jammed the brakes. Bad decision. The rear of the truck spun out. The car with camper clipped my left bumper. My truck, as if propelled by a slingshot, leaped farther off the road and headed nose-first down a ravine.

The truck bucked over bramble and stumps. I clenched the steering wheel. My torso batted the seatback. I avoided hitting a eucalyptus and a redwood tree, but I couldn't avoid the black oak. At the last second, I swerved and smashed into the massive tree sidelong. The engine sputtered and died. My head snapped forward and back. The strap of the seat belt held fast, pinning me to the seat. Searing pain shot down my spine. I tried to undo the seat belt; it wouldn't give. I clicked again and again. Finally, it released. I sat still as I ran myself through a number of tests. Fingers worked. Toes worked. I turned my ankles right and left. My muscles would ache, but I had no serious damage. I could move without going into a total body spasm. The wound on my arm hadn't opened up, either. Lucky me.

I peeked through the rear window. The Chevy Tahoe hadn't taken the plunge, but that didn't mean the kid wasn't following me on foot. If I were on the hunt, I would.

I shoved open the door and lurched out of the truck. My feet slipped on slimy foliage. My ankle twisted. A riddle of pain shot up my leg to my head. I ignored the jolt, regained my footing, and rather than going downhill—the easier route—I started climbing through tall shrubs of coyote brush and elderberry. I figured the kid wouldn't think that I'd go upward. Would he stop and get out or try to hunt for me while driving? What did he want?

Near a eucalyptus, I paused. I heard the skittering of creatures in the trees, the whoosh of traffic from the roadway, and the honk of a horn miles away. And then I heard something else—something human. Grousing. Thwacking bushes. At least three hundred yards to my left, off the path. Was it the kid? Had to be.

I hid behind a tree, steadied my breathing, and waited. In the Navy, during drills, we had learned to stay still and preserve our energy. Being invisible for hours was better than dying.

Soon the kid was moving down the hill, away from me, spewing curse words with every step. So much for stealth. When I was certain he was well below me, I dared to move again. Soft footfalls. Mindful not to step on dried leaves. The climb was tedious. When I reached La Honda Road, I stretched to loosen the kinks of tension in my neck, back, and legs.

The rumble of a mob of motorcycles yanked me to hyper-alert status. I swung around and, while smoothing my hair and trying to look normal, I grinned easily toward a pack of guys and women on Harleys. Most were donning helmets while revving their engines. None were paying attention to me.

Trying not to hobble, I moved toward the tiny town. Short of the gas station, I saw an alternate opportunity for escape. A black Cannondale mountain bike leaned against the exterior bathroom door. No chain. No lock. Indecision cut through me. I hadn't stolen anything since I was a teen.

Promising myself I would return the Cannondale the moment I could, I wheeled the bicycle to the road. I slung a leg over the bar, lodged my feet on the pedals, and tore south on Skyline Boulevard. The road traversed the crest of the mountains. My twisted ankle twinged, but except for the restriction I felt being dressed in khaki trousers, biking was a lot easier and faster than walking.

Wind slapped my face and sunshine bore down on me. Over the years, Barbie had warned me about the dangers of sun exposure and riding without a helmet. Too late for that. Would she let me borrow her car? Would she even speak to me after the way I had treated her yesterday? Her daughter had died for a second time, and I had acted like a jerk. How could I explain the things running through my head? Finding my mother in the trailer had cut me to the core. But now she was dead. For real. I couldn't bring her back. My father, on the other hand, might be alive. If I was interpreting my mother's last words correctly, I had to save him. When I found him, how would he react? He didn't know about me. Would he want to?

CHAPTER 15

While biking, I pulled out my cell phone. I know: *Don't text and ride.* Screw the rules. Besides, I wasn't texting, I was calling. I dialed my grandmother. She didn't answer. Neither did anyone at her office. I tried Kimo. Same deal. As I pedaled down Page Mill Road, I thought of another option. Holland said she had rehearsal this afternoon. Would she be at the Hole Theater yet?

Ten minutes later, I arrived there. Sunlight slashed through the towering trees. I blinked to counteract the strobe effect as I steered the mountain bike into the parking lot. The theater's sign was unlit and bare except for vowels indicating a change of program was in the works. A fake deer, studded with Christmas lights, stood with its nose near the sparse grass. A pair of trellises, each entwined with star jasmine, flanked the entry.

I headed toward the rear of the parking lot where trashcans, furniture, costumes, and garbage crowded the area. Back stage theater doors were propped open with bricks. A couple of cars beyond the opened doors were packed in like sardines. Which car was Holland's? The VW Beetle blocked by the yellow Camaro, I figured. She had always liked small cars. Or maybe hers was the water-spotted Prius. Was she still an eco freak? I recalled the time she had marched with a picket in her hand because the high school wouldn't stop overwatering the football field. Neither the Beetle nor the Prius would be proficient in a car chase, but I hoped I wouldn't be pursued again. I wanted to get back on track and interview the last exit patient.

I climbed off the bike, my legs heavy from exertion. My first step sent a shot of pain through my ankle and up my calf. In the dim light, I pulled up the trouser leg and inspected the injury. Not bad. At least my ankle hadn't swelled to the size of an elephant's. I set the bike alongside a pair of bikes that were leaning against the dumpster and paused again. Not from pain. To reassess my intent. Why was I turning to Holland? Because I required wheels and because, as I rode in the direction of Los Altos, I had rationalized the brilliant, albeit crazy, idea that I wanted someone else's opinion—okay, *her* opinion—about what just happened. Why did a maniac chase me and run me off the road?

Gathering my courage, I headed inside. The theater was dark. The seats were empty. A ladder stood in the aisle. A dim light lit the modest stage. I remembered seeing a play a year ago, involving a human boy born to bat parents; the play was *out there* but earned good reviews.

"Help you?" a woman in black asked. She descended the ladder while carrying a huge arc light under her arm.

"I'm looking for Holland."

"She's in the dressing room." The woman pointed to a door. "Rehearsal starts in thirty."

I thanked her and picked up my pace. I had felt a loss when Holland left this morning. No, it was more than a loss. It was a gut-wrenching ache. I knew the feeling was ridiculous, with all that was going on in my life, but I was falling for her. Again. Now I was excited to see her. I took two wrong turns before I found the women's dressing room.

It was a cramped space filled with racks of clothing and six folding chairs. *Break a leg* note cards were tucked into the ceiling-high mirror. A lit vanilla candle stood on the counter, its tip wavering from the blasts of heat being piped through the vents. A cell phone sat beside the candle. Her knit satchel and black leather tote rested on a chair.

A toilet flushed. A door opened. Holland stepped out and sucked in a breath. All she had on was a black bra and panties. "Don't you look preppy," she said, her eyes flat, distant, no humor.

Was she mad that I'd shown up? Was I crafty enough to convince her to lend me, a virtual stranger after all these years, her car? Maybe memories of our past would sway her; perhaps they would foil my plan.

She strode to the counter by the mirror and flipped over a piece of paper. Something about the move set off alarm sensors in my brain. Most women would have grabbed a robe to cover up. Who was she? She was so different from what I remembered. Back in high school, she was shy. Even in the dark when we groped each other with abandon, she always wore something—a shirt, a chemise, or tank top. Now she was worldly. I thought again of the rumor that she had become a narc. Was it possible that she was a police plant sent to keep an eye on me?

"What's that?" I asked.

"What?"

"The paper you turned over."

She gestured like a TV model. "Take a look."

I resisted the urge. I wanted to trust her. I needed to. "Tell me instead." Sure, she might lie to my face, but I was pretty sure I would be able to tell.

"It's my mother's death certificate, stupid. I'm burying her tomorrow. You should do the same for yours." Her eyes grew moist. Her shoulders shuddered ever so slightly.

A pang of guilt cut through me. How insensitive could I be?

Holland grabbed a black T-shirt and pair of black jeans off a hanger and slithered into them. When she was fully clothed, her face grew soft, her gaze warm. "What's up? Why are you here?"

I jammed my hands into my pockets. Truth or dare, now or never. Trust. It had to start someplace. I'd blown the chance back in high school.

Quickly I recounted the day: the list of exit patients I had contacted, my meeting with Kimo, and the drag race with the hefty kid that had pursued me up La Honda. Holland's eyes widened. Her jaw drew tense and the muscles in her neck pulsed.

I finished the story, and she crossed to the costume rack. Without saying a word, she fiddled with cuffs and collars of 1940's style clothing. She glanced over her shoulder once, eyeing me with suspicion. When she looked at me a second time, her chin was trembling, as if she were trying to hold her emotions in check. What was going on? Was she questioning whether or not she wanted to get involved with me? Maybe she thought I was a magnet for danger. I wished I could convince her that I lived a normal life. Usually.

"I need to borrow your car," I said. "I've got to contact the last exit patient."

"You should go to the police. Let them investigate."

"They suspect me."

"You don't know that."

"I don't have time to explain, but my gut instinct is that a cop was driving the car that followed us from the hospital, and a cop was in the parked sedan outside my duplex, too."

"A sedan was parked—"

"I think another cop was trolling the neighborhood," I went on, "and I would bet, dimes to dollars that the hefty kid who chased me up La Honda Road is a rookie cop. Of course, I could be wrong about one or all. Any could've been the person or persons out to get my father, hoping I'll lead the way. No matter what, that's my next step. I've got to find my father."

"And save him from people you believe might be after him." She looked skeptical. "People you can't identify."

"Maybe I can. My mom showed up at the trailer with a photograph. She kept others. They were in the box my grandmother gave me. I think the people in them matter. I know a guy who can run a digital program and age the people in the photographs. It's a start."

Holland jutted a hip. Her mouth curved up on one side. "You think you're pretty smart, don't you, professor?"

"Some days. May I borrow your car?"

She hesitated.

"If I find my father, I'll get answers. Answers that I can take to the police. Answers"—I swallowed hard—"that I've wanted to know for too many years to count."

"If I let you borrow my car, will you at least report the guy who chased you? Give the police a description of him and his car. Did you get a license plate number?"

"I caught a glimpse of the bumper sticker: *My kid's a genius*."

"That narrows your choices to, what, two million?"

"I'll need someone to move the Camaro that's behind the Beetle."

Holland smirked. "Chauvinist. I don't drive a Bug." She reached in her tote and withdrew a set of keys with a rabbit's foot attached. I spotted a Chevy key in the mix.

"The Camaro is yours?" I gaped. "You hate muscle cars. That was one of the reasons you walked away from—"

"Wrong. I didn't walk. You walked because I screwed around."

"Because I went drag racing."

"Let the past stay in the past." She wrapped her left arm around her body. Her right hand rose to cover her heart, as if protecting it. From me. "As for the car, my brothers converted me." All three were younger. One was a real pain, always stealing into Holland's room at inopportune moments. "It looks like crap, but it runs well. I tune it myself."

"You're a woman of many talents."

She dangled the keys in front of my face. "Contact the police."

"I will." Right after I visited the final exit patient. "Promise." I held up three fingers as a pledge. I was never a Boy Scout. I didn't worry that I was breaking some hallowed code.

Holland snapped the keys back and folded them into her palm. Her gaze turned flinty. "I don't believe you."

"C'mon. I said I will, and my word is my bond. May I please have the keys?"

"Holland, stage now!" a man's voice bellowed through a crackly loudspeaker.

"Yes, your holiness." Holland slid her feet into a pair of ballet slippers then moved to me. She placed the keys in my hand and inched closer, her lips parted. I felt a stirring stronger than anything I could remember. I wanted to grab her, throw her onto the makeup table, and take her hard and fast. But if I learned anything on my way to becoming an officer, it was how to be a gentleman. Not to mention, I had a job to do. I leaned forward to kiss her.

"Hey, Holland," a weathered, stout woman said from the doorway. "Practicing the love scene with a stand-in?"

Holland pushed me away and chuckled low. Her full lips curled up; impishness danced in her eyes. "Chase, this is our stage manager."

The woman gave me a curt nod. "Much more handsome than our leading man. He's a butcher who thinks he has talent. Ha! He butchers the lines." She eyed me. "Do you act?"

"No."

"Our loss." The woman hitched her head. "Let's go, leading lady. Richard's on the warpath, if you can't tell." She exited the room.

At the same instant, Holland's cell phone chimed. Even though she'd jumped on me for snooping the last time, I glanced at the phone. I caught a glimpse of the text that popped up: Need you now.

"Your director?" I asked.

Holland scooped up the phone. For some reason, she looked scared, wary. What kind of dictator was this guy? Holland wasn't getting paid. Why not walk away? She turned away from me to tap in a response, and suspicion cut through me. Was the person texting her really her director? I wished I could take her in my arms. Calm her fears. Calm my own.

She slid the cell phone into her pocket, spun around, and offered me a rueful look. "Gotta run."

"Maybe when I've found my father and the danger is past"—I waved my hand—"we could go on a date." The words sounded archaic. When was the last time I'd asked anyone out? Six months? A year? I was taking bachelorhood to a whole new level.

"Sure. Call me." She spouted off her cell phone number.

"You can call me, too." I pulled a business card from my wallet.

Holland pocketed it and ran out of the room.

Left alone, I eyed the paper lying upside down on the counter. Was it really a death certificate?

I resisted the urge to turn over the document and exited. I desperately wanted to trust Holland. After all these years, all the hurt, I was still in love with her. The turn of her mouth, the curve of her back, the length of her thigh. I wanted to know how the rest of her life had gone, each success and every failure.

Emerging into daylight, I instantly felt a presence. The birds and squirrels that inhabited the trees weren't making a sound. I ducked back into the building and peeked out. Was there someone in the bushes? I caught a glimpse of a shadow, a glint of metal. Who was after me this time? Was it the kid who tailed me on La Honda? No way he could have tracked me here. Whoever was hiding must have wiretapped my house and heard Holland and me talking about her acting gig. The cops might have had time to do that between the time I found my mother and when I returned home with Holland.

Another thought occurred to me. Was Holland mixed up with the people who were looking for my father? Was the person who texted her waiting outside, hoping to interrogate me? No, I was wound tight and seeing enemies at every turn.

A third notion struck me. What if the person lying in wait wanted to capture Holland? She had seemed agitated after receiving the text message. What if she hadn't become a narc or bounty hunter? What if, like my mother, she had led a less than pristine life? Someone could have picked up her tail at the hospital, followed her to my house, and then to here. I thought about racing inside to protect her. On the other hand, if I drove off in her car, her pursuer might think she was fleeing and follow.

No matter what, I had to move. If I ran down the driveway toward the Camaro, whoever was skulking in the bushes would intercept me before I could climb inside the car. I urged my breathing to steady and scanned the area. A trellis clung to the theater wall. Why not? I mused. Up and over. I stole around the corner and scaled the trellis. My ankle smarted near the top, but I willed away the pain and scrambled onto the slate roof. From the superior view, I caught sight of a vehicle concealed behind the bushes. A Ford Explorer. Was it the same one that had tailed me and Holland from the hospital? Was it the car that had made the U-ie outside my house?

Something cracked. A person groaned. I peered over the edge of the building. In the shadows, I made out a bruiser of a man climbing the trellis. A fedora obscured his face. The wood must have snapped beneath his feet. My lucky day.

Thrusting my arms out for balance, I scrambled across the roof. I reached the other eave and peered down. There were old mattresses wedged in between the discarded furniture. I leaped and landed on my back. I rolled off the mattresses and crouched to listen. I heard footsteps on the roof. No bullets. No sirens. I grabbed a woman's shabby coat from the discarded costumes to disguise myself if the guy was really after Holland, and I limped-ran to Holland's Camaro.

Barreling out of the driveway, I caught a glimpse of the guy again. still on the roof. His hat had fallen off, but he was too far away for me to make out features other than a massive nose. He leaped onto the mattresses, ran a meaty hand over his hair, then retrieved his hat, and jammed it on his head.

A mile down the road, when I was certain I was rid of him, scenarios churned through my mind. Was the guy acting alone? Was he tag-teaming with the kid that had chased me earlier? Were there more to come? I considered doing an about-face and taking the guy down to get answers, but I didn't want to delay my mission. Not for an iffy result. And the guy did try to pursue me, which meant that, for now, if he was after Holland, she was safe. I maintained my course. I would locate exit patient number five. If questioning him provided no answers, I would regroup.

CHAPTER 16

At a quarter to four, I stood on the porch of a nicely groomed home in upscale Palo Alto doing my best to look non-threatening. Late afternoon sun cast a glaring beam of light into the face of a withered Latina with wary eyes. She had parked herself behind the door, the chain still in place.

"*Qué*?"

"Ma'am, I'm trying to find Mr. Dalton." Exit patient number five. Numerous times I had called the telephone number that I had memorized. No one answered.

"No Mr. Dalton here."

"Gerry Dalton. The hospital brought him here."

"They wrong. No Mr. Dalton. The missus no here."

I didn't care a rap about the missus. I wanted the mister. The woman set her jaw. I peered over her shoulder, looking for movement. A Christmas tree twinkled in the room beyond her, otherwise the house was still.

"The missus no here," the housekeeper repeated. "Go. Leave."

I drew in a long, calming breath. *Be nice. Bees with honey and all that crap*. "I'm not looking for Mrs. Dalton, ma'am. I'm looking for Mr.—"

"Go away. It late." The woman started to close the door.

I blocked it with my palm. "Where is Mr. Dalton?"

"No Mr. Dalton."

"Gerry Dalton. G-e-r—"

"Mistake. The missus named Gert."

"Mrs. Dalton's name is Gert?"

"*Sí*."

I flashed on the records I had seen. Gerry Dalton was the patient's name. Gerry. Not Gert. No mistake.

The woman pushed on the door. I remained stalwart as I pondered what Saul Levine had said to me. My mother had spent time with a man that was in a coma. Levine thought the guy died. Was this mysterious Mr. Dalton-who-wasn't-Mr. Dalton the same guy?

"Where is the patient?"

"No."

"Is he here?"

"Not here."

Gotcha. "Is he in another hospital? Is he in a coma? Did he die?"

"Mr. Jack not dead."

I leaned forward. "Who is Mr. Jack?"

The woman's eyes blinked rapidly. "Go." She pressed the door harder.

"Where is Mrs. Dalton? Might I speak with her?"

"She at work."

"Where does she work?"

"I no tell you. High school be mad."

"She works at a high school? Which one? I've got to contact her. I'm doing a follow up for the hospital."

"I no believe. Go or I scream."

I smirked. Like she would do that.

But she did. At the top of her lungs.

The front door of the white house across the street from the Dalton's whipped opened. A woman who could have been the feisty Latina's twin was holding a telephone in her hand and stabbing in numbers.

CHAPTER 17

Adrenaline revved inside me as I tore away from the curb. What if the man the housekeeper called Mr. Jack was my father? I needed to know where Mrs. Dalton worked. I would get straight answers from her.

A mile from Dalton's house, it dawned on me that the high school wouldn't be open on a weekend. Did that mean the housekeeper had lied, and Gert Dalton was really at home?

Before I could turn around, the Camaro sputtered. The gauge read *Empty*. I was farther from a gas station than I was from home, and I kept a couple of gallons of gas in the garage for emergencies. At a brisk run, I could race home and return to the Dalton house in less than twenty minutes.

About a half-mile from the duplex, I broke into a sweat. A quarter-mile later, as I rounded the corner of my street, the hair at the back of my neck prickled. Not because the area was dark. Streetlights were switched on, as were Christmas decorations on a number of the lawns. A single light gleamed in the living room of my tenant's unit. The guy set timers on some of his lamps to ward off intruders. Nothing wrong there. I cut a look to the right. No movement in the bushes. I glanced at my place. The front door was closed. No windows were open or broken. But something felt off.

Maybe my worry was because Buddy wasn't barking. Usually when I arrived home, the mutt was ready to break down the door. He would scrape the floor with his claws and butt his head against the door while yowling. Perhaps he was silent because I hadn't pulled up in my truck.

My cell phone jangled in my pocket. The sound jolted me. I dropped to the ground, hands primed, toes dug in ready to sprint. I shook off the panic and scanned the phone's display: *Kimo*. Breathing high in my chest, I rose to my feet and scanned the area again. Still no movement. Not even a car roaming the street. Eerie but not out of the ordinary. I answered.

"You okay?" Kimo asked.

"Fine."

"What happened with that guy that was chasing you?"

"Lost him on the way up La Honda." No need to tell Kimo about my meeting with Holland or the bruiser in the fedora outside the theater. I didn't need to fuel his belief that I was paranoid on a grand scale. "What's up?"

"Lancelot was able to alter that drawing you gave me. He used facial recognition software called Pitter Pat or something like that. It's all Greek to me. Anyway, he got a name for the guy who killed your mother. Yuji Tanaka."

"Tanaka."

"He's a bodyguard and a jujitsu expert. He's won awards and stuff."

"That jibes." I remembered the guy's quick reflexes. Fortunately, I had been fast enough to counter. Just barely. "Who does he protect?"

"A woman named Noble. She's a wedding planner."

"Why does she need a bodyguard?"

"She's ultra high-end and pretty successful. Maybe she's afraid one of her Bridezillas will turn on her." Kimo chuckled. "Tanaka's worked for her for a long time. Speaking of brides, her daughter is getting married at Frost Amphitheater this Tuesday."

"Midweek?"

"Probably to save a dime."

"You just said she's successful."

"Yeah, but her husband—last name, Nichols; she must have kept her maiden name—died and left her in dire financial straits. My two cents? I would bet Noble has no clue that her bodyguard is doing another gig on the side."

"I'm not so sure." I told him about hearing the sound of high heels at the trailer and about the Polaroids my mother left me. "Did you see a photo of Noble?"

"Why would I have?"

It didn't matter. I had names: Tanaka and Noble. Maybe I could start piecing together the puzzle. Find my father. Stop the madness.

I headed for the front door of the duplex. "Kimo, do me a favor. Send a copy of Tanaka's picture to RCPD, attention Detective Philips, homicide division." Maybe a tip from me would get the cops to stop tailing me and make Philips believe I was innocent of my mother's murder. *Yeah, in the next century*. "And see if you can track down a woman named Gert Dalton. She works at a high school."

"Exactly how am I supposed to do that? By the way, Reggie is hurt that you didn't call her and tell her about your mom."

"Hurt as in angry?"

"Yeah."

Using my key, I opened the front door. I reached for the light switch, heard a muffled whimper, and froze. "Buddy, here boy."

The dog didn't come running.

"Hold on," I said to Kimo and shoved the phone into my pocket to free my hands. I could hear him asking me what was wrong. I didn't respond. He and Reggie, with her righteous anger, would have to wait.

The glow of streetlamps and Christmas lights provided enough light for me to look around. The entryway was empty. I tiptoed into the dining room. Also empty. No dog. No prowler. The mementoes I had laid out on the table were scattered on the floor. The students' papers, too. Someone had ransacked my place.

I stole to the kitchen door and peeked in. Vacant. I grabbed a knife from the knife block, thumb over the butt, blade down, and stole across the living room toward my bedroom.

Buddy whimpered again.

A pang of worry cut through me. I glanced inside the room. What I hadn't sensed, hadn't counted on, was that I would know the intruder. It was the hefty kid that had pursued me up La Honda. He was squatting beside the bed, one hand on Buddy's collar, the other holding a 9 mm Beretta to the dog's head. Perspiration soaked the neck of the kid's T-shirt. Buddy was sitting like a sentry, a sock stuffed into his mouth. His eyes pleaded for help.

Willing Buddy to stay cool—I believe in human-to-dog ESP —I set the knife down and raised my hands. "Don't hurt my dog. I'll give you whatever you want." I was pretty certain the kid didn't want to kill me because he didn't move the gun from the dog's head, but his eyes remained hard. I wasn't taking chances.

"You know what I want, Day."

"No, I don't."

"The exit patient list."

How the heck did he know about the list? I inched closer while shaking my head. "I don't know what you're taking about."

"From the hospital." The kid wiggled the gun. "It's not here. I've searched. Give it to me or I'll shoot the dog." His trigger finger twitched.

Steady, kid.

"What's your name?" I asked.

"Uh-uh."

"C'mon, you know mine. First name's Chase, by the way."

"I know that."

"What else do you know about me?"

"Your mother's dead. She saw your father."

"So you've got the inside track." Who had filled him in? Had someone bugged my duplex? I sauntered closer, palms open in friendship. "I like to start all negotiations with a name," I added, uttering the same corny line I used on reluctant students who would come into my office for a consultation. Using the word *negotiation* seemed to set them at ease. Not this time.

The kid's mouth twitched. "Nah, no way. I'm not that stupid."

I would wager he was. "How do you know about the list?"

"Someone at the hospital told me."

Nurse Darnell wouldn't have given information to this loser, and I was pretty sure nobody else saw me review the files. Of course, Darnell could have caved and told her superior, and the army tank of a nurse could have blabbed to the kid, or the kid could work for the guy who killed my mother. Maybe Tanaka saw my truck in the hospital parking lot, figured out I was searching for the same thing he was, and returned and strong-armed Darnell. I hadn't taken any paper. Did Darnell lie to Tanaka and say I did?

No. I was on the wrong track. Tanaka wouldn't send this punk to my house. He would come himself. So who was this kid? Was it possible he was acting alone? Why on earth did he want my father?

I glowered. "Try again. Who told you about this supposed list?" I ran my palm along the bureau and visualized my attack. No rash moves. A chop to the kid's wrist, a yank on Buddy's collar to pull him clear, followed by an upper cut to the kid's chin. I drew within a few feet. "I need a name."

"No names."

"No names? Really? None?" I cut a sharp look at the window, pretending to have heard something.

As I'd hoped, the kid's head swiveled, too.

I lunged. I banged his wrist with my elbow; he didn't release the Beretta. I looped my hand beneath Buddy's collar and tugged. The kid couldn't maintain his grip. With Buddy in tow, I landed an upper cut to the kid's jaw. He reeled back and swung up with the butt of the gun. He connected with my ear. Given how hefty he was, I hadn't expected him to wield any significant strength. Bad assumption. He had some muscle buried beneath the flab. I reeled.

"Buddy, go to the door," I ordered. "Sit."

I seized the kid's wrist. With my other hand, I pried his fingers off the Beretta. He moaned. I aimed the gun at his face and cracked my elbow into his cheekbone. He lurched and fell backward. His head slammed into the wall. He slumped forward.

I shoved the gun into the waistband at the hollow of my back and hurried to Buddy. I pulled the sock from his mouth. "You're such a good boy."

Next I fetched a couple of ties from the bureau. I dragged my dazed but not unconscious assailant to the living room, propped him on the floor against the couch, and lashed him to the frame. I rifled through the kid's pockets. No ID. C'mon. He couldn't be that good.

I grabbed the kid's chin. "What's your name?"

"T-T-Tommy."

"Who told you about the exit patient list?"

"H-Holland."

I released the kid as if he were red-hot. Holland? No way. And yet it held the ring of truth. I'd felt something was off the moment I saw her at the hospital, but I couldn't have trusted my instincts from the get-go, even if I'd tried. I had been blinded by my desire and by my past…*our* past.

The kid cleared his throat. His eyes flickered.

I scrutinized him. "Holland. You're sure?"

He nodded. Too enthusiastically. What if he was trying to dupe me? Maybe he had bugged my place. Maybe he was the driver who had driven past last night. I couldn't be sure the SUV was an Explorer; it might have been a Chevy Tahoe. Tommy could have seen Holland leaving my place. He could have followed her and figured out her name.

"Why would Holland tell you anything?" I demanded.

"She didn't. I overheard them on the yacht."

"Them? Them *who*? You're lying. Holland is at rehearsal, and then she's tending to her mother's burial. When would she have had time to go to a yacht?"

He didn't respond.

"Look, kid, I don't have any list."

"Yes, you do. Holland said so."

I thought about it some more. I'd told Holland about the list at the theater. Maybe her dressing room was bugged. "She doesn't know squat. Who are you working for, Tommy?"

Stubborn silence.

"Tanaka works for a woman named Noble. Is she involved?"

Tommy's eyes widened, his nostrils flared. Did he or didn't he know the name? He remained mute. The good news: whoever the kid's boss was didn't know where my father was. Yet.

"Let's go back to Holland," I said. "How do you know her?"

Tommy rolled his lip under his teeth, like he was regrouping.

"Where did you meet her?"

More silence.

I didn't have the time to break the kid down, and I sure as heck didn't have time to haul him to the precinct. "You said you saw her on a yacht. Talk!"

"No."

"Talk!" I raised a hand, prepared to strike.

"I didn't see her," he blurted. His eyes blinked repeatedly. "I heard her."

"Where?"

"They were in the office."

I thought about the guy outside the theater again. Maybe Holland wasn't involved. Maybe he kidnapped her. "Did Holland go to this yacht on her own?"

"Mine to know." Tommy's mouth curled up defiantly on one side.

A flurry of emotions flooded through me: anger at this kid, concern for Holland. I thought of the text message she'd received: Need you now. Had her director really sent the message? He had just summoned her to the stage via the stage manager. Had the guy in the fedora sent Holland the text? She had seemed scared. Who was he?

I moved closer. "Kid, I promise you, you do not want to feel the hurt of my fist. Did Holland go willingly to the yacht?"

Tommy started to quaver. "It's her dad's fault. It's always the father's fault, isn't it?"

"What do you mean? Her father's dead."

Tommy jammed his lips together.

"Tell me, or I'll knock you two ways from Sunday."

"No you won't." Tommy bared his teeth and offered a cruel smile. "Not if you want to save your grandmother."

CHAPTER 18

"My grandmother?" I lunged at the kid. He recoiled against the sofa. I grabbed the front of his T-shirt. "What have you done to her?" Barbie hadn't returned my call after I left a message asking to borrow her car. I thought it was because she was still mad at me. "Answer me."

Tommy's mouth thinned. His eyeballs darted back and forth. "What'll it get me?"

I released him with a shove. "You don't know anything."

"Yes, I do."

"Your eyes are playing Ping-Pong. You think you know something, but you don't have the whole story. You're a measly sneak."

"I'm—"

"Shut up. I swear, if you or anyone you work for has harmed my grandmother, I'll be back for you."

"Back?"

"I'm leaving. You're staying." I slugged the kid for good measure, the feel of my knuckles against his flesh, satisfying. Then I shoved the same sock Tommy had stuffed into Buddy's mouth into his mouth and secured it with a tie. "Buddy, let's go."

I seized the mementoes from the dining room floor and stuffed them into the cigar box. Then I grabbed Buddy's leash and secured it to his collar. Before dashing out of the house, I took one long look around. My gaze landed on the painting by the kitchen, the one Holland had critiqued. Where was she? Had she told the kid about the exit patient list? Was she in danger? I couldn't help her, even if she was. Barbie came first. I sprinted from the house.

Kimo's forest green Audi coupe screeched to a halt at the curb. He rolled down the window. His eyes blazed with concern. "Bro, are you okay?"

"How did you—?" I pulled the cell phone from my pocket. The line was still open. I pressed End.

"I got here as fast as I could. What the devil is going on?"

"My grandmother might be in trouble. I need a lift."

"Hop in."

Twenty minutes later, as day was turning to dusk, Kimo pulled up beside Barbie's one-story stucco house. My heart was pounding so hard I could feel its pulse in my throat.

I stared at the façade. The porch light was on. Lamps were lit inside the home office and my old bedroom. I scanned the neighboring houses. Some were dark. A number of them were adorned with Christmas lights. I didn't see any cars on the street. No one seemed to be lurking in the shadows.

"Looks okay to me," Kimo said.

"I agree."

Leaving Buddy in the Audi with a reminder to keep quiet, I stole up the brick path and tried the front door. Kimo followed. The door was unlocked, per usual. Barbie said criminals could get in if they wanted. I had told her on more than one occasion that locks were prevention measures. She wouldn't listen.

I slipped inside first. The house was warm. The heater thrummed. A pair of shoes stood, toes to the wall, by the front door. The Christmas tree in front of the picture window in the living room twinkled with blue lights. The scent of cinnamon hung in the air. I peeked into the kitchen. She had been baking, but there were no cookies cooling on the counter. The oven was turned off.

The hallways were empty. I inspected each room, primed for an attack. Were the people who were looking for my father as inept as the kid that had invaded my house? No, Tanaka was a pro.

Thirty-seven years was a long time to hold a grudge.

Pausing in the doorway to the master bedroom, I spied Barbie's suitcase open on the bed. Clothes still on hangers lay heaped on top. Light glowed from beneath the bathroom pocket door. I edged to the door, cupped my fingers in the pull handle, and drew the door open. The tiny room was empty, the shower dry. Makeup and other toiletries rested on the counter.

"Looks like your grandmother is packing for a trip," Kimo said.

"But she was interrupted." I returned to the kitchen. Car keys lay on the counter. I whipped open the door to the garage. Her Buick LeSabre stood in its normal spot. My gut wrenched. Where was my grandmother? If Holland had been abducted, then my grandmother could have been taken, too. By whom? Tanaka or the bruiser in the fedora or someone else?

"Nothing looks out of place," Kimo said. "There doesn't seem to have been a tussle of any kind."

Don't panic cycled through my brain. I pulled my mobile phone from my pocket and dialed my grandmother's cell phone number. She didn't answer. I called her office. Neither of her assistants had seen her all day. The male assistant added that Barbie didn't come to work because she needed to run a few errands before she left town to spread my mother's ashes—if and when the police would release her body. I hadn't missed his snide inference. Despite the fact that my grandmother had ordered me to do the right thing, she wasn't counting on me to do so.

I hung up and slumped into a chair by the kitchen table. Air wheezed out of the cushion.

"Well?" Kimo said.

I explained.

"Wouldn't she take her car to run errands?" he asked.

"Exactly. Someone's got her. Someone intends to use her to get to me."

"We should go to the police."

I cut him a hard look. "What if they're in on it?"

"C'mon, bro, do you hear yourself? Don't go wacko like Wonka." He wasn't referring to the Roald Dahl character; he was alluding to a sailor who went AWOL in the first week of training. "Look, we've got to start somewhere. Not to mention, we've got to tell the police you tied up a guy in your duplex. Let them bring him in and question him. It's a place to start."

CHAPTER 19

The Redwood City PD's interrogation room reeked of fresh white paint. I stopped pacing and stared into the mirrored wall. How many cops were standing behind the mirror staring back at my bruised face? Two, three? The police population in the precinct could be lean during Christmas season. Petty crimes required a lot more people on patrol.

"Four minutes have passed since Philips marched out," I said. "Where the heck is he?"

Kimo sat taller in one of the metal chairs. "Chill, bro."

"He thinks I'm lying." I orbited the room for the tenth time, trying to discharge the imaginary ants that were mounting a coup inside my veins.

Two minutes later, Detective Philips returned, dark eyes guarded, mouth grim. The glow of overhead lights reflected off his coffee-colored bald head.

Another cop who hadn't seen the better side of fifty in years entered the room after Philips. Barrel-chested, hangdog eyes, wide flat nose, graying hair thick with gel. He looked familiar, but I couldn't place him.

"Officer Hugh Vance, meet Chase Day and Kimo Cho," Philips said. "Gentlemen, Officer Vance."

The officer cleared his throat. "Los Altos PD has sent a patrol to your grandmother's house—"

"I told Philips I was just there," I snapped. "She's not home. Her suitcase is nearly packed. It looks like she was interrupted—"

"Let me finish, sir." Vance jutted his lower teeth then clicked his tongue. "I think you might be overreacting."

"Over—?" I shoved a chair out of my path.

"Mr. Day." Vance held up a warning hand. His eyes blazed with ferocity.

"Stand down, Day," Philips ordered.

I halted. What was I thinking? I would not accost an officer. Ever. I settled back on my heels.

Vance lowered his hand and continued. "Los Altos PD saw nothing to suggest foul play. In addition, following your lead, my colleagues at Menlo Park PD sent a patrol to your duplex."

Let's hear it for interdepartmental cooperation.

Vance added, "They didn't find anyone tied up."

"I bound the kid with a dozen neckties. He couldn't have escaped. They must have gone to the wrong house."

Vance recited my address. "Did I get that right?"

I nodded. Someone had freed Tommy. Who?

"Mr. Day, listen." Vance sucked in air; his nostrils flared with condescension. "You've been under a lot of stress. You might be suffering from—"

"Officer Vance, listen up. I'm telling you an overweight young man who called himself Tommy held my dog at gunpoint and warned me that my grandmother was in danger."

"And I'm telling you"—Vance jammed a finger at me—"that you're delusional."

"Why you—"

Kimo leaped from his chair and braced my arm.

Philips cleared his throat. "Vance, your people found no indication of any kind of altercation at Mr. Day's duplex?"

"None, sir."

"Philips," I cut in. "Pardon me, Detective, sir. This kid was the same guy that chased me in the Chevy Tahoe up La Honda."

"We only have your word," Vance said.

I threw him a blistering look then hitched my thumb at Kimo. "Mr. Cho saw him tear across the campus green."

Vance said, "Then what happened, Mr. Cho?"

Kimo glanced at me.

"You're not sure, are you?" Vance said.

"I saw the guy speed after Chase."

"Get a license plate?"

Kimo shook his head.

"Description?"

Kimo jammed his hands in his pockets.

I opened my palms. "Look, I'm telling the truth. He's a big kid, pockmarked face. Maybe five-ten. Early twenties. He forced me off the road. He nearly rammed into a Ford truck. Didn't anyone on La Honda report a reckless driver?"

"No, sir," Vance said. "We located your car in the ravine. There's no indication of any kind of wrongdoing by another vehicle. There's only a single set of skid marks. For all we know, you were speeding and swerved out of control."

"The car's been towed to the pound, Mr. Day," Philips said. "You can pick it up after we're through here."

"Were you drinking, Mr. Day?" Vance said.

I glanced between them. "What is this, good cop, bad cop? Is Vance supposed to make me lose my temper so you, detective, can label me a nutcase?"

Philips frowned.

"I'm telling the truth."

Vance said, "The truth isn't always as you see it."

I regarded the officer. His large nose. His bulk. And suddenly I knew where I'd seen him—at The Hole Theater. "It's you."

He cleared his throat. "Excuse me?"

"You chased me over the roof of the theater."

Vance splayed his hands at Philips. "I don't know what he's talking about." Perspiration broke out on his upper lip. He was lying. I had him.

I tapped my head. "You were wearing a fedora."

Vance's mouth quirked up. He shot a look at Philips. "Yeah, like I'd be caught dead wearing a fedora."

An uneasy feeling locked in my gut. Was Vance working for Philips all along, trying to pin the murder on me? I shot a finger at Philips. "You guys planted a locating device, didn't you? That's how you're keeping tabs on me. Where is it, in my car? In my duplex? Did Detective Bruno slip it into my wallet?" I yanked my billfold from my pocket and searched it, finding nothing. "Bruno is the one that tailed me to the hospital and home, isn't he? You had somebody hanging around my place last night, too." I eyed Vance. "It was you. In your Explorer. You drive an SUV, don't you?"

Philips eyed Vance.

Vance snorted. "You're delusional."

"You did a U-turn. Why? Because you saw another cop already in place?"

"Mr. Day," Philips said. "I only now asked Officer Vance in on this case because he's got connections with all the departments in the area."

I eyed Philips. "The fax."

"What fax?"

"The one I sent of the guy who killed my mother. I drew a sketch of him."

"Yeah, the fax," Kimo said. "Chase gave it to me. That's why I headed off in the other direction when the SUV tore after him. To take the sketch to a computer pal of ours. He's got a facial recognition program."

I nodded. "Our pal was able to ID the killer."

Kimo splayed his hands. "I sent the fax to you hours ago."

Philips shook his head "I haven't seen any fax."

He looked at Vance, whose jaw was ticking. Had he intercepted the fax and destroyed it?

"The guy's name is Yuji Tanaka," I said.

"C'mon," Vance sniped. "Where is this line of questioning leading? You have a picture created by some computer guy. That's not valid. You need to work with our artists."

"I sent it to your attention," Kimo said to Philips. "Homicide Division." He recited the fax number.

"Forget it, Kimo. They don't have—" I halted. "Wait!" I whipped my iPhone from my pocket and tapped the photo app. I clicked on the profile picture of Tanaka that I had taken at the hospital. I showed it to Philips. "This isn't a good picture. I only captured half the face, but this is him. Recognize him?"

"Excuse me." Vance tugged a cell phone from his trousers and checked the readout. I hadn't heard it ring; it must have vibrated. "Family emergency." He hurried from the room.

CHAPTER 20

I welcomed the time alone in the interrogation room with Philips. Maybe I could convince him I was innocent. I drew nearer, keeping my voice low. "What do you know about this Tanaka guy?"

"What do you mean?"

"You reacted when I mentioned his name. Vance did, too."

Philips pursed his lips, as if trying to determine how much he could say. "Tanaka applied to become a cop. He failed repeatedly. I heard he became a bodyguard."

"Does Vance know Tanaka?"

"How would I know?"

"Why did Vance just hightail it out of here?"

"His wife's got troubles. He—"

"Save your breath." I was on to something. Vance's presence at the Hole Theater couldn't have been coincidence. He was in this up to his eyeballs. Was he a dirty cop? Was he somebody else's minion? Did he kidnap Holland, or was she his partner? "You gave Vance a look when I said Tanaka's name."

Philips slapped the interrogation table. "Maybe Vance is right. You're suffering from—"

"I'm not delusional. I'm clearheaded."

Philips shifted feet. "Where did you say you took the photo of Tanaka?"

"At Keystone Hospital."

"What were you doing there?"

"Tell him, bro," Kimo said. "Everything."

Philips raised an eyebrow.

I blurted out an explanation. About my mother's locket. My suspicion that she had seen my long-lost father based on her final words. My belief that my father might be in danger. I didn't mention that my father might have stolen something, sticking to the KISS principle: *Keep it simple, stupid*.

Philips said, "Why have people been searching for him for more than thirty years?"

"I don't know. Look, after you released me, I went to my grandmother. She told me my mother was admitted to Keystone Hospital whenever she needed treatment. She was indigent. I thought the hospital might be where my mother saw my father, so I hurried there. When I arrived, I spotted Tanaka harassing a nurse, asking about my father. I considered taking him down, but a crisis on the ward occurred."

"What did you discover at the hospital?" Philips asked.

"I—"

The door opened. Vance returned. "Sorry for my absence. Where were we? Oh, right. You accused me of not doing my job, Mr. Day. Well, while I was out of the room, I asked Menlo Park PD to recheck your duplex thinking maybe my guy had given them the wrong address."

"I thought you had a family emergency."

"I can multitask." Vance's nose flinched as if he'd detected a bad odor. "Anyway, I was correct. No mistake. They did not find any sign of forced entry, and there wasn't any kid tied up in your home."

"That's just not possible. I don't mess up with knots."

"On that note, the officer in charge said your ties are hanging neatly in the closet."

"Gee, that's odd." I worked my tongue inside my cheek. "I don't hang ties in the closet. I keep them in a bureau. So who do you think did that, huh?"

Philips looked bewildered. Vance kept his gaze locked on me.

"Tell me something else," I continued. "Where did I come up with the name Tommy, huh?"

Vance shrugged. "From a psychedelic musical, I'd say."

"I am not making this up. What about Yuji Tanaka?"

"We have no confirmation that Tanaka is in any way involved in your plot. For all we know, your pal"—Vance hitched his head toward Kimo—"is merely covering your sorry butt so you won't have one more mark against you when it comes time for review at Weyford."

"Whoa." I stepped toward Vance. "How do you know about my review?"

"It seems you're not on the dean's most popular list. He's fed up with your anti-war rhetoric." He turned toward Philips. "Detective, this guy's head is filled with conspiracy theories. If I—"

"When did you have time to drum up my employment records?" I demanded.

"People are talking out there." He shot a thumb toward the main room of the precinct. "The dean says you're not a future thinker."

"Me? He's a dinosaur and should be stowed in a mausoleum."

"Is that a threat, Mr. Day?" Vance grabbed my arm and leaned in; his breath reeked of cheap pizza. "Maybe we should lock you in a cell until you calm down."

"That's enough, Vance." Philips gripped his cohort's upper arm and pulled him away from me. "I don't know what's gotten into you, but take the night off. There's obviously a little drama going on at home."

Vance tore himself from Philips's grasp and stormed out of the interrogation room. The door flew open and whacked the wall.

Philips said, "Sorry about that, Mr. Day. Like I said, his wife's got some issues."

And I didn't? I gazed after Vance wondering why he had brought up my employment record. As a ploy to steer the conversation away from Tanaka? Did he really have a family emergency that had made him run from the room earlier, or did he want to get rid of the fax—the evidence—that I was certain, for whatever reason, he had filched?

I glimpsed Vance standing a few feet outside the room. He had paused to talk to a buff, heavily tattooed cop. The cop listened, glanced over his shoulder at me, then nodded. What was up with that?

CHAPTER 21

Sitting in the passenger seat of Kimo's car, aggravation gnawed my insides. I dialed my grandmother for the sixth time. If she was okay, why hadn't she returned my calls? I thought again of the scent of cookies in her kitchen and smacked my thigh. "Of course."

Kimo cut me a worried look.

"Years ago, this guru friend of my grandmother's, Miss Margot, convinced her that a twelve-hour stint of total silence before any trip insured a successful, spiritual jaunt. The woman loves sweets."

Barbie had made me log Miss Margot's phone number into my cell phone registry. *In case,* she'd said. In case I ever wanted some spiritual guidance. I pulled up her number and dialed. After a few rings, she answered.

"Wishing you a lifetime of Eternal Peace," Miss Margot said. We had met once. She looked exactly as she sounded, kind and mellow. She always wore loose clothing and chain-smoked herbal cigarettes.

"Hi, ma'am. It's Chase Day. Barbara Day's grandson."

"Blessings upon your head." Miss Margot—not simply Margot—sounded like she was standing at the bottom of a well. I could only imagine where she was, some chamber she had designed to draw goodness and light into her soul. The place would be rife with incense and wind chimes and hunks of quartz.

"Have you seen my grandmother?"

Miss Margot didn't answer.

"Please," I pleaded. "I need to hear her voice. I have to know she's all right. There's some bad stuff going on. I…I thought a man might have hurt her. She left her place in a hurry. Her things—"

"You know very well she cannot speak until dawn."

"But she's there." Relief washed over me. My grandmother was alive and out of harm's way.

"You are letting her down, young man," Miss Margot said. "It is none of my business, but you should listen to her. Let her guide you. You must allow the past to die, and then move ahead with your own life. What is done, is done."

"Except it's not done," I said. "My mother was murdered, and she begged me to protect my father. People are after him."

Miss Margot snorted.

"They're after my grandmother and me, too. Tell her not to go home. Also tell her I can't rest until I've followed through."

"I cannot tell her these things. You know that is not the way."

Worry nagged at me. "Are you okay, Miss Margot? You sound different." What she sounded was stilted. She was using proper verbs and speaking in clipped sentences. The one time we had met, words flowed easily and quickly out of Miss Margot. She asked me everything about my job and my love life and how I was maintaining my own spiritual journey.

"I am fine. It is you who seem to be stuck in a quagmire."

"A quagmire?" I laughed and relaxed. *Quagmire* happened to be one of Barbie's favorite fifty-cent words. Miss Margot was merely channeling my grandmother. Was Barbie standing beside her, mouthing what she wanted Miss Margot to say? "Fine, yeah, whatever. I'm stuck. Look, I have some business in the morning, but I want to see my grandmother before she leaves town. Have her call me."

Miss Margot didn't say she would.

When Kimo and I arrived at the Outreach Hostel, Reggie was standing on the porch. We had called ahead to alert her of our arrival. She folded her arms and drilled the porch with the toe of her boot. Kimo didn't get out of the car. He offered to return to my house to grab some of Buddy's things. I said not to worry, Buddy could cope, but Kimo said it was no problem. He had other errands to run. In truth, the coward couldn't get away fast enough. He wanted love from Reggie, not fury.

Fifteen minutes later, I sat on a cot in one of the bedrooms at the top of the stairs. Reggie was checking out the wound to my arm. Buddy lay snoring on a mat at the foot of the bed. When I had come upon Tommy aiming a gun at Buddy, for a short while the pain in my ankle and arm had retreated to the back of my mind. Now the ache was raw.

"Gentle," I said.

"Are you looking to get yourself killed?" Reggie swabbed the wound with a solution of hydrogen peroxide, not an ounce of gentleness in her touch.

"Ow."

Buddy mewled.

"Hush, mutt," Reggie said. "You're here out of the kindness of my heart."

"You were a lot nicer when you were the lacrosse team's medic," I teased. Her brother, a lacrosse buddy of mine in high school, had returned from combat haunted by what he had experienced. Two years ago, he took his life. He was the reason Reggie had purchased the hostel. She had dedicated her own to making sure others didn't wind up like him. "Ow! C'mon."

"Pansy. This potion is watered-down."

Thinned or not, the stuff stung like mad.

"Is the other guy as beaten up as you, *idioto*?"

How I wished Kimo hadn't left. Two against one were the right odds whenever Reggie was mad. I would never forget her taking down a pair of girls outside the high school bathroom when she found them smoking. It wasn't the smoking that had bothered her; it was the fact that she would smell like a chimney if she stepped inside. *Dirty whores*, she had called them. The rest of her words had come out in Spanish. She wound up with a black eye; the other girls ended up much worse.

Reggie flicked a tangle of curly hair over her shoulder and jammed one hand against her narrow waistline. "Done. Put on your own stupid bandage." She cuffed me on the back of the head.

I smiled. If I had made a mess of my wound earlier, she would have hit me harder.

She set the peroxide solution on the chipped bureau beside the sink and washed her hands. Watching her from the backside, I was struck by the similarity in shape to Holland. Thinking about her sent waves of doubt through me. Where was she? What was the truth?

I must have grunted because Reggie said, "What?"

I hesitated.

"What?" she repeated as she approached with gauze, tape, and scissors in hand. "Don't hold out on me."

"I didn't tell you about Holland."

Reggie sneered. "Tate? What about her?"

"She's involved in this."

"Are you kidding me?" Holland and Reggie hadn't come to blows during high school, but Reggie hadn't cut Holland any slack. Holland had all the opportunity in the world to succeed. Despite her family situation, she had been blessed with brains. She could have gone to college on scholarships. Reggie had to fight tooth and nail for every chance. "What's her role in this?"

"I'm not sure. Tommy"—I had explained earlier about Tommy and going to the cops—"said she was the one who told him about the exit patient list. And yet…"

"Yet what?"

"She lent me her car."

"The one that ran out of gas."

"That couldn't have been on purpose. She couldn't have known I'd ask to borrow it." I scratched my neck. "I should call her."

"Uh-uh." Reggie wagged the scissors. "No way. You're not alerting anybody to where you are. Got me? This is a safe house."

While she redressed my wound, I thought more about Holland. Was Tommy scamming me about her? Was she in cahoots with him?

Reggie clapped her hands. "Are you listening to me? No, you are not. I want you to give these vets another art therapy class."

"I don't have time."

"Yes, you do."

"No, I don't. I have to track down this last exit patient. Face it, Reggie, most of the guys here are in good shape. They're getting out their anger. They're on the mend. Even Toothpick." Toothpick, aka Ted, was the one who had found Reggie's brother Ramón hanging by a rope from a second story balcony. Ramón was the reason I didn't press Ted, or Reggie, for that matter.

"You look parched. I'll be right back." She hurried out of the room. No doors slammed because there were no doors. Reggie didn't allow them. The vets held each other accountable. Trust was of major importance.

Buddy ran to my side and whimpered. I scruffed the dog's ears then struggled to my feet. While shrugging on my shirt, I thought again of Holland. Tommy said her involvement, if she was involved, was her dad's fault. Except he was dead. Or was he? Was she lying about that? Was her father looking for mine? No, that didn't make sense.

What about Officer Vance? If he was the leader, that would explain why the cops hadn't found Tommy bound and gagged at my house. He extracted Tommy and tidied up the scene. Except Vance wouldn't have had time to rescue the kid on his own, which meant he had men in the field who worked for him, men like the heavily tattooed cop. Did Tanaka work for Vance? His involvement was key.

I picked up the gilded cigar box and laid out my mother's mementoes on the chipped bureau. I looked at the Polaroids and assessed the people in the picture again. The blonde was beautiful and leggy. The thickset geek in the glasses looked familiar. I wracked my brain trying to figure out why.

Reggie reentered the room and offered me a bottle of water, the cap already removed. "Drink. By the way, where's your furry friend?"

"He moved to the far side of the bed."

"Not the dog. Where's Kimo?"

CHAPTER 22

Worry cut through me. I glanced at the clock. How long had passed since Kimo left? What errands had he needed to do? Why wasn't he back by now?

"Where's my phone?" I said to Reggie. "I should call him."

"If I didn't know better, I'd think you two had a bromance going." She smirked. "C'mon, he's a big boy. He probably stopped off for a burger. Drink your water. Hydrate. And follow me to the kitchen. I'll feed you."

I knew better than to argue. I drank the water as I moved behind her. The floorboards squeaked beneath our feet. I settled onto a stool beside the kitchen's center island. The white counter tile looked old but clean. Reggie moved from pot to pot on the stove, stirring each a couple of times.

"Smells good," I said.

"Leftovers."

"Still good." My stomach grumbled. When was the last time I'd eaten? I thought of Kimo again. He wouldn't have stopped off for a quick bite. He liked Reggie's food. He would have praised her, hoping to win her approval.

I dug my cell phone out of my pocket. At the same time, it rang.

Through the receiver, I heard Kimo yell a guttural war cry, followed by a rush of what sounded like flesh smacking flesh.

"Kimo!" My heart drummed my ribcage. "Where are you? What's going on?"

The phone connection died.

Reggie peered at me, eyebrow arched.

"It was Kimo. He—" What had happened? Had someone—Tommy

or the kid's associates—gone back to my place and encountered Kimo? Had they attacked him? I've got to go."

"Talk to me."

I replayed what I'd heard. The yell. The punches.

"You're overreacting," she said. "He probably forgot about returning here because he went to one of his tae kwon do classes. He's a good professor but a flaky friend."

I set down the bottle of water and tapped in Kimo's number. He didn't answer. I tried calling the dojo where he occasionally worked out. Three rings. Four rings. "Nobody's answering. Ah, heck"—I stabbed End, realizing it was Sunday—"the place is closed."

"Relax."

"I can't relax, Reggie, don't you get that? I was chased. My dog was held hostage. My grandmother was threatened."

"But Kimo isn't any part of that. He probably hooked up with some chick. You caught them in the middle of a hot moment."

"No way. He's into *you*, if you hadn't noticed."

"Give me a break. Me and every other woman on the planet."

"Are you pissed at him or something?"

She huffed and flicked her hair. Apparently, she liked him, and something he'd done or hadn't done had ticked her off. The love game—it sucked.

"Look," I said, "he called *me*, not the other way around."

"Pocket dial." Reggie pushed the bottle of water toward me. "Hydrate."

"Let me borrow your car. I—"

Reggie snatched the keys off the counter and wrapped them in a fist. "No, you need sustenance. You'll eat. You'll down the rest of that water, then I'll give you the car keys."

"Man, you can be infuriating."

"For good reason. I care about you. Drink."

"Fine." I took another sip. "But then I'm going to find Kimo, and after that, I'm going to track down this Dalton woman."

"What you need to do is rest. A full eight hours of sleep. Don't worry. Kimo will show up. He's like a bad penny. And you'll meet the Dalton woman in the morning."

"But my father—" A yawn welled up my throat. I couldn't fight it off. And my eyelids felt like lead. I glanced at the bottle of water and back at Reggie. "Aw, dang it, woman, did you drug me?"

❖

I snapped out of a nightmare and bolted to a sitting position. I was on a cot, the sheets wound around me like a cocoon. Buddy was howling like a banshee. The digital clock on the bedside table read: *11:45 P.M.*

"Shh, fella. Hush."

I wrestled with the sheets and tumbled to the floor. When I freed myself, Buddy straddled me. He lapped my face.

"Off!"

I hooked him with a free arm and held him still. I struggled to focus. I rarely had nightmares. Not like the one I'd had. Why—

And then I remembered. Reggie had drugged me. What had she used, a rufie? I'd taken Ambien before. It never worked that fast.

I shook my head to clear the fog. Portions of the nightmare felt significant: students yelling; my mother carrying her box of mementoes and a rifle; a phantom with long tentacles—Tommy—trying to squeeze the life out of Kimo.

I scrambled to a stand, switched on a bedside lamp, and paced the room. My father had appeared in the dream, too. Why did people want him so badly? Had he really stolen something of value? How had he eluded his pursuer or pursuers for so many years? Maybe he went underground. Maybe he entered the WITSEC program. Was that why Gert Dalton's housekeeper said *No Mr. Dalton*? Except WITSEC moved witnesses to different zip codes, didn't they?

Leonardo Da Vinci said: *Just as iron rusts from disuse, even so does inaction spoil the intellect.*

Clinging to that advice, I stuffed pillows into my bed in case Reggie came back for a bed check, and I padded to the hostel's office.

Without switching on a lamp, I sat at the desk, pulled my cell phone out of my pocket—at least Reggie hadn't confiscated that—and I dialed Kimo. No response. Incessant ringing. Not even the opportunity to leave a message. I texted him to call me pronto. The message zoomed into the stratosphere. And then my eyes felt heavy again.

Fight it, I urged, but I couldn't form thoughts other than a choppy to-do list: *Find Kimo, find Dalton*.

I slumped forward on the desk.

CHAPTER 23

I woke in the dark to the sound of pounding footsteps. "Reggie?" I called out. "Kimo?"

Something thudded. My pulse surged. Buddy mewled. I hushed him and inched up in the hostel's office chair. The insides of my head felt fuzzy. My sinuses throbbed.

Someone yelled, "Fire!"

Glass crashed. More footsteps. More shouting. The blare of a horn.

Buddy butted my calves and sniffed. I inhaled, too. I didn't smell smoke. I caught the odors of sweat and stale liquor. Had a homeless person stolen into the hostel? Was he raiding the refrigerator? I tore to the office door and peered into the foyer.

A vet in gray pajamas who I had dubbed Eggs, short for what everyone else called him, Scrambled Eggs for Brains, bolted toward me waving a foot-long US flag and blowing a kazoo. "Fire!" Eggs pointed the flag toward my room down the hall. "It's the pigs. Stinkin' pigs." He jogged in place; his bare feet smacked the floor. "Get 'em, Chase."

I grabbed the baseball bat that Reggie kept by the check-in desk and sprinted toward my room. Buddy yipped his support. The blob of pillows I had mounded to resemble my body were tossed on the floor. Nothing was on fire. The window was broken but wedged open. Shards of glass lay on the sill and floor.

Eggs dashed in behind me. "I scared him away."

"Who?"

"The pig."

"Pig?"

"Cop."

Reggie, dressed in robe and slippers and fighting a yawn, hurried into the room. "What's going on?"

I studied the mess. "We had an intruder." I addressed Eggs. "What did he look like?"

Eggs pressed on his nose. "Flat and wide." He plucked his hair. "Black and gooey."

I stiffened. Eggs was describing Vance. How had he found me? I flashed on Vance conversing with the heavily tattooed cop outside the interrogation room. Did Tattoo Guy tail me and report back to Vance?

"Give the vet a job!" Eggs did a St. Vitus-type dance. "I yelled, 'Fire!' That's what scared him off." He tooted on the kazoo. "Did you hear me, Chase? I screamed real loud." He demonstrated; his screech could have wakened the dead.

"Yes, I heard you. Barely." I glowered at Reggie. "You drugged me."

She held up a T for *time out*.

"No time out," I hollered. "How could you do that to me?"

"You needed sleep."

"And almost died because of it. Good thing I moved to the office between drug-induced nightmares."

"Why did you go there?"

"To get answers. Call me crazy, but I thought sitting at a desk would keep me awake. Guess I dozed off again."

"I'm sorry, I—"

"Save it."

Reggie addressed Eggs. "Back to bed. Good job, soldier." Eggs scuttled out of the room.

I called Buddy and hooked his leash to his collar. "C'mon, we're getting out of here, fella."

Reggie frowned. "Where are you going?"

"I know who the intruder was. A cop I met at the precinct."

"Don't be ridiculous."

"Eggs described him. He's not the lead investigator; he was brought in as a consultant." Earlier, when explaining things to her, I hadn't mentioned my fear that Vance was involved. I didn't want to presume.

"This is nuts." Reggie slumped against the doorjamb. "You think this is a conspiracy because of some age-old vendetta against your father?"

"Buddy, sit." The dog obeyed. I retrieved my mother's mementoes and slipped a couple of photographs into my shirt pocket, then shoved the cigar box between the mattresses. Call me crazy, but out of sight, out of mind. If Vance wanted my mother's things, he'd have to search hard for them. "I need your keys." I strode to Reggie, hand open.

"You need to cool down, get perspective. Let's call the police."

"Didn't you hear me? They could be in on this."

"One cop."

"One could mean there are more."

A thick layer of silence fell between us.

I broke it. "I know you care, but I can't sit idle. Kimo's missing."

"You don't know that."

"Here we go again. Show a little concern, will you?"

She shoved herself off the doorjamb and folded her arms.

"I need to regain control of my life, Reggie. I need to get a handle on where everyone is. I don't know about Holland, either, where she is or what her role is in all of this. I'm sorry. I have to go." I reached out for her. She came into my arms. As tough as she pretended to be, she was shivering. Buddy broke command and loped to us.

Reggie wriggled free. "I'll track down Kimo."

"And I'll locate the Dalton woman. Maybe I'll learn from her where my father is, and if I find him, maybe I'll get answers and end this madness."

Reggie rolled her teeth over her lower lip. "What if Dalton can't help you?"

I couldn't face that possibility. Not right now. I picked up Buddy's leash. "Keys, please."

"I'll give you my car on one condition," Reggie said. "Go to Manuel. He's got resources." Manuel was Reggie's older brother. Like their younger brother, he had seen the darkest side of battle, but he had survived the emotional fallout. He and his wife owned a diner near the airport. "While you sleep, Manuel will figure out where the Dalton woman works."

"I can't sleep—"

Reggie laid a hand on my shoulder. "The school where Dalton works won't open until the morning. Also, while you sleep—truly sleep—I'll call a pal at the police department and ask a few discreet questions about...what's the cop's name?"

"Officer Hugh Vance."

"Division?"

"Redwood City PD. But don't stir a hornet's nest."

"Me, *chico?* I am the epitome of grace under fire." She jutted out her hand. "Give me the dog. Buddy doesn't need to tilt at windmills with you."

CHAPTER 24

I didn't slow down even though Reggie's Chevelle rattled and groaned. Headlights from the few oncoming cars flared in the windshield as I sped toward San Jose. Despite the early hour, I called Kimo again. Still no answer. No possibility to leave a message. I tried Holland, too. Same result. I stabbed End and cursed. While dodging cars with the efficiency of an ambulance driver, I rehashed what I knew.

In the interrogation room Detective Philips had kowtowed to Vance at first, but when Vance left, Philips seemed genuinely concerned about my plight. Due to Vance's closing attack, I didn't finish telling Philips everything. Should I have?

I would bet my life that Vance was a dirty cop. He had broken into The Outreach Hostel. To kill me? To scare me? I replayed the meeting at the precinct. Vance got edgy after hearing Tanaka's name. He must have filched the fax with Tanaka's face on it. And what about the kid who wasn't found tied up at my duplex? Did Vance's colleagues free him, or were there more players in this drama?

Tommy had come looking for the exit patient list. Only two people knew about that—Nurse Darnell and Holland. I replayed the moment when I ran into Holland at the hospital. Coincidence or synchronicity? Was Holland's story a lie? Was her mother alive? Was her father? We ran from the hospital. Someone followed us. Was it a cop, or someone looking for my father? Or was it someone keeping an eye on Holland? Maybe Vance tailed Holland and me from the hospital, and when Holland left my house, he followed her. He went to the Hole Theater with the specific intent of wringing information from her. On the other hand, Tommy said he overheard Holland on a yacht. Whose yacht? Vance didn't seem like he could afford one. Did Holland go willingly, or had Vance kidnapped her?

My head hurt. There were too many unknowns.

An airplane zoomed overhead. To the south of the San Jose airport laid a series of runways. Large aircraft were awaiting instructions. I veered down an off ramp and into a parking lot. Three semis and a couple of campers occupied spots closest to Manuel's Diner. A red neon sign on the front of the diner read: OPEN 24/7. Posters in the windows, outlined in cheap tinsel fringe and Christmas lights, boasted the best coffee and breakfasts in the Bay Area.

Before entering the diner, I scanned the parking lot for familiar cars. If I was going to be paranoid, I might as well use a schizophrenic's heightened senses to remain alert, right? I didn't recognize any of the vehicles, but I still felt on edge.

The diner was a junkyard owner's paradise, with tables that didn't match and walls filled with tires, dented bumpers, road signs, and pictures of abandoned cars and trucks—all of which were outlined with strands of Christmas lights. *Tis the season, ho, ho, ho.* A family of eight occupied two of the tables. The children, all under ten years of age, looked dog-tired and were acting up. I remembered my mother keeping me up past midnight a couple of times. I was just as cranky as these kids were. A swarm of truckers filled the rest of the tables.

"Hey, dude. Welcome." Manuel moved from behind the Formica counter, his hair Navy-short, his brown skin weathered, his smile easy. He was about the same size as me, same athletic build. He whacked my arm. Hard. "Coffee?"

"Black."

"Babe, coffee." Manuel gestured to his wife Nita, a buxom Latina waitress in a bright blue uniform. She gave me a thumbs-up sign. "Sis wasn't lying. You look like crap."

"No worse than you."

"I've got a few years on you. I ought to look like crap. Sorry about your mom."

I nodded my thanks.

"Hungry?"

"Toast, dry." Anything to soak up the acid stewing in my gut. "And eggs." I needed protein to fuel my brain.

Manuel repeated the order to Nita. "Follow me." With a hitch in his step—thanks to shrapnel—he led me through the kitchen to the office at the rear. "Reggie said you might need some shuteye."

"I need answers."

"She said that, too. She gave me some names to run down."

"Did she mention whether she'd been able to track down Kimo?"

"At this time of night? What's going on?"

I told him as much as I knew.

"I agree with my sister," Manuel said. "Kimo can be a flake sometimes. He makes plans and cancels at the last second." Manuel, Kimo, and I had knocked back plenty of beers on Kimo's sloop over the past few years. Kimo and Manuel were always going at it over some sport. Kimo held a fanatical interest in the America's Cup races; Manuel tried to convert Kimo to football. "But if anyone can find him, Reggie can. She's got her sources."

The office was sparsely furnished with a desk, a desktop computer, a file cabinet, and a seedy-looking couch that Manuel must have acquired on one of his junk-buying sprees. Manuel never paid retail if he could help it.

"Sit, take a load off. Catch a show." He indicated the couch. A TV sat on a bureau opposite the couch. A muted rerun of *NCIS* was on. Manuel picked up a remote controller and flung it to me. "Not much to watch after midnight."

I set the controller aside.

Manuel took a seat and hit a key on the keyboard to wake up the desktop computer. "Reggie told me to start with this cop Vance that blew into the hostel." Manuel had served as an information expert in the Navy. Though he was a skilled computer hack and eminently employable, he wasn't hard-wired to sit in a cubicle. He liked to cook and preferred being his own boss.

The door opened and Nita entered with a tray of food. She set a plate and silverware setup on the desk, and then placed a pot of coffee and a mug beside them. "Hey, gorgeous." She eyed my bruises and clucked her tongue. "You've seen better days. Want catsup?"

"No, thanks."

"A cold steak for your face?"

"I'll survive."

"Then I'll leave you two to business. Sorry about your mom." She exited. The door swung shut.

Manuel said, "I hear this Vance dude made no bones about keeping quiet when he broke in."

"He might have intended to, but the vet that scared him off is one crazy sucker. Three tours of duty, only half of his brain left."

"So far, all I can find on Vance are commendations."

"You pulled up his file?"

"Public records. He's lily white. Nothing illegal."

"Until now. What does that tell you?"

"He's in it for the money? Or a woman."

I downed the eggs and toast in a few bites. The coffee burned my throat, but I didn't care. Pain meant I could still feel. "Run me through what you've got."

Manuel read from an open page on the Internet. "Vance saved a kid from a car accident."

"He's a hero?"

"He also saved a fellow cop named in a squabble with a drug dealer. The perp was aiming at the cop's head. Vance was on his beat. Saw the fracas. Leaped in front. Took two to the chest and got off one. The perp went down."

"Who was the cop?"

"A guy named Pete Philips."

Well, didn't that explain a lot? Detective Philips owed Vance. Did he know Vance was a bad cop? Maybe not. Was Vance the major player in this scenario? I said, "Philips is the guy in charge of my mom's murder."

"Small world."

I thought about Tommy's disappearance from my house and again wondered whether Vance had orchestrated that. Perhaps Philips had let Vance in on the investigation earlier than he claimed.

"I see wheels turning," Manuel said.

I explained my theory. "Vance ran out of the interrogation room shortly after Yuji Tanaka's name was mentioned. I think he wanted to warn him. What can you pull up on him?"

Manuel typed in a string of words in his search engine. A Wikipedia page and photos emerged. "Yuji Tanaka is a celebrated comedian."

"No. Not him. We're looking for another guy who is the bodyguard of a wedding planner named Noble."

Manuel added words to the previous search. "Aha, got him. He's worked for Uma Noble for thirty plus years. He—"

"Hold it." I threw up a hand as the final moments with my mother slammed into me. "Did you say Uma?"

"Yeah."

"My mother…when I found her"—my chest tightened—"she moaned *ooh*."

"Okay."

"'Ooh,' she said. 'I told her. I saw…' And then she hummed. What if she was trying to say a woman's name that started with the letter *U*? 'Uma. I told her. I saw…' Him," I added, certain I was right. "She saw my father." I jabbed a finger at the console. "Are those pictures of her?"

"Yeah. There are tons of images. She's gorgeous." Manuel clicked on a YouTube link. A video emerged of a classy blonde woman, mid-fifties, sculpted hair, sculpted body.

I pulled the Polaroids from my pocket and held one up to Manuel. "Do you think this is the same woman?"

"Definitely."

In the YouTube video, Uma Noble paced a room filled with a tearful bride and frantic bridesmaids. With the calm of an army general, Noble spoke into a headset advising a colleague that the bride was nearly ready. When a lean younger woman entered, upset that the parking attendant hadn't shown up for the gig, Noble kept her cool. I could see how my mother would have been drawn to her. Had they met when the Polaroid was taken or before? What was their relationship, friend, mentor, rivals for my father? I could also see how this woman, fully in control, might lose it if someone rocked her world. Had she thought my father was dead? Was she surprised when my mother showed up and said he wasn't? What did he steal? How had that altered this woman's world?

"Seen enough?" Manuel said.

I nodded. "Now at least I know a few of the players, but I don't know the game, and I sure as heck don't know the rules. My father holds the key. I've got to find him before anyone else does." I didn't add: *if he's still alive*. "Which means I need to locate Gert Dal—"

"Chase." Manuel punched my arm.

I blinked and realized I must have drifted off for a second.

"Dude, you need sleep. You're spacing out."

"I'm fine." I rotated my head to remove the kinks. I described Dalton's relevance and my encounter with her housekeeper. "She works at a high school."

"I need more than her name."

"She lives in the Palo Alto area. Let's start with nearby schools. You can pull up employment rosters, right?"

Manuel grinned. While his fingers clicked the keyboard, I drank a cup of coffee. Then I stood and paced the office. The caffeine took a minute to kick in.

A short while later, Manuel said, "Gertrude Dalton is a guidance counselor at Gunn High School."

"On my way."

"Whoa. Have you lost it?" Manuel, even with his injured hip, was fast getting to his feet. He grabbed my shoulder. "You're not going anywhere."

"Don't be your sister." I shook him off. "'Lead me, follow me, or get out of my way.'"

"Look, man, I can quote Patton, too, but be real. It's two A.M. Nothing and nobody's going to be at school at this hour. Not even the cleaning crew."

Exactly what Reggie had said.

"Catch forty winks. I'll wake you at seven. You can get a move on then."

My cell phone rang. I answered. The caller sounded garbled, like he or she was calling from a tunnel. The whoosh of wind or static made it impossible to identify the voice. The call broke up and ended. Thinking it might have been my grandmother using her guru's phone, I pulled up Miss Margot's contact information but didn't dial when I saw an incoming call. I answered.

Reggie said, "Chase."

"Have you tracked down Kimo?"

"Not yet. Listen up. A cop named Tibbs came looking for you. He woke everyone up with his pounding on the door."

My gut tensed. "What did he look like?"

"Buff. Spiky blond hair."

Tattoo Guy. It had to be.

"He said your duplex had been broken into. He needs you to come to the precinct right away."

Fat chance. I didn't trust Vance; I wouldn't trust his pal. And I wasn't going to contact Detective Philips at this point, not until I had something concrete, like my father in tow.

"Second thing," Reggie continued. "I called a friend at the police department. He was part of the detail that Philips took to locate Tanaka."

"Philips believed me? He checked out Tanaka?" Maybe showing him the photograph of Tanaka in profile had helped convince him.

"Tanaka wasn't there. My friend said they met with Tanaka's boss, a woman named Noble."

"She's involved," I said. "Manuel and I just figured it out. She's the woman in my mother's Polaroids."

"She said she fired Tanaka."

"Fired him? Why?"

"My friend didn't say."

To preserve her pristine reputation? Was Tanaka fleeing town, or had Noble disposed of him permanently? Was she capable of murder?

"About Kimo," Reggie said. "Don't worry. I'm still looking for him. I've put out feelers."

"Thanks, Reggie. Be safe."

"You, too."

We disconnected, and I drew in a deep breath. Did the latest news mean Philips could be trusted?

CHAPTER 25

I slept in fits and starts, hearing every tick and hum. When I awoke at six A.M. Monday morning, I was groggy but hungrier than ever to find the father who had never made an appearance in my life. How many times during my youth had I asked about him? In my teens, I had wanted to rip off his cowardly face. In the Navy, I did everything I could to forget him. After I graduated grad school, his memory resurfaced. I considered hiring a detective or one of those groups that help orphans locate parents through DNA. In the end, I didn't. Now I wanted answers. I wanted to look into my father's eyes and ask why he left. Ask why he never showed up for one day of my sorry life. Show him that I had made something of myself without an iota of his help.

After a quick shower and hearty meal, I drove to Gunn High School. I scrambled out of the car and pulled the hood of Manuel's raincoat over my head. A new weather front promised a hearty storm. Rain battered me as I ran beneath the banner slung across the entry praising the school's Titans for a great football season.

Inside the main building, I followed the strains of Chuck Berry's "Run, Rudolph, Run" to the administrative offices. A sign sitting on the receptionist's desk reminding students that all independent work was due before the holiday—*no ifs, ands or buts*—made me stop short. I felt a pang of guilt for not attending to my students' term papers but pushed the feeling aside. Grades didn't need to be turned in until after the holiday. I would do my duty if I survived the holidays and if—*big if*—the dean didn't fire me after the way I blew him off. Was that only yesterday?

"Good morning," I said to the middle-aged receptionist.

She grinned with warmth. "Bad day for ducks."

I brushed rainwater off my jacket. "And humans."

The woman chuckled, which gave me hope. Maybe she wouldn't be as unsympathetic as Dalton's housekeeper.

I swooped the hood of the raincoat off my head. The woman gasped.

"What? Oh…sorry." The bruises on my face had turned deep purple. Luckily, I had dressed nicely—slacks, clean shirt, and tie, compliments of Manuel. "I was in a scrape. Not my fault. Long story."

The secretary nodded knowingly. "That's what all the boys say, including my sons. What's up?"

"Is Mrs. Dalton in? It's about…" My grandmother's warning, *Tell one lie, shame on you*, gave me pause, but I pressed ahead. "One of your students applied for acceptance at Weyford University. I'm a professor there."

"Sure thing. Step on in, hon." She hitched a thumb at the door to her right. "Gert isn't booked for student meetings until nine." She leaned forward as if to impart a secret. "While you're in there, maybe you can convince her to turn off that awful music."

"You don't like it?"

"I'm a Bono gal. Gert is the Berry fanatic."

I nearly did a fist pump. Gert Dalton and I had something in common. I had strummed "Maybelline" along with Chuck Berry so many times during high school that my fingers had bled. I couldn't sing a lick, but I could pick. I strode into the office.

Gert Dalton stood at the filing cabinet, her back to me. She wore her steel-grey hair in a short-cropped style; she had a penchant for red—red scarf, red jewelry, red off-the-rack suit. She had decorated her office in red, too; it went nicely with the Christmas glitz, which included a fake three-foot tree draped with tinsel. Red lights blinked with regularity.

"Ma'am." I rapped on the door.

The woman turned. She stiffened and bit back a gasp.

"I was in a scrape," I explained. "You should see the other guy. May I come in?"

"What's this about?"

"I'm a professor, and—" As I strolled into the room, I scanned the pictures around the room. The ones that hung on the wall were school-oriented. An eight-by-ten frame sat on the desk facing away from me.

Dalton gestured to a chair opposite her desk.

I sat. "I like your choice of music." I air-strummed a guitar and sang along with the music.

Dalton frowned.

I laughed. "Sorry. I've got a tin ear, but I can keep the beat."

Dalton glanced at the iPod tower sitting on the credenza behind her desk and back at me. "I should turn the volume down."

"Not on my account, but if you want to earn the goodwill with Miss Merry Sunshine out front, you might consider a minor reduction in volume."

She grinned. So did I.

"Call me Gert."

Excellent. I liked being on a first-name basis.

"What can I help you with, Mr…?"

"Day."

"You said you were a professor."

"At Weyford." I glanced at the door and wondered if the secretary was listening in. "Actually my visit doesn't have anything to do with school. You signed a patient out of Keystone Hospital."

Gert sucked in a quick breath. A normal person would have missed the hiccup, but right now I felt anything but normal. My emotions were hot, my nerves wired. Her warm gaze turned chilly. She crossed behind her desk but didn't sit. "What business is that of yours?"

"The patient's name read *Gerry Dalton*, except your housekeeper said, 'No Mr. Dalton.' She called him Mr. Jack."

"You're the one who came to my house?" She fingered the telephone on her desk.

I rushed to continue. "Ma'am, my father, Luther Marcussen, was possibly one of the exit patients Saturday. I don't know him. I've never met him. I believe, due to a number of reasons, that he might have changed his name. I came to your house to see if your husband—"

"Is your father." Gert forced a smile, but sincerity didn't reach her eyes. "I'm sorry to disappoint you, but my housekeeper was right. There is no Mr. Dalton."

"Ma'am, Mr. Dalton was released to your custody."

"No, there is no Mr. Dalton. My maiden name is Dalton. Just so we're clear, my ex's name is Battle. Jonathan Battle."

Battle. The name sounded familiar. I tried to place it, but I couldn't.

"What was your father's name?"

"Luther Marcussen. Ma'am, you signed a form."

"Yes, I went to the hospital to sign a release, but an ambulance delivered my ex to my son, Jack, or Mr. Jack, as Maria calls him." Again with the phony smile.

A quote by Twain—or was it Churchill?—zinged through my mind: *A lie can travel halfway around the world while the truth is putting on its shoes.*

"The hospital had your ex written down as Dalton."

"An honest mistake."

Honest my foot. "Hospital's need ID ma'am. Did your son bribe someone to keep your ex's identity a secret?"

"No, of course not. He—" Gert gripped her desktop and eyed the framed photograph that faced her. "Look, young man, I'm sorry for your disappointment, but you don't know my son. He would never bribe anyone. Yes, he wanted privacy for his father. He paid for that anonymity. His father can be…could be…"

"Could? Is he dead?"

"No, it's just—" She traced a finger along the lower edge of the picture frame. "My ex has a dark side. He carries a secret burden. He served in the war. He struggles with nightmares. When he ran off to join the Navy thirty-seven years ago—"

"Thirty-seven?"

"Yes."

"Why did he run off? To escape his past?" *Like the fact that I existed*?

"Don't put words in my mouth."

"Maybe he changed his name."

"No."

"Does he have other children?"

"Why are you asking all these questions?" Gert looked beyond me, as if ready to flee if she could figure out a way past me.

Suddenly the name *Battle* registered. "Is your son Jack Battle, Jr., the dot.com guy?"

Gert blinked.

"He runs Young Warriors," I said.

"Yes."

When I stopped playing the guitar, I turned to video games. I excelled at many of the Young Warriors' creations: *Urban Hobo Power*, *Cyborg Vigilante.* "I've read all about your son and his rise to fame. He was a wunderkind at Stanford. When not creating new video games, he likes to play tennis or compete in triathlons."

"I'll have you know my son was going to be a concert pianist before he got into all that gaming stuff." She toyed with a strand of gray hair that cupped her ear. "Johnny B. Goode, that's what I liked to called my son. He hated the nickname. He hated Chuck Berry music, unlike me, but he loved Chopin and Debussy. The music world lost a true talent."

Jack Jr. had talent, all right, to make a buck. He started out as a gamer and game designer, then he created software that made Apple hunt him down and pay him millions. Using that money, he built Young Warriors. My friend Lancelot had tried to get a job at the place.

But enough about the son.

"Where is your ex-husband now?"

"Jack moved his father to another facility."

"What's the name of it?"

"It's time for you to leave." She motioned to the door.

"Is he ill?"

She didn't answer.

"Gert, my father ran off thirty-seven years ago. The timing of your story…" I pulled my mother's locket from my pocket, popped open the lid, and displayed the photograph to her. "This is him around twenty years old."

Gert's gaze flew from the locket to the photograph on the desk and back to me in a matter of seconds. Again, the untrained eye wouldn't have caught the move because it was fleeting, but I had learned in the Navy to notice the slightest nuance.

I gestured to the photo in the locket. "You know this man, don't you? Whatever you tell me will be held in the strictest confidence. I won't hurt your son or your ex-husband. I promise."

Gert rounded the desk. "I asked you to leave." At the corner, she faltered and gripped the desk. Her breathing quickened.

I bolted toward her. "Are you all right, ma'am?"

"Don't touch me." She steadied herself. Her eyes grew flinty. "I'm fine. Leave."

At my new position nearer the desk, I was able to glimpse the photograph on her desk. Within the frame was a collage of pictures. In one photo, a teenaged boy stood shoulder to shoulder with an older man. They had the same strong jaw, the same riveting eyes. They reminded me of *me*. A pang squeezed my heart as I realized the man standing with Jack Jr. in the picture was, indeed, my father, Luther Marcussen. He had changed his identity and had become Jonathan Battle. Both father and son wore scouting uniforms. Jack Jr. was pointing proudly to the badges on the sash across his chest.

Gert caught me looking at the picture. She grabbed the frame and flattened it on the desk. Through gritted teeth, she said, "Leave. Now."

"Where can I find your ex?"

"You can't. He's very sick."

"Is he in a coma?"

"Why would you—"

"Gert…Ms. Dalton, I don't mean to hurt you or your son—" I paused as the notion hit me; I had a half-brother. *Don't dwell.* I pressed on. "Your ex-husband is my father. You know it, and I know it. My mother recognized him at the hospital. She spent time with him. Someone saw them together. He said the man looked like he was in a coma. He thought he'd died. He didn't, ma'am, but my mother did. She was murdered."

Gert gasped.

"As she lay dying, my mother told me I had to save my father. Before I was born, he went off the grid. That must have been when he joined the Navy. When he came out, he assumed a new persona: Jonathan Battle. I believe there are bad people after him. I have to find him before they do. Where is he?"

Her lips began to tremble. "Leave."

"I have to see him."

"Go." She pointed at the door. Her arm shook with the force of her anger.

"At least tell me where I can find your son. Please. My father…Jack's father…is in danger. I have to protect him."

"Marge!" Gert yelled, her panic razor sharp.

The receptionist appeared at the door.

"Call security. This man—"

"Don't bother." I stormed toward the door. "But, listen up. I'm going to find your son, and when I do—"

I glanced at the flattened picture frame. A notion jarred my brain. I strode to the desk and snatched the frame. In one of the pictures in the collage, Jack Jr., now a grown man, stood with his father in front of a four-story, avant garde building that I recognized. It was located a block from the Fairmont Hotel in downtown San Jose.

CHAPTER 26

I sped through Monday morning traffic, swearing at the idiots who cut in front of me despite the rain and slick roads. Minutes later, I pulled in front of the black-windowed building and peered up at the Young Warriors' logo. A crack of lightning pierced the bloated clouds and flared like the blade of a sword. How appropriate, I mused, given the circumstances that Jack Jr. and I might find ourselves at war. I parked at a nearby meter and charged through the rain into the building.

Posters of Young Warriors' most famous game covers hung on the entry walls. I approached the burly security guard and stated that I had an appointment with Mr. Battle. A plaque on the wall listed Jonathan Battle, Jr. as president.

"Driver's license," the guard said. "And sign this log." He pushed a black book with a pen attached at me.

Surprised but pleased at the lack of security measures, I jotted my name then took the elevator to the top floor. I exited into the circular reception area set with one desk. At the desk sat a whip-thin assistant, her tawny hair pulled into a ponytail. Behind her stood a bureau, arced to match the curving wall. A slew of schooner replicas rested on top. There were three doors in the reception area. One led to the stairwell. Another was narrow and looked like a supplies closet door. A security panel was embedded in the wall beside the third door, which I assumed opened to Jack Battle's personal office. So much for easy access. Unless his code was the default 1-2-3-4, I would have to resort to charming his assistant.

Pictures of Jack Battle with leaders of the community filled the walls, as did photographs of Jack in various athletic events. I looked for more similarities between us. We had the same rugged jaw, the same oval-shaped eyes. In one series of snapshots, the photographer had captured Jack at a triathlete event: running, swimming, biking. Seeing the photos made me think of Kimo, who intended to compete in the next Iron Man triathlon in Hawaii. Why hadn't he returned my call? Had Reggie tracked him down? And what about Holland? Had someone kidnapped her or was Tommy lying about that? Why hadn't she returned my call? I hate loose ends.

Stop. Focus. One task at a time.

I strode to the assistant. "Good morning. I have a meeting with Mr. Battle."

The woman tightened her ponytail. "I don't think so." She ran her finger along the edge of a stack of what appeared to be swirly sketches. I spied brochures beneath the artwork. For travel? Was Jack intending to leave town with our father? "Try again," the young woman said.

"Try a…" I summoned a boyish smile. It felt tight. Swell. "Hmm, let's see, I *should* have an appointment with Mr. Battle."

"Sorry, nope."

"I would *really appreciate* a meeting with Mr. Battle."

"To discuss…?"

"A merger." It wasn't a total lie.

"Are you a dot-com business?"

"No."

The woman had a brittle smile. "Then why should Mr. Battle bother?"

"I'm a designer."

"What do you design?"

"Triathlete techno training movies." I couldn't believe how the words tripped off my tongue. I hadn't really lied since I was a teen. Was this how my students felt when they attempted to tap dance their way out of turning in a project on time? "It's an interactive platform. It encompasses the preparation for athletic events, the diet challenges, and meditation." A year ago, Kimo had proposed a similar program. I had made fun of him. Today it sounded like a good idea.

"Mr. Battle is a triathlete."

"I actually know that. He'll love my design. Can he squeeze me in now?"

"No." The assistant reviewed the calendar on her computer. "How is two weeks from Tuesday?"

I glimpsed the telephone on the assistant's desk. A light was on. "Are you sure he can't see me? Two minutes, that's all I ask. He and I have a lot in common." Like DNA. "I'm assuming he built those model ships on the credenza."

"He and his father."

There was so much I wanted to know about my father. Not just his current location. I wanted to know his likes and dislikes and what the heck he'd been doing the past thirty-seven years, not to mention why he had changed his name.

"I'm a hobby geek," I said. One more lie wouldn't hurt, would it? "Are those Mr. Battle's designs for larger boats?" I indicated the swirly artwork.

With magicianlike speed, the assistant swooped up the drawings and rolled them into a tube. I got a clearer view of the brochures below. Antigua, Barbados, and a third with the partial word LANS. I reached for it. The assistant grabbed my hand. While we struggled for possession, I read the letters: MENT and caught the last letter of the last word: M. The woman yanked hard. I retained a paperclip and a corner of the brochure.

"You fool. You damaged it," she cried and tucked it and the other brochures into a drawer. "Leave."

"Look"—I jammed the paperclip and torn corner into my pocket—"you're probably thinking I'm a corporate spy. I'm not. All I want—"

"Go."

Above the replicas hung a rendering of a sleek whaling ship. Vamping and desperate for a connection, I said, "Hey, that's the *Niantic*, isn't it?" I knew it was. After my stint in the Navy, I had not only studied history—naval battles, in particular—but I had immersed myself in the lives of war heroes, the nature of civilization, and the spectacular beauty of ships. All of it seemed to help my trivial life make sense, in the grand scheme of things. "It's a nice rendering."

The assistant regarded me and softened ever so slightly. "Mr. Battle painted that. He's very gifted." She rose with the tube of drawings in hand and crossed to the narrow door that I had presumed was a supplies closet. She opened it and fetched a mailing cylinder. She inserted the drawings into it, laid the cylinder across her desk, and resumed her seat. "He's an artist at heart."

"And a fine pianist, I heard."

"That, too."

I laughed at myself for being a slow on the uptake. The assistant was in love with Jack Battle. So much for hoping that flirting with her would get me a meet and greet. Maybe joking would. I said, "I'll bet he charts out his life. Get it?" I jutted a finger at the mailing tube. "*Charts*?"

"He's not obsessive-compulsive, if that's what you mean."

I grimaced; I had lost her. No sense of humor. The icy frost had returned. "Come on. I'm sure he can squeeze in a meeting with an old friend."

"Ah, you're friends now, are you?" She raised a cynical eyebrow. "Well, then he'll be very sorry he missed you, Mr.—"

"Missed me? He's in there. The phone line is lit."

"That was a good ploy, don't you think? Just before you arrived, his mother called to warn him about you. He split." She jutted a finger at the door to the stairwell. "Right about now he should be pulling out of the parking lot."

CHAPTER 27

I rushed to the window and peered out. A black BMW sped out of the Young Warriors' parking lot and made a hard right. At the same time, the telephone rang.

The assistant answered. "Yes, Gert. He's here. No, ma'am. Jack Jr. left in time. You did what? You called the cops and they're on their way?"

I swore under my breath and flew to the stairwell. I bolted downstairs, taking them two at a time. My lungs ached as I rounded the third, second, and first floor landings. A minute later, I burst out of the building into the rain.

The wail of a siren pierced the air. The sound came from the direction where I had parked Reggie's car. I pressed myself against the wall and peeked around the corner. A black and white patrol vehicle was pulling alongside the Chevelle.

My insides tensed. If a policeman caught me, he might turn me over to Philips, or worse, Vance. Would my life depend on the outcome? I did a one-eighty and jogged in the opposite direction, keeping to the shadows of the buildings. I picked up my pace and checked over my shoulder for a tail. No one was following me. Yet. My cell phone hummed. I pulled it from my pocket and, protecting it from the rain, scanned the display: *Reggie.* I slid my finger across the prompt to answer. "Hey."

"Kimo showed up. Luckily he's okay."

My insides snagged again. "What do you mean *luckily*?"

I heard Reggie and Kimo fighting for possession of the phone. Kimo won. "Bro, listen up."

Reggie yelled from a distance. "Someone beat him up."

"Scratches," Kimo said.

"He had to swim two miles in the ocean," Reggie added. "Some bozo dumped him overboard."

"Cut it out, Reg! Chase, it was a guy named Zorn."

"Zorn?" A few years ago, I'd met a man with the same name, an entrepreneur of the highest magnitude. His company, Zorn International, was at the center of the computer revolution. He'd come to Weyford to speak. "First name Karl?"

"I didn't catch it. His henchman called him Mr. Zorn."

"Describe him."

"Silver spiky hair, feral eyes."

"A hyena on the hunt."

"That's him."

Karl Zorn. It had to be him. He had reminded me of Gordon Gecko, the villain in the movie "Wall Street," lean and mean, but oh, so charming. He had come to Weyford to advise the faculty and students about the phenomenal things that were happening in the digital world. I recalled how he stood on the stage before one thousand of the university's brightest and finest, positioning himself in front of the lectern instead of behind it. He regaled us with tales of his rise to fame. He joked that, as a young man, he was an insatiable reader, a conniver, and a chemist—not necessarily in that order. After he spoke, he approached me at the snack table. He grinned, exposing lots of teeth, and asked how I had liked his presentation. I got the distinct impression that he wanted my approval. I also sensed his father never failed to tell him he was worthless.

"I went to your house," Kimo continued. "To get Buddy's things. Zorn and his guy, a muscular Australian covered in scars, were there. They wanted the exit patient list."

"How did they—" I stopped myself. *Tommy*. What had he said? *It's her dad's fault.* Then he'd added: *It's always the father's fault*. The first part related to Holland. Did the second part relate to himself? Was he Zorn's son? Had he chased me on the road and invaded my house at his father's bidding?

Another brief moment of my initial meeting with Zorn surfaced. While at the snack table, he dined on carrot sticks and coffee. He told me he never drank anything other than coffee—black. Had he been fat, like Tommy, at one time?

"I told them I didn't have the list," Kimo went on.

"Good."

"Zorn didn't trust me. He ordered his guy to attack. I fought. I thought I could take him. Man, was I wrong."

"What happened?"

"He pinned me and Zorn said, *Get rid of him*. Then he doused his eyes with—"

"Eye drops."

"Yeah. Can you believe it? He had just ordered my execution. Talk about a cool cucumber."

Zorn had used eye drops at the lecture. He said having to wear contact lenses irked him, but powerful men had to keep up powerful appearances. Glasses, he claimed, weakened a man's look. Had he at one time worn glasses? Was it possible that he was the thickset goggle-eyed geek in the picture with my mother and father?

"Chase?" Kimo said. "Are you still there?"

Zorn had known a lot of my history, like my time spent in the Navy and my rise to fame in the field of history. He had pointed out things about the other professors, too, so I didn't question his interest in me. Thinking back, he had called me Day, not Professor Day.

"Chase, what's up? Do you know the guy?"

"Maybe."

Why would Zorn take the risk of breaking into my house and putting a hit on my friend? Because he was desperate to get his hands on my father. Was Zorn working in tandem with Tanaka? With Noble?

"What else did you learn?" I asked.

"Not much. He left. He said he had a Christmas cocktail party to attend on his yacht."

Reggie yelled, "Tell him the rest! Zorn's goon tied him up and took him for a boat ride on the ocean."

"I roused just before he pushed me overboard, but I didn't let on."

"The idiot drove away without making sure Kimo stayed under," Reggie added.

"Good thing you've got lungs," I said. During training Kimo was the best at water challenges. He could hold his breath for nearly three minutes; he could escape any kind of bonds they put on him; and he had excelled at the sunken helicopter trial. He had considered becoming a SEAL, but he settled for officer instead. And then he got booted out.

Kimo said, "After Reggie patches me up, I'm going to the police. I'll file a complaint."

"No, don't."

"Why not?"

Good question. Why not? Zorn must have kept tabs on me all these years hoping I would lead him to my father. Was Holland in his employ? Had she been paid to follow me? Were there others, like Vance? He could have alerted Zorn to his son's capture.

"Chase, talk."

"No police. Not yet." I explained my theory. "Think about it. What are the odds that people would try to off you and me right after we visited the precinct?" I told him about Vance's raid at midnight.

"But I can ID Zorn and his lackey."

"No. Lie low. I don't want to let Zorn know I'm on to him."

Kimo sighed. "What's your plan?"

"I don't have one. Yet." I wished I did. "Are you sure you're okay?"

"Nothing a shot of whiskey and polysporin won't cure."

I heard Reggie struggling for possession of the phone. "Watch your six," Kimo said before she got control.

"Chase, get your rear back here so we can talk." She hung up before I could tell her that I had abandoned her car.

CHAPTER 28

I raced down the street, seeking anonymity in the shadows while contemplating my next move. My cell phone rang. Thinking it was Reggie again, I swiped the prompt to answer without checking the readout. "What?"

"Hey, fella, didn't you like my wheels?"

I tensed at the sound of Holland's voice. The thoughts I'd had moments ago about her working for Zorn flicked through my mind. The text she had received when I was in the theater dressing room read: Need you now. Did Zorn send it? Holland had looked conflicted. After I left, did she go to his yacht to tell him she was through helping? Did he force her to tell him about the exit patient list?

"I found it where you ditched it," she went on.

"You're free?"

"I'm not free, and I'm not cheap, but I can be had." She laughed low and sexy.

"Holland, what's going on?"

"What do you mean? Why am I flirting with you? Do you need a road map?" Her tone was jaunty and flippant. If she'd been held against her will and she had escaped, shouldn't she be blathering to me about the experience? No, she wasn't a blatherer. She never had been. Conversation, even back in high school, was limited. Her mother's departure made her cautious and pensive. What if she was still in custody and someone was sitting beside her, forcing her to call me with a gun held to her head? I ached for the truth, but I wasn't sure if I asked, that I would get a straight answer. If only there was an ESP lie detector test.

"Luckily, I installed a GPS system," she went on.

"Holland, I can't talk right now."

"Why not? Where are you? At the gym? You sound out of breath."

"I'll get the keys to you."

"Don't bother. I can start a car without keys."

A horn bleated. I whipped around expecting to see a cop. A testy VW driver was waiting for me to step off the curb. I waved it past and then, seeing the entrance to San Jose University, hustled across the street. I would lose myself in the anonymity of the sprawling campus until I could figure out a plan.

"Chase, are you okay?"

"Fine. Just wet. You?"

"I'm okay." No artifice to her tone. "Do you need a lift? I filled up the tank."

I hesitated.

"I could come get you. How about we grab a midmorning coffee, and I'll fill you in on every facet of my life? Say, did I tell you? I'm on hold for a commercial. I auditioned for it last week. Cool, right? Say yes."

She sounded normal, unruffled. If she was guilty, could she pull that off? If I looked into her eyes, would I be able to read the truth? I wanted to trust her, and I needed wheels, sooner rather than later.

"Chase? You there?"

Barbie said I was impulsive. Maybe I was. "Yeah, sure. Pick me up. I'm car-less. South parking garage at CSU San Jose, near 7th and San Salvador." If Holland was working for Zorn, it would be safer to meet her somewhere public.

"I'll be there in ten minutes."

I hid in the shadows of the parking garage, checking my cell phone every few seconds for the time. My phone buzzed. Insistent. I read the display this time but didn't recognize the number. To answer or not to answer? I couldn't risk missing a call from someone with information. I stabbed Accept.

"Chase," my grandmother said, her voice barely a whisper.

"Barbie. Where are you calling from?"

"Shh. Don't talk. I'm—" She sucked in air. "Oh, no."

My breath caught in my chest. "What's wrong?"

"Red won't stay put."

"Red?"

"I'm at her house." Red was my grandmother's next door neighbor.

"I thought you were at Miss Margot's."

"I left there a half hour ago. I came home to finish packing. Minutes after I arrived, two guys showed up."

"Cops?"

"They're not in uniform."

"Is one of them black and bald?"

"No."

Not Philips. I said, "Barrel-chested with a wide, flat nose?"

"No."

Not Vance, either.

A Toyota Celica approached. I tucked into a recess. The driver didn't glance my way.

"One is a big Caucasian," Barbie said. "Linebacker size. Tight T-shirt, huge muscles. The other one is older. Silver hair. Too many facelifts."

Zorn. He had intended to nab my grandmother before, except she had gone to Miss Margot's.

"When they were climbing out of their Mercedes," Barbie went on, "I got a bad feeling, so I raced out the back gate to Red's." In Barbie's backyard, right behind a stand of camellias, there was a hidden gate.

"Good," I said. "These could be bad guys. There are people looking for my father."

"Don't start—"

"Listen to me, Barbie! It's true. I don't have time to explain. Mom tried to warn me. They killed her. They hurt Kimo."

"Lord." She liked Kimo; she considered him sassy. "Is he all right?"

"He'll recover, but now they're after me. If they get their hands on you—" I didn't want to think what Zorn might do. "I want you to hang up and call 911."

"Oh, no, Red's going outside. Red, wait!"

"Barbie, don't yell." My heart slammed my ribcage. Talk about feeling powerless. "Barbie."

"She didn't hear me. She's walking down her driveway," Barbie said, like an announcer on a sports program, giving a play-by-play account. "She's picking up her newspaper. It's okay. Wait. No. It's not okay. He's walking toward her."

"Which one?"

"The older one. Expensive suit. Talks with his hands."

Definitely Zorn. He had acted like a master conductor during his presentation at the university.

"The window is open. I can hear them. He's saying something about a contest." Barbie's delivery was choppy. "He's telling Red I've won a contest."

"It's a scam."

"I wasn't born yesterday. He's too slick. He's pointing to my driveway. He's asking Red if she knows where I am. I'm going out there. I'll put an end to this."

"Barbie. No. Don't. No heroics." My gut twisted with dread. Would Zorn risk hurting Red in the open? "Hang up and call 911."

"Hold on. Red is shaking her head. She's saying I drove away. She's walking back toward the house." Barbie gasped.

"What?" I felt sick to my stomach, like I was listening in on a live-action crime happening on the radio, with no ability to stop it.

"He's following her. He grabbed her elbow. I've got to help her."

"Barbie—"

"No, it's okay. She pulled away. She's shaking her newspaper at him." Barbie hiccupped out a laugh. "She's got spunk. Once a nun, always a nun. He's backing up. Oh, no. Lord, he's putting his hand in his pocket. Does he have a gun?"

"Barbie, is there anybody around? On the street? A gardener? Anybody?"

"I don't see a soul." She blew out a quick burst of air. "Phew. He didn't pull out a gun. He's waving cash at her. Red's taking it. Her mouth is moving."

"What is she saying?"

My grandmother was silent for a few seconds. "She told him I drive a white Honda, not the LeSabre. License plate LUV TRVL. Love travel. Ha! Can you imagine me with a vanity license plate? That Red is good. And they're off."

"Off?"

"The two men are running to the Mercedes like someone said, 'Drivers, start your engines.'"

"Barbie, I need you to get out of there."

"Okay, don't shout. Red has a car. We'll go to her sister's house. She's married to a tough guy. An ex-Marine. Where are you?"

"In limbo. Text me when you get situated."

She hesitated, then said, "I knew your father was trouble from the moment your mother told me about him. You remember I said that." She hung up.

The silence was deafening.

CHAPTER 29

While waiting inside the parking garage for Holland, I called Manuel. Reggie had touched base with him. I asked him to drum up all he could on Karl Zorn. I explained that Zorn was also in the Polaroid pictures my mother had kept. In addition, I asked him to dig up whatever he could on Jonathan Battle and Jonathan 'Jack' Battle, Jr.

"Will do," he said and disconnected.

As I contemplated what my father could have done to require that he change his name—stealing a book seemed too tame—I received a text from my grandmother: Safe.

At the same time, Holland's yellow Camaro appeared. I tensed, but I was determined to proceed. I slid into the passenger's seat and gasped at the sight of her. Her left eye was swollen. The skin on her cheek was red and slightly cracked.

"You're soaked," she said.

"I'll dry out. Who did that to you?"

"I walked into a door."

"A door with a four-inch hand span."

Holland steered the Camaro out of the garage and into traffic. "Old boyfriend." She was lying. Her eyes were tight, her mouth firm.

So much for hoping for the truth.

I took the plunge. "Is your boyfriend a guy named Tommy?"

"Who?"

"Thick neck. Bad skin. He came by my place and held a gun on my dog."

"Crap. Is Buddy—"

"He's fine." I studied her face. "Tommy said he knew you. Do you know him?"

"No." She didn't blink. No inkling of a lie in those eyes that had haunted my dreams for years. She was an actress; was she that good?

I pressed on. "How about a guy named Zorn?"

"Who is he? A creature from the planet Xenon?"

"Don't joke. Did he kidnap you?"

Holland coughed out a laugh. "That's ripe. And then what, this Zorn let me go?" She brandished her right wrist. "No hackles, no handcuffs. Look, Chase, I have a history of bad choices. The guy that did this to my face is one of those bad choices." Her eyes moistened, as if on cue, but her mouth remained firm.

Sirens blared. I glanced over my shoulder but didn't see any flashing red lights. No one was signaling us to pull over.

Holland eyed me with concern. "What's going on with you?"

"Cops are searching for me. It's a long story. Let's swing by the Outreach Hostel." Granted, Reggie had declared the hostel a safe house, but I couldn't follow her order. I'd given up all confidence in my ability to recognize duplicity in Holland. I needed someone with a keen eye—specifically Reggie—to give me an opinion. "I'll bring you up to date." I gave her directions.

"What's the Outreach Hostel?"

"I told you that I give veteran's art lessons."

"Right. The angry art."

"Reggie Ramirez—you remember Reggie?"

"Do I ever." Holland snorted. While Reggie had disliked Holland because of her idiotic choice not to go to college, Holland had despised Reggie because, well, she was pretty sure Reggie had a thing for me, way back when. "Should I be jealous?"

"Not then; not now. Reggie's the owner of the hostel." I explained quickly about her brother dying. "She gives her heart and soul to vets. She also makes the best coffee in town. We might have to sneak in through the back." I explained about Vance's attack. Holland didn't react to the name.

"Cops might be watching the place."

"Get real."

"Another cop, an associate of Vance's, came looking for me after midnight on trumped up business."

"Are you kidding? Chase, what are you messed up in? Tell me everything. From the beginning."

Her alarm seemed genuine. Keeping to basics, I recounted the last twenty-four hours, from the moment she left my house, to Vance pursuing me over the roof at the theater, to Buddy being held hostage. "Kimo picked me up. We went from there to the precinct." I didn't tell her about Kimo and his run-in with Zorn's henchman. If she was in league with Zorn, I didn't want him to discover Kimo was alive.

"You're not making many friends, are you?" Holland turned right and stepped on the gas. "Why were you in San Jose?"

I hesitated. I didn't want to tell her about my lame attempt to interrogate Jack Battle, Jr., either, because if I gave her Jack's name, then she would have something to hand over to whomever she was working for. *If* she was working for anyone.

"Enough." Holland pulled to the side of the road and jammed the car into park. She twisted in her seat. "You don't trust me. What's going on? What did I do?"

I drummed my fingers on the car door.

"C'mon. I deserve the truth."

"Do you?"

"Yes! You and I have a history. We're in this—whatever *this* is—together."

I drew in a deep breath then pressed forward. "The guy who showed up at my house—Tommy—said he overheard you telling someone on a yacht about the exit patient list."

"On a yacht? Are you kidding me?" Her voice skated upward. "First of all, I hate boats. Second of all, I hate guys named Tommy. Chase, you've got to believe me. I would never do anything to purposely hurt you." She reached for my hand.

I wrapped my fingers around hers and felt the same connection I had experienced with her before…until I replayed the words she'd just said. She would never *purposely* hurt me. I pulled my hand away.

Her eyes welled up. "What?"

My breath snagged in my lungs. I couldn't remember seeing a more beautiful, vulnerable woman in my life. If only I could rewind my life. See my mother alive. Meet Holland before all the tragedy.

"What?" she repeated.

"Nothing."

"Do you trust me?"

"Yes," I lied. I didn't. I couldn't.

"Have you located your father?"

"Not yet. I've got a friend in San Jose who is good with computers. He's working on an angle." That was all I offered. It seemed to be enough.

Holland steered the Camaro north on the 101 Freeway. She took the turnoff at Embarcadero. Minutes later, following my directions, she drove past the hostel. "I don't see any police cars."

"That beige sedan looks suspicious." I sank down into the seat. "Drive past and turn right. Drop me off around the block. I'll go in by myself."

"I'm not dropping you off anywhere." Holland pulled to a stop in front of a row of rundown houses. "I'm not leaving you until I know you're safely inside."

"I'll be fine." I thanked her for the ride and hurried out of the Camaro, not sure when or if I would ever see her again. Doing my best not to look back, I limped up the path—the jog down the stairs at Young Warriors had made my ankle ache again.

"Chase. Wait."

I whipped around. Holland was following me.

"Why didn't you tell me you were hurt?" she asked.

"Go back to the car."

"I see a break in that hedge." She pointed. "Think you can hobble through there without making a sound?" She didn't wait for a reply. She led the way. At the back entrance to the hostel, Holland stepped aside. "After you."

I shuffled into the kitchen. Reggie was feeding Buddy. The dog charged me while howling a greeting. His feet scrambled beneath him. I stopped his progress and scratched his ears. "Yeah, I missed you, too."

Reggie pivoted and regarded Holland with outright contempt. She flipped her curly hair over her shoulders. "Well, well, Holland. You're older for sure. Any wiser?"

"Not yet." Holland extended her hand to shake.

Reggie didn't reciprocate. "Chase, I warned you not to bring anyone here."

"I know."

"Then why did you break protocol?"

"I needed a ride."

"You had my car."

"I had to abandon it in San Jose. Police were roaming the area." I gave Reggie the street address where I'd parked her car.

"Why were you in—"

I flipped her the key to shut her up. She caught it and bunched it in her fist, her eyes smoldering.

"Which reminds me..." I pulled Holland's keys from my back pocket. "Here are yours."

A solemn moment passed between the three of us.

Holland cleared her throat. "I can see you're in good hands. I should be going."

"No, don't. We can have coffee in the kitchen."

"Uh-uh." Reggie wagged her head. "The kitchen is not open twenty-four-seven. I closed it at nine-thirty. Besides, we just gave our last cup to yet another friendly cop who wanted to know if I'd seen you, Chase."

"Another cop?" Holland said.

"None of your business." Reggie folded her arms.

Holland offered a tired smile. "Chase, you've got a lot on your plate, and I've got rehearsal. We'll make a date for that coffee. Good luck finding your dad. Call me when you do. Let me share your joy." She hugged me then released me, running her fingers under my shirt collar to lift it around my neck. I remembered her doing the same thing in high school. She said I looked tougher that way, like something out of *Grease*, which was her favorite musical and movie. She pulled a business card from her purse, scribbled something on the backside, and handed it to me. "Be well."

After she exited, I whirled on Reggie. "Could you be any nastier?"

"I don't trust her." She planted her hands on her hips. "I'm getting a vibe."

"You don't trust anyone."

"Excuse me, but Holland just *happened* to be at the hospital when you were? And she just *happened* to call when you needed a lift?"

Her suspicion fueled my own. I had wanted her honest assessment. I got it. But if Holland was working for Zorn or even Vance, wouldn't she have lingered to find out whatever I had learned? The uncertainty made my head hurt. "Where's Kimo?"

"In the yellow room." Each room in the hostel was painted a different color. Reggie claimed the variety of colors helped the vets feel special and individual.

I headed upstairs. Buddy bounded after me.

Reggie pounded up the stairs behind us.

I entered Kimo's room and winced at the sight of him. He sat propped on the pillows, eyes closed, his face a mass of bruises. His wrists were chafed raw. I drew near. "Are you awake?"

Kimo's eyelids fluttered. He worked hard to open them then grimaced with pain.

Reggie leaned against the doorjamb, keeping her distance.

"Man, I'm sorry," I said.

"No sweat. Just proves I've got to up my workouts. What've you got?"

I pulled the Polaroids from my shirt pocket. "Is this Zorn? It's an old photo."

Kimo nodded. "What's going on?"

I told them about my one and only introduction to Karl Zorn. I also gave them a rundown about finding Gert Dalton and locating—then losing—Jack Jr.

"That's when Holland called," Reggie said. "She gave him a ride here. They're going on a date." She sounded so snide.

I glanced at the business card Holland handed me. I recalled that she had written something on the back. I flipped it over. *Beware of Zorn,* her message said. I flinched as if I'd been sucker punched.

"What?" Reggie snatched the card and scanned what Holland had written. "I knew it."

"You don't know anything."

Reggie shook the card. "Don't be naïve."

I grabbed it back. "Listen to me, we need to know Zorn's plan. You know how in the game *Battleship* you sit on opposites sides of the table trying to figure out where your opponent has put all his ships? In this game we have a lot of players—Zorn, Zorn's son, Noble, and Tanaka." I elaborated.

"Don't forget about Vance," Kimo said.

"And Holland," Reggie added.

Kimo aimed a finger. "I told you before, you've got to steer clear of her, bro."

Reggie pumped her fist. "Exactly what I've been telling him. Don't you remember how it went down in high school?"

I glowered at them. "That was my fault, not hers. Stay on track. What's important is finding out why they're all in the game. Why do they want my father?"

"The book," Kimo said.

"Right. The blue book. Whatever is inside it has to matter, right? So my primary goal right now is to track down Jack Battle, Jr. He's got to know where his father is."

"*Your* father," Kimo said.

"*Our* father."

"*If* this Jack guy is really your half-brother," Reggie said. "That's a big *if*. Are you positive?"

I would never forget the look on Gert Dalton's face. She said my father lived with a heavy burden. I would bet it was the weight of leading a double life. Just knowing that I was close to finding him sent a tremor of anxiety and also hope through me. What would I say when I faced him? How would he feel? Would he remember me? Would he remember my mother?

"I've got to get back to Manuel. I need his help. Reggie—"

"Another car. Got it." She huffed. "Man, you're an insurance company's nightmare."

CHAPTER 30

At half past ten, I sat slumped in the booth at the back of Manuel's diner, my stomach as knotted up as the rope hanging on the wall behind me. A mug of steaming coffee and a plate of toast swathed in peanut butter rested on the Formica table in front of me. I took a bite of the toast and pushed it aside.

"No good?" Manuel was sitting beside me, his laptop computer open on the table. He looked as ragged as I did.

"No appetite."

"You've got to eat."

"Don't mother me."

"If I don't, my wife will." He aimed a finger at the computer screen. "Here's what I've got on Zorn so far."

In 1980, Karl Zorn graduated at the top of his class at UC Berkeley. He then became an entrepreneur, rising to instant fame with his invention of the Hub, one of the first interactive computer software programs. Next, he created the Hi-Wire, a forerunner of today's cellular phones. Along the way, he invested well, including in Google. He turned his millions into billions. He owned a house in plush Los Altos Hills and another in Lake Tahoe. A yacht. A sailboat. A few luxury cars. According to various articles, Zorn eschews politics, he loves the America's Cup races, and he is a major philanthropist who donates to charities and museums.

One photo that Manuel drummed up was of Zorn and his family standing in front of a black-and-white Benetti yacht. Zorn had married a handsome younger woman, although her face was pinched. She looked tired. Of him? Beside her stood a pair of twin Asian girls and a thickset youth with pockmarked skin. Tommy.

"Do you have anything that might link Uma Noble to Zorn?"

"As it so happens"—Manuel leaned back in his chair—"Noble went to UC Berkeley, too."

"It's a big campus. They might not have run into each other."

"True. Zorn was Zeta Psi. Noble was a Delta Gamma sorority girl. They didn't reside in the same dorm. Zorn studied computers and business; Noble earned a degree in English. No crossover there, either."

"You were able to pull up their syllabi?"

He grinned. "People have been inputting data for decades now. Information is up for grabs. It's insane.

"Hold it." I yanked the photographs from my pocket and tossed them like a folded hand of cards onto the table. I tapped the one with the magnificent columns. "I thought this was a mansion. What if it's a frat house? I'm no architect, but those are Doric, aren't they? Except why would my mother have crashed a frat party?"

"Kids do it all the time. Free booze." Manuel typed: ZETA PSI > UC BERKELEY > IMAGE into the search line. Hundreds of images emerged. He chuckled. "Wow. Party hearty, man." He scrolled through two pages of images. "Hey, take a look. There are the columns. See the window in the background?" He compared the Polaroid to the one on the screen. "Same window. This is the place."

"How would my mother have known about the party? She didn't go to college."

"Maybe she knew Zorn or Noble, you know, from high school or something."

"Where were they born? Where did they grow up?"

"Zorn is from Michigan. Noble is a local."

"From where?"

"Menlo Park."

"My mother lived in Los Altos. That's a bust."

"Wait a *minuto*." Manuel's fingers flew across the keyboard. A new Internet page emerged. "There's an article dated back in the seventies that says Noble's parents divorced. One of her parents moved to Los Altos. She might have attended Los Altos High." Yet another Internet page appeared. "Bingo. She's a Los Altos High alum. Your mother and Noble could have been friends. They look about the same age."

I nodded. "Okay, so Noble told my mother about the party. Mom went. How did my father end up there? According to my Internet search, he didn't go to college, either."

"I'm telling you, free booze." Manuel fingered the corner of the photo. "Zorn seems *into* Noble, doesn't he?"

"What went down that night?" I said. "Do you think they all hooked up?"

"More importantly, why did your mom keep this commemorative photo?"

"Because it was the night I was conceived."

"Or perhaps that was the night your father stole the blue book. Afterward, he vanished and changed his name."

I nodded.

Manuel said, "How about this scenario? Karl Zorn was a cutting-edge scientist. What if whatever is in the blue book is scientific in nature, like supersonic spaceflight or the cure for cancer?"

"Then my father should have handed over the book to the proper authorities. Think of the acclaim. He would have become a hero." I shook my head. "We're missing something."

"Maybe what's inside is a diary or a record of an event."

"What event? A mass murder? A coup?"

Manuel drummed the table top. "Until Noble's husband died, she donated a lot to Republican causes. Maybe the book holds age-old secrets that could bring down a regime. You know, the dirty laundry of up-and-comers."

Dirty laundry made me think of Officer Vance.

I slapped the table. Customers at the counter swiveled and stared at me. I held up my hands and explained. "Sorry, folks, the computer froze. Amazing they work at all, isn't it?" I lowered my voice to address Manuel.

"When I did an Internet search on my father, I found him referenced in some articles. He was an orphan and, as a teen, involved in a petty theft crime spree. What if Vance—"

"The cop who tried to attack you at the hostel—"

"Knew my father. He is the approximate age of these four. What if he came to the party with my father? Maybe he's the one that took these photos."

Manuel peered at the picture. "Difficult to say."

"Maybe Vance knows what happened because he was part of it."

"Dude"—Manuel pushed the computer away and leaned back—"your father changed his name. He went into hiding. Shouldn't these people rest assured that he has no intention of outing them for whatever it is that went down?"

"Precisely. They don't care about him. They want the book." I glanced at a picture of my mother again. Why did she, who had been fake-dead for so many years, decide to come back to life? "My mother saw my father at the hospital. Maybe she thought there was money in it for her. She went to Noble—"

"Or Zorn or both."

"She said she told *her*. I'm assuming she meant she told Noble about my father. Noble was at the trailer."

"Makes sense."

"My father had abandoned Mom. Maybe, all these years later, she wanted to get even. She went to the trailer, ready, willing, and able to turn him over for cash. But something happened. Either Noble opted not to pay, or my mother asked for more money. If that was the case, the bodyguard would've told Noble not to negotiate. He was packing a Glock. He threatened my mother. They struggled. The gun fired. In her last breath, Mom one-upped them. She told me to save him."

"Do you think Zorn has a clue that Noble is after your father?" Manuel picked up one of the photos and flipped it over. "Hey, what's this date?"

He displayed the back of the photograph. My mother had written

5/18/80. Back in the day, photograph printers had included the developing date on a photograph. The developing date on that particular photograph, May 20, 1980, didn't match the handwritten one. Was May eighteenth the day of the frat party? It wasn't my mother's birthday. Counting ahead forty weeks, it could have been the date of my conception.

"May," I said. "That's near the end of a school year. What if the party at the fraternity was in honor of a Berkeley graduation?"

"I'd buy that."

Had the foursome—or fivesome, if Vance was involved—partied all night? Had they gotten drunk and done something that they needed buried in order to preserve their reputations? Where? What? Why?

Manuel's wife Nita appeared. Her face was bathed in perspiration. "*Mi amor,* I need you. We just got slammed. Twenty truckers."

"Go," I said. "I'll keep at this. Truckers have to eat."

Manuel rose and said over his shoulder, "By the way, when do I get another of your grandmother's home-cooked meals? I'm still waiting for her to hand over her recipe for meatloaf."

The mention of Barbie jolted me. Even though she had texted me, I needed to hear her voice. I dialed her number. Busy. I pressed End and tried again. As I listened to the phone ring, I tapped in a string of words on the Internet browser, seeking information about any crime in the Bay Area in May of 1980. I added the words: THEFT, COLLEGE STUDENT, and FRATERNITY.

A link to an article about the murder of a student on the Berkeley campus appeared.

I was opening the link when my grandmother answered. "Chase, my sweet boy. I'm so glad you called. I was rude when I hung up before. I know you need closure. Remember, and I quote, 'No matter who your enemy is, there's a chance you'll need him tomorrow.'"

"Gandhi?" I said.

"Michael Westen, *Burn Notice*."

I laughed. She and her TV reruns. She was an addict. I blew her a kiss. "I love you, Barbie." Before hitting End, I said, "Wait. One last question.

May 18th, 1980. Was that the day my mother met my father?"

Silence.

"Barbie, please."

"Yes, it was." She hung up.

I stared at the computer screen. The student who was shot was named Geoffrey Gaynor. His roommate was Karl Zorn. The police believed it was a case of robbery. Gaynor had a history of carrying a lot of cash on him. The police never found the killer. Zorn was not a suspect because he was attending a graduation party at his fraternity at the time of death.

CHAPTER 31

Energy thrummed inside me as I headed across the Golden Gate Bridge toward Sausalito where Gaynor's parents lived. Rain pelted the windshield. I had visited the area a couple of times with my grandmother. I had boarded tall ships, taken the tour and learned about the hippies that had inhabited the area, and visited the nearby giant redwoods. I made the first right and drove down the ramp. I followed the line of cars moving along Lateral and Bridgeway. A gray gloom surrounded the island of Alcatraz in the bay to the right.

A few minutes later, I stood inside Gaynor's parents' house, which was a brilliant blue and white Victorian-style home that looked freshly painted. On the drive over, I had called Mr. Gaynor and claimed I was a reporter who worked for the *San Jose Mercury.* The paper was doing a story on cold cases. Gaynor had seemed eager to talk about his son.

"My wife isn't up to chatting today. Hope you understand." Gaynor was a tall man and had the unkempt look of a studious person who didn't care much for fashion. Shaggy hair. Rumpled shirt. A hawk's piercing eyes. He stood by the bay window, looking out, a cup of tea in his hand. He had poured me the same. One sugar. "She's never fully recovered. Post traumatic stress syndrome, the doctors said. Geoffrey's death hit her hard."

"I understand." He had no idea how much I got it; for years after my mother's initial death, I would break out in sweat just thinking about it. Now that she was not only dead but murdered, breathing was coming harder, and fury hovered just beneath the surface.

"His death hit me hard, too," Gaynor said. "But I'm tougher. I served in the army. I saw action."

"Navy," I said. "Lieutenant."

Gaynor saluted. "Sir."

"Forget about it."

He lowered his arm. "It's nice of you to ask about Geoffrey. After all these years. He deserves recognition." Gaynor's breath popped out of him, as if he were holding his emotions in check. "You asked where we came from. Ohio. Holmes County. Land of the Amish. We aren't Amish. We're Presbyterian." He wagged a hand as if to bring himself back on track. "When Geoffrey chose to go to Berkeley, we were surprised, but we didn't say no. How could we? Full scholarship. California. Such a lure. I was an inventor. My income was modest. Geoffrey was an inventor, too. He had such high hopes."

"He was an inventor?"

He motioned for me to take in the room. Gadgets filled every space. The bookshelves, the tabletops, the floor. There was a miniature solar windmill, a towering mechanism with a slew of silver balls in the bottom-most feeding loop, a variety of colorful whirling objects that would have been considered art in any other setting. Zorn had excelled in the technology industry. Had he stolen Geoffrey's designs? Was that how he had made his billions?

"Was he technologically savvy?" I asked.

"Yes, Geoffrey was what people now call a techie. He was…different. When he went off to college, we moved to the Bay Area to be close to him. The wife and I could live anywhere. I never thought we'd remain here." Gaynor had mentioned at the outset that Geoffrey was their only son. "After the tragedy…" He sighed. "We chose to stay to help the police. They kept looking. For the killer. They never found him."

I thought of what Manuel had said earlier. Maybe the blue book held something scientific in nature. "Sir, was Geoffrey working on any particular project when he died?"

"Geoffrey never shared. With anyone." Gaynor pivoted, a ghostly smile on his face. "He thought I might steal his idea."

"Really?"

"He was paranoid. Diagnosed in his teens."

Welcome to the club, I mused.

"It's part of what made him brilliant." Gaynor approached an object that looked like a bunch of loopy wires. "See these?" He ran his fingers along the wires to a doorknob on a door that must have led to a closet. "Open the door, a dog barks. No dog, of course. Merely to panic an intruder. Geoffrey designed it when he was five. His mind never rested. He only slept for four hours at a time. He had the Einstein problem, his psychiatrist said. How he idolized Einstein."

I sat taller. "Your son saw a psychiatrist?" Perhaps Geoffrey told the shrink what he was working on.

"Back in Ohio. Not here. My wife…she worried. Geoffrey could...He would prattle." Gaynor smiled. "Like me. But then he might lash out."

"He was violent?"

"Only to himself. A side effect of depression." He studied a button on his shirt for a second then looked up at me. "What were we talking about before the psychiatrist?"

"Geoffrey didn't sleep. You said he had the Einstein problem."

"No, that's not it." Gaynor snapped his fingers, then pointed. "You asked what Geoffrey was working on. I don't know exactly. He took so many classes, kept so many notebooks."

I recalled the test books we had used in college for final exams. "Were the notebooks blue?"

Gaynor nodded. "Yes. We found a pack of the darned things in Geoffrey's dorm room safe."

The kid had a room safe in college? He was more suspicious than I was.

"Many of his inventions were ready to go." Gaynor waved his hand at the gadgets in the room. "Each of these is a prototype. In Geoffrey's notebooks, we discovered a few software ideas, too. Computers were so new to the world. I didn't understand. I didn't think they would last. I was wrong. After Geoffrey died, we—my wife and I—sold his designs. The money the designs earned put enough in our pockets to retire for life."

I shifted in my chair as I imagined the night Geoffrey died. I would bet Karl Zorn, not my father, was the instigator. Geoffrey might not have told anyone what he had created, but that didn't mean Zorn, his roommate, hadn't pried. Did Zorn bring Noble and my parents to his dorm room to watch him seize and conquer? Did he coerce my father, a petty thief, to break into Geoffrey's precious safe? Maybe Zorn already knew the combination. Geoffrey came home and caught them mid-heist. He went ballistic. He accused Zorn. They struggled. Things got out of control. Geoffrey died. My father panicked and ran with the blue book in hand. Why he'd had hold of it was anybody's guess.

Even now, all these years later, if the police discovered Zorn killed Geoffrey to get his hands on the designs, he would go to jail for life. If someone found out that Uma Noble was an accomplice, she would be ruined, too. The two of them had believed my mother was dead. When she reappeared, did that throw them into a tailspin? When they learned my father was alive, did they panic? If he surfaced with the missing blue book in hand, no matter what was in it, he would reveal their guilt.

"The roommate, Karl Zorn. What can you tell me about him?"

Gaynor tilted his head like an inquisitive bird.

"What did he say happened?" I asked.

"Karl wasn't sure. He was out that night. With friends. It was graduation. He said Geoffrey went off by himself."

"Didn't you go to the ceremony?"

Mr. Gaynor paled. "My wife was sick. I couldn't leave her. Geoffrey told us he didn't mind. He was such a loner. If only—" He sucked back a dry sob. "Karl believed Geoffrey went to a bar and flaunted his money."

That was in the article I'd read.

"Geoffrey did that sometimes. As a teen, he sold a few inventions. We didn't deny him immediate access to his money. He liked carrying hundred dollar bills. Me? I like twenties. They're easier to make change." He rubbed the bridge of his nose as if regrouping. "Someone must have followed Geoffrey back to the room."

"He was robbed and shot."

Gaynor nodded curtly.

"Which bar did your son frequent?"

"The police never figured that out."

Because Karl Zorn misled them, no doubt.

"Go on, sir. What else did Zorn say happened?"

"He said the killer must have taken advantage of the fact that he and the rest of the dorm were out. The robber—the killer—was able to follow Geoffrey without someone else seeing him. He got the jump on our son. The killer even used Geoffrey's gun."

"Your son owned a gun?"

"Like I said, he was distrustful."

"Paranoid."

"Yes."

"Were there fingerprints on the weapon?"

"None."

"Was there any other evidence?"

"The room was in total disarray. The bed tossed. The closet ransacked." Gaynor moaned. "Such a stupid, senseless act. He was a good boy. Never hurt a fly."

I thought again about the notebook. Has the invention that was outlined in it been created yet? What if Karl Zorn still wants what Geoffrey formulated? Is it meant for good or evil? If evil, did my father realize what it was? Did he run off with it to save the world? Did he realize Zorn would continue to hunt for him? Was that why he returned to society as an entirely different person?

Gaynor said, "I'd give all this up to have my son back, you know."

"I'm sure you would."

"In the end, it's relationships that matter. All this"—Gaynor gestured to the view and things in the room, the life he and his wife led at the expense of his son—"is worthless."

CHAPTER 32

Steady rain fell from the dusty gray clouds and made the road slick. I took the road slowly; the wheels on the Ford Escort that Reggie lent me were nearly bald. My cell phone buzzed. I fumbled to read the text. The dean of students was demanding to know where I was. I didn't respond. Seconds later, the phone rang again. It was Manuel. I heard lots of noise in the background.

"Dude, I got a fix on Jack Battle." Manuel chuckled. "Just goes to show that former girlfriends have their talents." I heard a *thwack*. Manuel yowled, then laughed again. "The wife's not a fan of my traffic patrol pal. Ow! Nita, cut it out! Enough with the newspaper, woman. Chase, you still there? Where are you?"

"On the freeway, near Marsh Road." I scanned the rearview mirror. I didn't spot a tail.

"You're not too far from where Battle is. My traffic pal pulled up Battle's license plate and tracked him to a chichi section of Palo Alto. She saw him parking his Beemer. Here's the address."

"Thanks."

"Wait. Nita's nagging me. Did you eat the sandwich she fixed you?"

"Yes," I lied. It was sitting on the passenger seat. I would eat it. Soon.

Minutes later I drew alongside Jack Jr.'s BMW X6. Jack wasn't inside it. I would wait.

As I was parking in a nearby spot, I caught sight of something that sent a jolt through me. Zorn International headquarters were just down the street. The building was understated and didn't look high-tech in any way. Was Jack inside negotiating on behalf of our father? Did he plan to turn over the notebook in exchange for our father's freedom?

Quickly I exited the car, eager to nab Jack as he left the building, but I stopped short when I spotted Tommy Zorn, with an umbrella in hand, swaggering or, rather, staggering along the sidewalk. A cigarette hung from the kid's thick-lipped mouth. He held a cell phone to his ear. Tommy paused in front of Zorn International, tossed the cigarette into the gutter, pocketed his phone, closed his umbrella, and swung the door open with force. He lost his grip. The door whacked the doorstop. Tommy disappeared inside.

At the same time, I detected movement out of the corner of my eye. Jack Jr. was heading toward his car. No umbrella, no raincoat, nice suit. Where had he come from? Maybe he had exited a side entrance of Zorn International.

I burst from my car and raced toward Jack. Before he knew what was happening, I shoved him against the Beemer's driver door.

Jack was about my height. Leaner. All muscle. He pushed back. I looped my car keys around my index finger and gripped his jacket lapels.

"What the blazes?" Jack smacked my hand. My keys flew into a puddle.

Rain drenched us as I took a firmer hold on his jacket. "What deal did you cut?"

"What?"

"With Karl Zorn."

"I don't know what you're talking about."

"You know who I mean."

"I've heard of him. Never met him."

"Don't play coy with me."

"Get off me." Jack wedged his arms and elbows in between him and me and heaved.

I couldn't maintain my grip. I staggered back a foot, skidding on the wet pavement.

"Look, fella." Jack stabbed a finger at my face. "You must have me mistaken for someone else. Back off."

"You're working with Karl Zorn."

"Who are you?"

"Chase Day. You ran off when I came to your office earlier."

"You're the guy who scared my mother?" He hauled back with his right arm and shot it forward, his intention to ram my chin with his fist.

But I was quicker. I had dealt with guys like Jack in the Navy. They fought with their heart, not their brain. I grabbed his forearm mid-punch, wrenched the arm behind his back, and shoved his face against the window of his car.

He snarled. "I told you, I don't know Karl Zorn. We don't do business together. I'm an independent entrepreneur. A gamer. I make games."

"You just exited his building."

"I did not."

"I saw you—"

"Coming out of Gaming Galore."

I glanced quickly at the terrain. There was a Gaming Galore store to the east of Zorn International. Jack made a move to reach inside his jacket. I seized his wrist before he could grab hold of a weapon.

"Cool it, man," Jack snapped. "I purchased a game. I'll show you. It's in a bag. Let go of me."

His tone was earnest. Reluctantly, I released him.

Jack withdrew a plastic bag with the store's logo on it. He pulled a game from the bag: *Memory.* "Our latest design. This is the first on the shelves. I buy a first every time. We have over sixty titles. Okay?"

I didn't know what to make of him. He seemed straightforward. "Did your mother mention that I'm your half-brother?"

"Yeah, right." Jack screwed his head sideways. "A stalker who claims kinship." In a surprisingly quick move, he broke free of my hold. He spun around and thumped my chest with the heel of his palm. "Listen up, pal. I don't have any brothers, half or otherwise, got me?"

"My mom and your father had an affair."

"Buzz off."

"Way before he got together with your mother. He never knew about me. He split town before my mom could tell him. Back then, his name was

Luther Marcussen. Your mother recognized his picture in my mom's locket."

"Ah, this is rich. You're saying my father lives under an assumed name?"

"It's a long story."

"Tell it to your kids, and don't plan on me writing you into my will." Jack cut past me and opened the BMW's front door. He tossed the bag holding the game onto the passenger seat.

I grasped his shoulder and spun him around. "People want our father dead."

"Our. *Our*? Are you certifiable?" Jack gave my hand a disdainful look. His gaze traveled to my face. When he got there, he paused. Was he curious, after all? Did he note the same color of eyes and skin? The same bone structure? Heck, we even had the same cadence in our speech—one of the first things I had noticed. Could that be passed along genetically?

"I think our father might have witnessed a murder thirty-seven years ago," I went on, running with the theory I had devised in Sausalito. "He took something from the crime scene. I have to find him before Karl Zorn does."

"My father is not a thief."

"There's no mention of Luther Marcussen anywhere on the Internet after that night. He went off the grid. My mother claimed she saw your father...*our* father...at Keystone Hospital. She was recuperating there before she was murdered." Saying the last word hit me with an intensity that shocked me. I gagged down the acid flooding my throat. "Before she died, she told me to save my father." I didn't elaborate how I'd come to that conclusion. "I've poked around and figured out Zorn and possibly a woman named Noble are the ones who want to harm him. Years ago, our father took a book—a notebook, I think—that contains an invention."

Jack wiped rain off his face. "Why should I believe you?"

"I've been followed and attacked, and Zorn's kid, who just entered Zorn International, held my dog at gunpoint."

"Sounds like you'll need a few therapy sessions. *Adios*, bro."

"Our father—"

"*Your* father," Jack said.

"—is in danger. Zorn also tried to kill a friend of mine and almost kidnapped my grandmother."

"This keeps getting better. The Zorn Conspiracy. Good-bye, Mr. Day."

I reached for him. "You're not getting it."

Jack jabbed with his right. This time I wasn't prepared. His fist met my nose full on. I retaliated with a punch of my own but missed. I barely scathed Jack's jaw. He countered with another mind-numbing blow, which sent me staggering. I slipped on the slick pavement. Jack charged me and swung again. Pain shot into my skull; humiliation ran a close second. How could I have let a non-com like Jack get the jump on me? With the heel of his palm, he rammed me hard in the chest then kicked my keys into the middle of the street.

I reached for them at the same time a Toyota veered toward me. The driver wailed on his car horn. I rolled out of the way. A rooster tail of water hit me and knocked me off balance. Before I could scramble to my feet, Jack leaped into his car and tore off.

CHAPTER 33

The rain continued as I drove angry, my movements erratic. Headlight flares shot into my skull and made my brain ache.

Karl Zorn. Everything came down to him. He had ordered his man to kill Kimo. He had tried to kidnap my grandmother to use her as bait to lure me. When Zorn's roommate was found murdered, Zorn had a pat alibi. Why hadn't the police been able to prove otherwise?

I rounded a curve and thought of Holland. What was her connection to Zorn? Relative? Employee? Her warning had been clandestine. Had he threatened her? I pulled out the business card she gave me, and against the rules of the road and all the warning signals blaring in my brain, dialed her on my cell phone. I reached a voicemail. When her message ended, I said I needed to meet. *Urgent.*

Rather than wait for a return call, on impulse, I headed down El Camino Real toward Los Altos. I recalled Holland saying she had rehearsal. To get to the theater, I needed to pass the house where she had lived as a teen. A *For Sale* sign was planted in the overgrown grass in the front yard. I remembered stolen moments—wonderful moments—in her bedroom, when her father wasn't home. We had made plans and talked about our future together. If only I could turn back the hands of time.

When I arrived at the theater, my jaw was locked so tightly it hurt. The theater looked closed. No lights were switched on outside. Had I misunderstood? Maybe Holland meant she had rehearsal tomorrow night. A rundown Chevy was parked near the rear entrance. The Canondale bicycle that I had borrowed and vowed to return still leaned against the dumpster. A miracle. In this day and age, most big-ticket items left out in the open wound up stolen within twenty-four hours.

The stage door was ajar. A sliver of light gleamed through the opening.

I pulled in beside the Chevy and slogged across rain-soaked gravel to the theater door. Hoping to wrangle Holland's current home address from whomever was working within, I entered. I didn't hear a sound. Running lights provided a dim glow backstage.

"Hello," I called. "Anybody here? I don't want to startle you. I'm looking for Holland." I moved past the green room, into the wings, onto the stage. A halo of light filled the technical booth, which was located behind the tiers of loge seats. A silhouette moved inside the booth. "Hey, you, there. The door was open. I'm looking for—"

Floorboards on the stage creaked. I swung around. Out of nowhere, three guys hurled themselves at me. Before I could register faces, the beefy one in the middle smashed my jaw with a fist. I reeled backward. I couldn't gain traction. Couldn't get my fists up. Was the tech guy in the booth aware? Would he call the police?

The beefy one nailed me again. I slammed into a dividing wall. Suddenly, all three were on me. One pinned my arms. Another shrugged a burlap bag over my head. I tried to fight back but couldn't. They spun me around. One landed a blow to my kidneys. The pain shot up my spine. I felt something being girded around my middle, constricting me. Whoever had control of the cinch nudged me at the knees. I buckled.

One of the three hefted me over a shoulder and started running.

A second guy ran alongside. With boozy breath, he said, "You lose, man."

I recognized the squeaky voice. Tommy Zorn. Had he followed me from downtown Palo Alto? I thought I had paid attention looking for a tail.

"Holland," I yelled. My voice sounded muffled beneath the burlap.

"Yeah, blame it on her, dufus. You had no clue she planted a tracking device on you, did you? You are dumb as a rock."

I flashed on Holland: fingering my lapel; her good-bye kiss; the note on the business card. She had warned me, but I had slipped up.

"You're Karl Zorn's kid," I said.

"Two points, idiot." Tommy snorted. "I got wind of the bug at my dad's place. For the past half hour, I've been on you like grease on cement, in real-time, using my smart phone. Take that."

Someone whacked my head with something. Hard.

CHAPTER 34

I woke to the rumble of thunder. I tried to open my eyes but couldn't. A blindfold held them shut. I lay face up on what felt like a leather couch. My ankles and wrists were bound with rope. I wriggled but couldn't get either bond to give an inch. I heard Metallica-style music and announcers on ESPN Sports Center. What time was it? Already nine at night? Man, my head ached; my mouth was dry; my stomach felt empty and sour. How had I let myself get kidnapped by the likes of Tommy Zorn? I remembered that much.

"Bro, this pool table is awesome," a guy with a deeper voice than Tommy's said. His speech was slurred. Pool balls clacked and thudded against the felt.

"Hands off, Schtick," another guy—not Tommy—burped then corrected himself. "Stick. That cue's mine."

"How am I gonna compete in the World Championship of Pool if I don't practice?" Stick asked.

"You aren't," his buddy said. "When are you going to get that through your thick skull? Give me the cue and drink up."

Metal caps popped off something fizzy. Glass clinked glass.

Someone approached me and kicked my calf. "Hey, you." It was Tommy. "Knock, knock, anyone home?" He yanked off my blindfold and kicked me again. His lips were pulled back over his teeth in a malicious sneer. "You"—he rapped a cue stick on my forehead—"are going to make my papa proud of me." He twirled the cue like a ninja pro. How long had he been perfecting that move? He prodded me with the tip. "Sit up. Oh, right, you can't. You're as useless as a slug." Tommy poked me again. "But you can talk, slug, so talk. Where's your father? Where's Luther Marcussen?"

I spit at him.

"I told you we should have gagged him." The beefy one rammed the tip of his cue into a ball, which scudded off the table and nearly hit the third of the kidnapping team—a matchstick thin mess of a guy—bad skin, bad hair, bad posture, a definite candidate for osteoporosis.

Stick swooped up the ball and slammed it down on the table. "Watch it, Beef Brains."

"My name's not Beef Brains. It's Ben."

Tommy whacked me again with his cue. "Talk. Luther Marcussen."

"You first," I said. "Tell me how you know Jack Battle, Jr."

"Who?"

"Your dad and Jack Battle, the video game honcho. Are they in negotiations?"

"For what?" There wasn't a flicker of recognition in Tommy's face. He didn't know Jack. The bag Jack had shown me with the *Memory* game inside wasn't a ploy. Where did that leave me, other than tied up?

"Should I track down this Junior guy?" Tommy tapped the butt of his cue on the floor.

I moaned. Me and my big mouth. If only I could touch base with Jack. If only I could convince him that our father—that all of us—were in danger.

"Where's Luther?" Tommy sauntered around the couch while poking me with the cue stick. "Huh, huh?"

"Eat me," I muttered.

"Big talk, slug," Tommy hissed. "I've got to pee. You two, watch him. And, Day, when I return, we'll continue this interrogation." He jabbed me hard in the solar plexus with the pool cue.

A shooting pain cut clear to my back. Tommy entered the bathroom and slammed the door.

Seconds later another door creaked open. Soft footfalls followed. Someone was tiptoeing into the room. I craned my neck but couldn't see beyond the end of the couch. And then I detected her scent.

Holland. She sprinted past me, across the hardwood floor, leading with a Beretta fitted with a silencer. She aimed it at Tommy's buddies. "You two, turn around. Hands up!"

"Tommy!" Ben reeled back, wielding his cue like a lance. "Stick, get Tommy." Ben charged Holland.

She fired. The bullet, which sounded like no more than a spit, ripped through Ben's thigh. A flesh wound. No bone. He crumpled to the floor.

Stick ran at her next. I tumbled off the couch to stop his progress. Stick tripped over me and careened, shoulder first, into a chair. A bone snapped. Stick howled.

I said, "Tommy's in the—"

The bathroom door flew open. Tommy raced out, pool cue in hand. "Bitch."

Holland spun around. Too late. Tommy jabbed her with a pool cue then used the cue to whack the Beretta out of her hand. Holland grasped the pool cue with both hands and tugged. Tommy didn't lose his hold. Showing more grit than I realized she had, Holland powered him toward the pool table and shoved. Tommy landed against the table at the small of his back. Air spewed out of him. His hands loosened. Holland thrust the butt end of the pool cue into his belly.

"Stay," she ordered.

"My father will kill you," Tommy sputtered.

"I don't think so. I'm doing him a favor." Holland wielded the pool cue like a baseball bat; she wailed into Tommy's shoulder. Another crack. She followed with a jab to his belly. Tommy doubled over, coughing uncontrollably. "What the devil were you thinking, Tommy?" Holland demanded. "Did you think you kidnapping Day would make you a big man in your daddy's eyes? Did you think he would love you? That's never going to happen, you dimwit." Holland retrieved the Beretta and hurried to me. "Hold still." She pulled a jackknife from her pocket and cut the rope from my wrists then handed me the knife. "Get your ankles then lash Tommy to the pool table."

"Who are you?" I said. "Really?"

"One of the good guys."

"Liar," Tommy said. He was still coughing. Holland must have dealt him a mighty blow. I bound him to the pool table leg.

I ran my fingers under my collar and found the tracer Holland had placed there. "Why did you put this on me?" I said.

"I'll explain, but right now we need to get you out of here. Destroy it." Holland raced to the beefy kid, who looked green at the gills. "Take off your shirt."

"No."

"Do it." She barked out the order, teeth gritted. The meanest commander in the Navy hadn't looked half as fearsome.

Ben obeyed.

Holland twisted the shirt, and using it as a tourniquet, tied it tightly around his thigh. "You'll live. You," she barked at Stick. "Take off your shirt and sit on your rump with your back to your friend."

"My shoulder," he whined.

"It'll heal. Do it."

He complied.

Holland wound the shirt as she had the other and looped it around their necks. "If either of you move, you choke to death. Got me?" They blinked their response. To me, she said, "Let's go."

"I'm telling my father," Tommy said as we reached the front door.

"You have nothing to tell," Holland said.

"But Day does. Ask him about Jack Junior."

CHAPTER 35

Water splashed up either side of the car. The wipers whipped rain off the windshield. Light from streetlamps strafed Holland's face as she drove like a skilled racer, zipping in and out of traffic. Memories of our blowup in high school ripped through me. If only she had taken to drag racing back then, how our lives might have turned out differently.

"Where are we headed?" I asked.

"To the theater to get your car."

"That means there's plenty of time for you to explain."

She glanced at me and back at the road. "It won't be quick. It's my life story since high school."

"I love history."

"By trade, I'm a bounty hunter."

Rumor confirmed. It felt good to know the truth. "How did you get into that line of business?"

"A man approached me with an offer I couldn't refuse."

"Zorn?"

She hummed.

"How long was I your prey?"

"On and off for seventeen years."

The number jolted me. All those years, feeling like someone was watching, telling myself I was nuts.

"A year after we graduated high school, Zorn got his hooks into me."

"How—"

She held up a hand. "Let me finish. He put me through training. I learned from the best. I watched you join the Navy. I saw you graduate college. There were others on your tail, in addition to me. Your entire life."

"Ever since my father split."

She nodded.

I couldn't imagine the kind of obsessive commitment Zorn had made. I calculated the cost of paying employees to follow me for that many years. Could whatever was in Geoffrey Gaynor's notebook be worth that much?

"Was his son Tommy his employee?"

"No. Zorn didn't authorize that. Tommy has a few crossed wires. He's an alcoholic. He went after you on his own initiative. He badly wanted to impress his father. He blew it when he chased you up La Honda. I thought Zorn would blow a gasket." Holland swerved around a truck.

"Tell me how Zorn lured you."

"I put off going to college because my dad needed…" She drummed the steering wheel. "My father—" She swallowed hard. "You know, after my mother ran out, Dad cleaned up his act."

"He stopped drinking. He found religion."

She nodded. "But once an addict, always an addict. He started playing poker. At first, he was good at it. But then he started betting on anything. The horses. Raindrops tracking down a window." She rolled her lips together. "He was weak. He thought he could beat the odds. Sadly gambling isn't an exact science. He started losing. Big time. Zorn approached him and gave him a good paying job."

"It's always the father's fault."

"What are you talking about?"

"Tommy said that to me. 'It's always the father's fault.' Yours. His. Mine. Go on. Sorry I interrupted."

"With Zorn's help, my father racked up even more debt." She drew in a long, slow breath. "When Dad was so far gone and there was no way he could get out of the hole, Zorn came after me. I think that was always his plan."

"Because of me."

"To save my father and pay off his debt, I agreed to work for Zorn by tailing you. What could I say? We had split up. You had moved on. I didn't know Zorn's endgame." She honked out a bitter laugh. "You want to know how God mocks the prideful? The day I paid off my father's debts, he died."

"Why didn't you quit then?" I asked. "Don't tell me you had no other options. You're smart. You could have—"

"Zorn threatened to kill my mother."

I weighed her response. Since her teens, she had pretended her mother meant nothing to her, same as me. "Now that she's dead—"

"She's not. She's alive. I made that up to connect with you at the hospital." She glanced at me, her eyes filled with regret. "There's no excuse."

"Where is she?"

"Running the diner in Texas."

"Have you communicated with her?"

"No. Not ever."

"Does she still send you cards?"

She chewed her lower lip. "You remember that?"

"I remember everything." I stared out the window for a moment, then turned back. "Tommy said you met with Zorn on his yacht. That's how he learned about the exit patient list."

"I didn't meet with Zorn. He hijacked me at the theater."

"After you and I talked. Why?"

She blinked back tears. "I don't think I've ever stopped loving you, Chase. For seventeen years, I've watched you make something of yourself. You're a good man. After you left the theater, I called Zorn and told him I wanted out."

Could I believe her? Was she playing me? To what end? She had bruises that corroborated part of the story.

I said, "He wants my father. Why balk at that?"

"Don't be naïve. He wants your father dead, which means he'll kill you, too. I know he's capable of it." She moaned. "All those years, I convinced myself that your father was gone. Dead. Zorn was paying me to do virtually nothing. I could live with myself. But when your father surfaced…" She shook her head. "Zorn is a vengeful man. He doesn't like the word *No.* He captured me and strong-armed me."

"Which is why you gave up the information." I stroked her shoulder. "Was he the one who hit you?"

"His man Eagleton did it."

"Big Australian guy? Lots of scars?"

"Yes. How do you—"

"He and Zorn went after my grandmother to get to me."

A wave of emotions crossed Holland's face: disgust, fear, rage. She pounded the steering wheel. "No, no, no!"

"Don't worry. She's"—I hesitated, unwilling to share where Barbie was—"fine."

"Thank heavens." Holland massaged the steering wheel for a good minute.

"Is there anything more you want to tell me?"

"Yeah." She grinned. "You blew it with Tina."

Tina, the last woman in my life, was a child advocacy attorney. We dated for nearly two years. She had a quick smile and easy manner, but two months after she had a bad skiing accident, she changed. She became abusive and uncommunicative. A month later, she revealed that she was hooked on painkillers. She grew zipper thin and went into rehab. We lost touch. I hadn't heard from her in three years.

"Why didn't you pursue her?" Holland asked. "Was it because of the drugs?"

"Yes."

We drove in silence for a while. I broke it.

"When Zorn took you to his yacht, is that when he threatened your mother?"

"He said I was weak. I had to prove myself. In order to be welcomed back into the fold after my error, he made me put a tracker on you. If I didn't, he promised he would, without a doubt, end my mother's life, and it wouldn't be pretty." Holland gazed at the road ahead.

"You tried to warn me with the note on your business card."

"It was the least I could do. Later, when I was at Zorn International getting a status update, I saw Tommy and realized he and his pals had found out about the tracker. I knew what he was going to do, but I couldn't break away. I found you because of the tracer." She sighed. "Zorn will come after me, Chase, and—" She blew out a short burst of air. "I'm quitting. For real this time. I'm dropping you at your car, then I'm going to Texas." She veered left on San Antonio Road. "I'll convince my mom to move. We'll go into hiding and change our names. I've called my younger brother. He's on his way to protect her until I get there."

Something snagged in my chest. Could I simply let Holland disappear? Yes, I had to.

"By the way," she whispered, her eyes moist. "Just for the record, Zorn had no hand in killing your mother."

"I know. It was a guy named Tanaka. He works for Uma Noble. Do you know that name?"

"No."

I explained the connection between Zorn and Noble and how they had known each other in college. I told her about the night Geoffrey Gaynor wound up dead. "I think one of them shot Geoffrey."

"Your father stole a book?"

"I'm not sure what's in it. Geoffrey was a genius. An inventor. Whatever is in the notebook might not matter at this point. Even so, I think Zorn and Noble can't afford to have my father surface because if he exposes them as killers or accomplices to murder, their lives, families, and careers will be ruined."

"I disagree. Your father stayed in hiding all these years. He wasn't coming forward. Zorn didn't worry about that." She worked her jaw backward and forward. "You said Geoffrey kept his inventions hidden in a safe. Zorn, being his roommate, must have known that."

"Right."

"Whatever is in that notebook has driven Zorn's obsession. Maybe it's something that could change the world. Maybe it's a formula for an invention that will make Zorn millions. He's power hungry, Chase. He's like no one you've ever known."

"My father ran off with the notebook. If the formula in it could benefit mankind, why wouldn't he have brought it to light?"

"Perhaps he didn't understand its value." Holland veered right again, nearly sideswiping a standing vehicle. She steadied her course. After a long while, she said, "Can you ever forgive me?"

I didn't know, honestly, so I didn't answer.

"I deserve that," she said. Following another poignant silence, she said, "Who's Jack Jr.?"

"Nobody. A friend." I knew my answer was curt. I wished I could tell her about Jack. But I couldn't kid myself. Holland had put a tracer on me. To save her mother, she would doubtless do it again. To test her, I said, "What do you know about Kimo?"

"Kimo Cho? Your buddy from high school?"

"You must have observed him with me over the past few years. Have you seen him lately? Because I haven't." I hated to lie to her, but I had to know what she knew.

"Kimo's missing?"

"I've tried calling him. Last I knew, he went to my place, then he went off the grid. Did Zorn get to him?"

"Why would Zorn—"

"To get the exit patient list."

"Is it possible Kimo went sailing? He loves that boat of his."

"Possible, not probable."

Holland blew out a gust of exasperated air. "Look, we really need to talk."

"What do you think we're doing now?"

She glanced in the rearview then zigged into the right lane. "There's a twenty-four-hour diner a couple of blocks away. Let's get a cup of coffee."

"Can't," I said. For all I knew, Zorn was at the diner waiting for Holland to deliver me to him. I couldn't risk it.

"But I'm leaving town tonight. If we don't talk—"

"Travel safely." Man, I sounded cold.

Holland shot me a caustic look. "You're never going to forgive me, are you?"

"What's to forgive? You followed me. You lied to me. It was your job."

Holland swerved to the curb. Tires screeched. She parked and left the engine idling. She reached for my hand. "I'll stay in town. I'll help you."

There it was. The play. The con. Despite the rush of passion I felt, I removed my hand from hers. "Go to your mother. Keep her from harm."

"I hate that you won't trust me." Holland bit back a whimper.

Her pain pierced me more than I had expected. "Look, my mother lied to me my entire life. If you and I had been straight with each other from the get-go, maybe we could have started up again, fallen in love, but we can't." I had too many bad memories of Holland from the past few days. Given time, could the good ones outweigh the bad?

"Is that enough reason for us to—"

"End it? Yes." The vehemence in my voice startled me.

Holland acknowledged me with a blink. She ground the car into gear and tore back onto the road. When we reached the theater, the lights in the parking lot were dim. Rain had subsided. The Escort was still where I had parked it. Luckily, Tommy hadn't thought to steal the key from my pocket.

"Good-bye." I opened the passenger door and slid out.

Holland pushed open the driver's door and yelled, "Wait."

She sprinted around the car. I put my hands up to keep her at bay. No more tracers. No more deceit.

I loaded the Cannondale bicycle into the trunk of the Escort, tied the hatch down with a stray piece of rope, pulled out of the lot, and regarded Holland via the rearview mirror. She stood outside the Camaro with her cell phone pressed to her ear.

I waited for my cell phone to ring, but it didn't. Was she calling Zorn? Admitting defeat? I put her from my mind. No more diversions. No more wrong turns. I had to keep to my path. Find Jack Battle Jr. before Zorn did and convince Jack to reveal the whereabouts of our father.

CHAPTER 36

I returned the Cannondale bike to the spot where I'd found it outside the gas station bathroom in La Honda. As I headed back to the car, my cell phone rang. The readout said: *Manuel*. I had called him on the drive over, desperate to track down Jack Battle, Jr.

I answered. "What've you got?"

Manuel gave me Jack's home address.

I drove like a speed demon to Atherton and surveyed the area. Jack's modest home—modest for an ultra successful dot.com guy; one level stucco and brick—was dark inside. Only a porch light and low-level garden lights glowed. There were no holiday candles in windows or poinsettias by the door. Apparently, Jack shunned his mother's fixation for Christmas décor. Catching sight of a pile of old, plastic-wrapped newspapers in the driveway, I began to wonder if Jack had moved. Maybe, prior to me accosting him outside the game store, he had learned that our father was in danger. But how could he have? I was the first to mention any connection. Maybe my father realized my mother had recognized him at the hospital. Maybe he told Jack the truth—about the night the roommate died, about the blue book he stole, about me. Maybe that explained Jack's fierceness in our scrape. On the other hand, exit patient Levine thought my father might be in a coma.

A lot of maybes.

I waited in the Escort all night, lights doused, ignition switched off. At times I closed my eyes, but any sound jolted me awake. Jack never appeared.

By dawn, I was chilled to the bone. I considered passing by Gert Dalton's house to see if Jack had crashed there for the night, but I knew I wouldn't get past Dalton's sentry of a housekeeper. I also considered going to Weyford and making an appearance for my students' sake, maybe even having a conversation with Dean Hyde to patch things up, but I decided I was too emotionally wrung out. I would wind up doing something I regretted, not to mention that if Zorn's people had been watching me for years, one of them might expect me to go there. Hoping Zorn wouldn't guess I was collaborating with Manuel—we saw each other so infrequently—I headed toward the diner.

All the way there, I thought about Jack. Where could he be? Was he hiding? I replayed my visit to his office. His assistant had been so cagey. Why? There had been sheets of loopy artwork in the stack of items on her desk. Beneath them, the travel brochures. When she saw me eying the artwork, she quickly bundled them into tubes. What if the artwork wasn't artwork? What if the swirly drawings were maps? Not just any maps. Topographical maps. What if Jack had been planning to go into hiding with my father? He was a triathlete and a Boy Scout with multiple badges. He could probably live off the land for weeks. If I recreated the topmost map, would it give me a clue to Jack's location?

Manuel intercepted me as I entered the diner. "You look like garbage."

"Feel like it, too."

"Did you eat that sandwich?"

"Not yet." One truth. I was on the mend.

"Nita, food!" he yelled.

I plowed ahead. "Just coffee."

Manuel ordered a full breakfast and followed me to the office. He was apologetic. Though he had been able to pin down Jack Jr.'s home address, he hadn't been able to locate a cell phone number. No one was answering at Jack's office. There wasn't an *In case of emergency* number provided on the business line.

"Do you have a pencil and paper?" I asked.

"Sure." He pointed to the desk. "In there. I'll be back in a minute." He exited.

I fetched drawing tools and set to work. I wasn't a sketch artist; I swiped oil paint onto a canvas and hoped I could create something. However, I had a good eye for detail. It was why I had done so well in history. I could memorize facts and data. I could visualize every facet of a battle.

While I was roughing out a picture, I heard from Barbie. She was at the airport. Red was traveling with her. They were heading to Red's other sister. The older sister's ex-Marine husband thought it was a good idea to keep on the move. Their plane was boarding in thirty minutes. Without asking about my quest, she said she loved me and hung up. Her call made me eager to touch base with Reggie and Kimo. Reggie answered. Kimo was sleeping. She would have him call me when he awoke.

"All's quiet on the western front," she added, "except another cop showed up."

"Who?"

"Detective Philips. He's the one in charge of your mom's case, right?"

"Yeah."

"He asked where you were. I told him I didn't know. Chase, he seemed on the up and up. Genuinely concerned."

"Time will tell."

"By the way, I clued him in that an officer named Vance had come looking for you. Philips grew tense, if that's worth anything. He exchanged a look with his colleague."

"Bruno?" I described him.

"Yeah. Philips thanked me and they left."

"Reggie, you're a saint."

"Don't you forget it."

I hung up wondering about Philips. Could I trust him? How had he figured out the connection between the hostel and me?

"Dude," Manuel entered. "I'm back."

Nita followed carrying a tray of food. She set it down and pointed. "Eat."

"Not hungry."

"Eat," she ordered, "or I'll cram it down your throat."

I gave her the evil eye. She gave me an equally caustic look. I took a bite of the eggs, but my stomach rebelled. A pang shot through me. I gulped down half of the coffee and shoved the plate away.

"I did not poison you," Nita said. "Eat a French fry."

"I can't. It's—" I shook my head.

"You need nourishment."

"I'll be okay. Thank you for trying."

She exited, shaking her head with concern.

I picked up the pencil and resumed sketching.

"What're you doing?" Manuel asked.

"I'm drawing a topographical map." I explained my theory. As I did, I gazed at what I'd drawn so far, and I thought again about Jack being a Boy Scout. I turned the sketch to view it from another angle. "When I was ten, I'd wanted to go to camp, but my grandmother said we didn't have the cash to cover it."

"Your point?"

"What if Jack Jr. removed my father from danger by taking him camping?"

"Are you kidding, dude?" Manuel stole a French fry from my plate. "Would you take a comatose patient into the bitter cold for a little father-son bonding? No way."

I told him about Jack Jr.'s assistant literally taunting me with the maps, as if daring me to understand their meaning. "Then she rolled them up and whisked them away. Take a closer look. Do you see a road?"

Manuel rose from the chair and peered at the drawing. "Fill it in."

I did. I added some crosshatch marks to the sketch. A road took shape.

"Is that a mountain on the right?" Manuel asked.

"More like a chasm."

Manuel tapped the map. "I think that's a ridge, and that's the ocean beyond."

I stared hard at the drawing. Something about the features looked familiar. I stood up and placed a palm on either side of the drawing. That was when I saw something, if only for a second. I picked up my pencil and darkened the ridgeline. Suddenly the map wasn't just familiar, it was obvious. "You won't believe this. See the road with all the switchbacks? That's La Honda." I tapped the spot. "And this is where La Honda veers to the ocean. Right here, there's a park."

"Sam McDonald County Park."

I set the map aside and pulled the computer keyboard forward. I typed a string of words into the search engine. The names of three Boy Scout camps came up. "I'll be darned."

"What?"

"There were travel brochures on the assistant's desk, beneath the topo maps. The assistant covered those up, too, but I caught a glimpse of the first word on one. LANS. There's a Boy Scout camp with the name Lansing right here"—I stabbed the map I'd drawn—"except, according to this site on the Internet, it's defunct."

"Dead end. Too bad."

I paced the room then came back to the computer and typed in Lansing Boy Scout Camp hoping to find a director's name or a forwarding address. "Aha."

"What did you find?"

"Gert Dalton said that her ex is a sick man. Maybe she meant mentally sick. The other letters I spied on the flyer were MENT and a word that ended in M. Maybe Jonathan Battle isn't in a coma. Maybe he was doped up at Keystone Hospital. Maybe he's staying in another kind of facility. Look." I swiveled the computer screen so it faced Manuel. "Lansing Boy Scout Camp has been transformed into a mental asylum."

CHAPTER 37

Before leaving the diner, I took a shower and changed clothes. Dressed in Manuel's Old Navy camouflage jacket and a pair of jeans, my face yellow and purple from all the beatings I'd taken, I looked liked a guy who had survived a bad night on shore leave. Years ago I had crafted a fantasy about the first meeting I'd have with my father. This was not how I was supposed to look. At least my hair was combed.

Harsh sunlight glared through the windshield of the Escort. The skies were clear; the pavement, dry. I drove north on La Honda Road and turned into the lushly treed park. Two miles in, I veered onto the drive leading to the defunct Boy Scout camp, now called Lansing Mental Asylum according to a nearly indecipherable sign. If I hadn't known the place existed, I would have driven past.

Morning moisture dripped from the trees that flanked the driveway. The scent of eucalyptus hung in the air. I parked the Escort in a visitor's spot and scanned the other vehicles. There were over a dozen cars, but none were BMWs, which most likely meant Jack Battle was not present. Where he was, was anyone's guess.

The U-shaped building was one-story and understated. I entered the lobby through a glass door. I paused inside to take in my surroundings. A bleached-blonde nurse in a peach dress and matching cap stood behind the welcome desk, her back to me. She was writing on an erasable board with a black marker. A young couple sat on a beige sofa in the waiting area. A plate of cookies, a pitcher of red liquid, and plastic cups sat on an end table to the right. The woman looked miserable, as if she had been asked to give up her first-born child. Wadded tissues sat in her lap. The soothing music being piped through speakers didn't seem to be helping her mood.

Though my insides roiled with tension, I strolled to the welcome desk. Calm. Cool. A total façade. I cleared my throat.

The nurse spun around. Her eyes were a brilliant blue and devoid of emotion. The nurse in *One Flew Over the Cuckoo's Nest* had nothing on her. "May I help you?"

"I'm here to visit a friend."

"Your name?"

"Adam Smith," I lied, in case Jack had put the staff on high alert for a man with my name. The alias came out easily. I had written a thesis paper on Smith's *The Wealth of Nations*. "The patient's name?"

"Jonathan Battle."

The woman's thin smile hardened. "I don't believe we have anyone here by that name."

"Are you sure? Older guy, close to sixty years old? Maybe he goes by the name Jack."

"No, sir." She didn't glance at the registry. "If you don't mind, I'm very busy. Please leave or—"

"Do you have a patient by the name of Luther Marcussen?"

The nurse let out a sigh and reached under her desk. Seconds later, a hulk of a guard in a starched brown uniform appeared through the door beyond the waiting area. Would more arrive?

I hadn't planned to fight. I wasn't armed, my body ached, and I didn't have a battalion of buddies in uniform to back me up. The nurse gestured to the guard. Had Jack, Jr. instructed her to thwart visitors, or was she following the hospital's privacy policy? Had Jack discovered the missing notebook and figured the best way to reap its benefits was to stow good old Dad in an asylum? Was the hospital holding my father against his will?

The guard clutched the butt of the pistol that was slung into his hip holster.

Vamping, I said, "This is Happy Haven Retirement Home, isn't it?" I had seen a sign for that place along La Honda. I backed up a step. Toward the exit.

The nurse arched an eyebrow. “No, sir.” Through taut lips, she said, “This is Lansing. We are a private facility.”

“Aw, gee, my mistake. I’m looking for Happy Haven.” Two steps. Three. Four. “My sister must have given me the wrong directions.” I pulled a cell phone from my pocket and waggled it at the nurse and guard. “I don’t have a clue how to work GPS. What a joke, huh?” I pushed backward through the door.

As I tore to the Escort, I saw the guard charging after me. I hopped into the car, jammed the gear into reverse, and sped out of the lot.

CHAPTER 38

While heading out of the park, I spotted a road leading to hiking trails. I made a snap decision. If I couldn't go through the front door of the asylum, then I would go through the rear. I stowed the car in a stand of trees, exited, and trudged through bushes and brush, glad I was wearing the camouflage jacket that Manuel had loaned me. If a Lansing guard was on the lookout for me, he might miss me.

The overgrown path to the asylum took about fifteen minutes. A simple eight-foot chain link fence surrounded the rear of the U-shaped building. In spots, the fence sagged beneath the weight of overgrown ivy. I was prepared to climb over one such spot when I came upon a gate with no lock. Someone was going to be mighty ticked off at the lax security measures, but I wasn't going to be the guy who blabbed.

After slipping through the gate, I found myself facing a courtyard with fountain. No one sat in the courtyard; though the rain had passed, the temperature had turned bitter. Four windows and two glass doors faced the patio. The Levelor blinds on all were closed. When I approached the entrance to the asylum, I had noticed security alarm stickers on the windows, but I hadn't seen any security cameras. I didn't see any now, either. Were they tucked out of view?

I had to risk exposure. Time was of the essence for three reasons. First, I had no doubt that Zorn, if he wasn't already clued in, would soon learn of Jack, Jr.'s existence, thanks to me mouthing off to Tommy. Zorn would force Jack's assistant to talk. He would learn that Jack was hiding our father in the asylum hospital and break speed limits to get here. Second, there was Jack Jr. to consider. No doubt the asylum's admitting nurse would contact Jack and tell him that someone had come looking for his father. The nurse would describe me. Third, Uma Noble. Who knew how she played into all this?

Move, jerk. Tick tock.

Quickly, I jogged across the courtyard. No sirens blared. I tried to open one of the doors. Locked. I tried the other. It, too, was impenetrable. I stole around the corner of the left leg of the building and searched for a door. There was one—no access. Dang. I hunted for an open window. None. All the windows looked new and updated. I retraced my steps and examined the right wing of the building. One access door—locked. None of the windows hung open, but the windows looked older. Paint peeled from the frames. Like many establishments, the asylum was undergoing renovations in stages. The third window, an old hand-crank style, was textured and small, no more than two feet square. The lower corner of the window was warped and bent out of shape. I grabbed the ledge beneath the window and hoisted myself up for a peek. The textured glass prevented a clear view into the room beyond, though I figured it was bathroom. I didn't see shadowy movement inside. Hoping the room was vacant, I pried the bent corner of the window. No warning bell rang out.

After loosening the window a half-inch, I wedged my fingers beneath the wood. Five sturdy yanks later, the window opened with a groan. I listened for a human response to the intrusion. Nothing. No one raced from the building to arrest me.

Confident that I could proceed, I forced the window open all the way and slithered through the opening, head and hands first. The scent of sterility made my nostrils twitch. I landed with a smack on a pale green Formica counter. I scrambled to a squat and dusted myself off.

Silence.

I opened the bathroom door a crack and peered out. I truly believed my father was in the facility. Why else would the admitting nurse have acted so confrontational? Was he hidden in this wing or the other?

A variety of music resonated from a number of rooms. A food cart stood at the far end of the hall. No attendant was nearby. Down at the other end of the hall, an old man moved with the help of a metal walker. No nurse accompanied him.

I slipped out of the bathroom and drew in step with the old man. "Do you know Jonathan Battle?"

The guy gazed at me with sad, rheumy eyes.

"Jonathan Battle," I repeated.

The old man laughed at something. I looked over my shoulder. No one was around. I patted my new friend on the shoulder. If a witty brain had once resided within his gray-haired head, none of it was left.

I moved on, footfalls as silent as possible. No charts hung on the doors. There were no nameplates for patients. I opened each and peeked inside. In one, I found an old woman. In the next, I discovered an even older woman and an ancient man. As I neared the ninth room of my search, I heard the sound of Christmas music. It wasn't just any Christmas music, however. It was Chuck Berry singing a bluesy, soulful "Merry Christmas, Baby."

Gert Dalton said that her ex-husband loved Chuck Berry music.

Hopes high, I raced toward the sound and burst into the room. It smelled of oatmeal and Clorox, and it was sparse. A bed, a table, a CD player. Beige curtains, beige rug. A gaunt man with wispy salt and pepper hair, wearing pajamas the same color as the décor, sat in a chair by the hospital bed. I recognized him instantly. There was no doubt in my mind. The face, though much older than the face of a man nearing sixty should appear, matched the face in my mother's locket. My father wasn't in a coma. He didn't appear to be sick. But he wasn't being held hostage, either. His fingers tapped rhythmically on the arm of the chair. He didn't glance at me; he hadn't noticed my intrusion. He stared at the television hanging on the wall, even though the TV wasn't on.

I had prepared for this moment the past few days, and yet I felt torn, disturbed, anxious. A pulse beat wildly in my head; my mouth turned dry. Would my father embrace me? Shun me? Would I like him? Would he like me?

In a whisper, I said, "Luther."

My father turned. His gaze, which was penetrating in the locket photograph, was now dull. He muttered, "Luther is dead."

"No, he's not."

"I buried him. Evil."

"You buried his identity."

My father returned his gaze to the television. I drew closer. He didn't flinch. He didn't seem frightened of me.

I said, "I like your choice of music."

He didn't respond.

I drew alongside him. "Should I call you Jack or Jonathan?"

"Jonathan," the man whispered, giving a marginal nod.

"Jonathan Battle."

"Always at war."

"I'm Sybil Day's son. Do you remember Sybil?"

Jonathan's fingers drummed the chair with agitation. His jaw worked back and forth. Was he searching for an answer buried deep in his brain?

"You knew her when you were Luther."

"Luther's gone."

At least this time Jonathan didn't say Luther was dead.

"Sybil had a son. Me."

Jonathan turned his head. I jabbed a thumb at my chest and smiled. His eyes grew narrow, as if he was searching his mind for a memory.

"I'm your son."

After a long moment, he reached toward me. "Johnny?" Over the Christmas music, Jonathan lit into Chuck Berry's song, his voice gravelly. He sang of Johnny B. Goode who never learned to read or write. He paused, as if he couldn't remember the rest.

I finished the lyric.

He grinned. "She didn't like the name Jonathan."

"Who? Your wife?"

"Sybil."

My breath caught.

Jonathan scanned the room as if taking it in for the first time. He stopped on me. "Where am I?"

"The Lansing Mental Asylum."

"Why am I here?"

"You're in treatment. Shouldn't you be here?"

More drumming with his fingers. He waggled his head. "No, no, no."

I glanced at the door. How long had I been in the room? The guard—maybe more than one—might be bearing down on us. We had to move. "Are you being held against your will?"

"I don't have a will."

"No, I meant—" I worked my lip between my teeth. Was my father prematurely senile? "Can you walk?"

"I've got legs."

"Good." At least a sense of humor existed somewhere in the nethersphere of my father's addled brain. "I think you're in danger. I need to get you out of here."

"Danger?"

I heard footsteps in the hall. "Want to go for a ride?"

"I'm hungry."

I hurried to the door and listened. Whoever was outside didn't stop at my father's room. He or she kept moving.

"I want eggs," Jonathan said.

I rushed back to him. "Let's get you on your feet. I'll take you someplace and make you some eggs. An omelet."

"No yogurt." He screwed up his nose.

A sense of something intangible struck me. Just like my father, the only food I didn't like was yogurt; the texture made me gag. Maybe he and I had other things in common. Would I find out what they were once I got him off the meds the hospital was feeding him? Was he even on meds, or was his condition more chronic and irreversible?

I grinned. "No yogurt. Deal. Now on your feet."

"No legs."

"A minute ago you had legs."

Jonathan looked up at me, helplessness in his gaze.

"How about I carry you?" I bent down to lift him.

He flinched. His eyes narrowed with suspicion. “Who are you?”

“I’m Johnny. Johnny B. Goode.”

CHAPTER 39

Worry shot through me as I scooped my father out of the hospital chair because he was lighter than a bantamweight. When had he last eaten a hearty meal? Had Jack ordered the hospital to intentionally starve him?

"Put your arms around my neck," I said.

He didn't comply.

"Come on. You can do it." I helped him. "Hold tight." I started for the door.

Jonathan moaned. "Down." The moan turned into a deep groan. "Put me down."

"Shh," I said. "I'm not going to hurt you. I promise. I'm going to take you to eat. You're hungry, remember?"

Jonathan started to hum. "Oh, Come All Ye Faithful."

"That's it," I said. "Hum, but quietly." I cranked open the door, wondering what I was getting myself into. I was kidnapping a guy who wasn't sure where or who he was, a guy who couldn't tell me whether or not he wanted to be rescued.

I peered into the hallway—empty, except for one older woman accompanied by a Minnie Mouse-sized nurse. The old woman was bending over a water fountain at the far end, away from the exit to the courtyard. Minnie twisted the fountain's knob and coaxed her patient to drink. I nudged the door open wider and slipped out. I ran heel-toe toward the exit.

Just as I pushed down on the lever, a man yelled, "Stop!" It was the guard from the foyer.

I wondered again if other guards were on site. I didn't see backup.

"Stop!" He charged toward us while pressing a walkie-talkie to his mouth. He plucked at the strap of his holster to release his gun; the strap resisted. Lucky for me. "Stop! Now! Or I'll shoot!"

Despite the extra weight of my father, I dashed across the courtyard and through the gate. The bramble, still wet from rain, squished beneath my feet.

"Stop!" the guard yelled again.

Not on a bet.

By the time I reached the Escort, I was panting like I had run a marathon. I inserted my father into the passenger seat. He fumbled for the seatbelt but couldn't accomplish the task. I pushed his hands out of the way and did it for him, then slammed the door. Hustling to the driver's side, I gazed through the trees and searched for the guard. The man appeared in a clearing, his face beet red, his chest heaving. He was still struggling to release his gun, and he was shaking the walkie-talkie angrily, as if it had run out of juice. Poor fool.

I switched on the ignition and bolted up the access road. As I drove, I dialed Manuel. His phone was busy. I ended the call and glanced at my father who was staring straight ahead. "I heard you like sailing, Jonathan."

"General MacArthur liked sailing."

"Yes, he did."

"MacArthur said, 'We are not retreating, we are advancing in another direction.'"

It took me aback that he knew the quote. Did we have the habit of spouting inspirational quotes in common as well? "That's what we're doing today, Jonathan."

"MacArthur also said, 'Age wrinkles the body; quitting wrinkles the soul.'"

I grinned. "You're a man after my heart, Jonathan. I like MacArthur, too."

"Who's MacArthur?"

"He's—" I glanced at my father. He wasn't kidding. How I wished I could lock onto his odd mental rhythm. What was wrong with him? Why wasn't our first meeting like I had dreamed? We were supposed to be talking about football or ESPN or the Giants' bad season and how they were screwing around trying to get big hitters instead of good pitchers. The momentous ending of dawning recognition between father and son at the end of the movie, *Field of Dreams,* had not been lost on me. I wanted that. No, I craved that.

"The Bartons had a dog named Arthur," Jonathan said.

I recalled the name *Barton* from the accounts I had read. They were Luther Marcussen's last set of foster parents.

"They didn't care for me. They loved Arthur."

I cut another look at my father. He was undoing and refastening the buttons on his shirt. I said, "Do you remember your life as Luther?"

"Luther's dead."

"I know. Dead and buried. What happened to Luther?"

"Evil." Jonathan screwed up his mouth. "He had no focus. No drive. I am an architect. I build things."

I forged ahead. "Do you know Karl Zorn?"

He blinked rapidly.

"Zorn," I repeated.

"Nuclear."

I gaped. Was he trying to tell me that the notebook he stole held an invention that had something to do with nuclear power? "What do you mean nuclear?"

Jonathan shook his head.

"What about Uma Noble? Do you remember her?"

He started to tremble. "I went sailing."

"With Uma?"

Jonathan started humming Christopher Cross's song, "Sailing."

I gritted my teeth. This was harder than anything I imagined. Would I have to peel away the layers of my father one slice at a time?

He stopped humming and said, "'It is of great use to the sailor to know the length of his line, though he cannot fathom all the depths of the ocean.'"

"You're quoting John Locke."

"Locked inside." Jonathan tapped his head, then resumed humming.

"You like sailing. Got it."

"I like the Navy."

I veered around a corner and pulled to a stop. "Of course you do." I recalled a conversation with Jack Jr.'s assistant. "You were in the Navy, Jonathan."

"Luther."

"Right. Luther was in the Navy." I did my best to follow his train of thought.

Jonathan sang, "'Anchors aweigh, my boys, anchors aweigh.'" He drew in a sudden gulp of air. "I'm tired." He leaned his head back against the seat rest and closed his eyes.

I gazed at him and a notion struck me. Had Luther enlisted in the Navy that fateful night? Was that why he had disappeared? When did he return? He must have enrolled in college afterward. He became an architect, a builder. If only he could frame thoughts fully in his mind. Would Jack Jr. know the diagnosis? Would he share it with me?

Jonathan opened his eyes. "The eye of the needle."

"Are you quoting the Bible now?"

Jonathan shook his head as if he didn't understand.

I recited, "'It is easier for a camel to go through the eye of a needle, than for a rich man to enter the kingdom of God.' Is that the phrase you're quoting?"

"The eye of the needle."

I gave up and dialed Manuel again. I waited through three rings. Finally a woman answered. "*Buenos dias*. Manuel's Diner. How may I assist?" Not Nita. They never answered the café's phone that way. But I knew the voice.

"Reggie?" I said.

"*Sí, sí.*"

"What are you doing there?"

"*Sí*. We are open." Reggie whispered, "Yeah, it's me. Nita called me for support."

"Support? Why?"

"Where are you?"

"Driving. I've got him. I've got my dad. I'm bringing him to the diner."

"No. Don't. Zorn's here."

My insides tensed. I knew it was just a matter of time before Zorn's people tied me to Manuel and the diner. One of the many surveillance hounds that had tailed me over the years must have told him. Had Zorn found his son Tommy tied up in the guesthouse? Had he learned about Jack Jr.? If so, it was only a matter of time before Zorn located the asylum and learned that I'd kidnapped my father.

"I can't go home," I said. "And I can't go to the hostel."

"*Qué*?" Reggie raised her voice. "Nita? So sorry. She is here, but she is busy."

"Is he listening in?"

"*Sí*. Nita will meet you for drinks at five o'clock. Where? You know how Nita loves fresh air. Why don't you meet at the Calypso Bar and Grill?"

I wasn't familiar with a restaurant with that name, but then it dawned on me what Reggie was trying to communicate. Kimo's boat was named *Calypso*. We'd meet there. "How's Kimo doing?"

"Girlfriend, the drinks will knock you out," Reggie said. I deciphered her code. Kimo was still recuperating; he was sleeping. And from the lightness in her tone, I assumed Zorn didn't realize Kimo was alive. "See you soon," Reggie added breezily and hung up.

CHAPTER 40

With caution I approached the Coyote Point Marina where Kimo stowed his boat. I didn't see anyone lying in wait. I pulled into the parking lot and parked between an SUV and a truck fitted with an empty boat trailer. I hurried to the passenger side and asked my father—Jonathan—if he needed help getting out. Despite his inability to buckle the seatbelt, he proved adept at unbuckling it. He slung his feet out of the car, stood to his full height, and drew in a deep breath. The quick movements startled me.

Though frail, Jonathan stood an inch taller than me. He was lean and ropy and had eyes the color of the sea, the same as mine.

"Smell the salt." He drew in another deep breath. His sunken chest swelled with the effort. "You never forget the smell."

"When were you in the Navy?"

"I wasn't in the Navy."

"Right. *Luther* was in the Navy."

"Luther is dead."

I winced. Was there some kind of clinical depression going on? If only I could contact Jack Jr. and get answers.

Jonathan shivered.

I gripped his elbow. "When we get to the boat, I'll find you something warmer to put on." I ushered him down a ramp leading to twenty boat slips. Sailboats of all sizes and a few motorboats bobbed in their slips. Kimo had taken such care with *Calypso*, a twenty-two foot pocket cruiser. Every weekend, he checked her out. He polished and painted the moment any chip appeared, no matter how small.

My heart wrenched as I stepped onto the *Calypso*. What would I have done if Kimo had died? Family wasn't always related by blood. I guided my father over the rim. "Have a seat." I indicated a bench with a blue leatherette cushion.

Jonathan sat. Air hissed out of the cushion. He stretched his legs and turned his toes up, heels balanced on the deck. "I love to sail."

"So you said." I opened the combination lock on the storage bin, then rummaged through the contents. I found a fisherman's vest and a tattered zippered sweatshirt. I chose the latter and slung it on my father, zipping the sweatshirt to the neck.

"I left my life behind when I joined the Navy."

"Luther's life." I held up a hand. "And don't tell me Luther's dead. I know. Jonathan's alive."

"A needle in the haystack."

"We're back to needles again?" Was my father a former junky like my mother? Maybe that was why he was obsessed with needles. I hadn't noticed any scars on his arms.

"I'm hungry."

"Great. I'll get you some food. Lucky for you, the guy who owns this boat is a health addict." I shuffled downstairs and rummaged through the small refrigerator that Kimo kept stocked with juice, nuts, veggies, and fruits. He didn't have any eggs, but by now I expected Jonathan to have forgotten about wanting them. I grabbed almonds and one of every fruit and climbed up the steps. I sat beside my father on the blue cushion and popped open the bag of almonds. "Can you feed yourself?"

"I have hands."

I smiled. Jonathan scooped out a few nuts and chewed them slowly, emitting sounds of pleasure between bites as if the nuts were manna from heaven.

"Let's discuss the needle in the haystack thing. Are you saying you're the needle? You've been hiding."

"In plain sight."

"Indeed." What I couldn't understand was why Jonathan had chosen to hide in the Bay Area while his enemies continued to look for him. Had he really believed he could evade them this long? And yet he had, living under an alias.

"You let Luther die and you became Jonathan. You have a son and an ex-wife."

"Good woman. Didn't like sailing. Told her about the *Niantic*. She didn't want to hear."

"Didn't want to hear what?"

His jaw ticked with tension. "I joined the Navy that night."

A seagull squawked overhead. The sound of a powerboat motoring up crackled in the air. The engine rumbled. The driver moved the boat out of its slip and headed out to the waterway. Quiet resumed.

"Which night did you join the Navy?" I asked.

"The night I met her."

"The night you met Gert?"

"Sybil. I—" Jonathan shuddered. His eyes grew filmy.

I stiffened. For a second time, my father had remembered my mother. I thought of the date they met. I swiveled slightly on the cushion to get a better view of him. "You met Sybil on May 18th, 1980."

Jonathan repeated the date.

"Was that the date you joined the Navy?"

He nodded.

"Did something else happen that night? Did you and Sybil and a girl named Uma and a guy named Karl—"

"Zorn." Jonathan's nose twitched.

"Zorn's roommate Geoffrey died that night. Did Zorn or Uma—"

"Evil woman." Jonathan hissed. "Evil." He mashed his lips together and stared at the other boats in the marina, all idle.

"Did one of you shoot Geoffrey?" I braced for the answer.

He didn't reply.

"Did Zorn shoot him?"

"Nuclear."

That was the second time he'd mentioned the word *nuclear.* "Was there something about nuclear power in the notebook you stole?"

"Evil."

"Did you take the notebook because you thought Geoffrey had created something that could hurt people?"

He snarled.

"That night Luther ran away and joined the Navy."

"Luther is dead."

"You became Jonathan Battle."

"I took his name. He didn't mind."

"He, who? Did you know someone named Jonathan Battle?"

"My best friend. An orphan."

"An orphan like you. Was he in foster care, too?"

"He died so young. Car crash."

"And you assumed his personality." That was how he'd kept Zorn from finding him.

Jonathan turned his chin toward the sun and closed his eyes. "No one should leave love and life behind."

"What did you do with the blue book you took?"

"The past is buried. Forgiveness is hard." He grew quiet.

In the stillness, I thought of my past, my choices, Holland. Yes, she had betrayed me, but she had no choice, if her story was true. Could I forgive her?

My cell phone buzzed. I fished it from my pocket and glanced at the readout. I recognized Holland's cell phone number. Had she sensed I was thinking about her? I couldn't help myself. I craved another chance to hear her voice. I swiped the screen to answer.

"Are you halfway to Texas?" I said in an effort to keep things light.

"Still in town."

"Why?"

"Long story." She sounded strained. Had Zorn recaptured her? "I couldn't stop thinking about you. I hate how we ended it."

I did, too, but I couldn't form the words. "What about your mother?"

"She's not answering my calls. Neither is my brother. I'm worried."

"Have you tried calling local police?"

Holland coughed out a laugh. "Like they'd take me seriously. Adults have to be missing more than forty-eight hours before authorities start the hunt. Did you hook up with Jack Battle? Did he help you find your father?"

I glanced at Luther, aka Jonathan. He sat beside me, worrying his hands together as if working out a puzzle.

"Chase?" Holland said.

"No."

"No, you didn't find him, or no you can't tell me because you don't trust me?"

"Holland, I've got to go. I—"

My father burst into the chorus for "Anchors Aweigh."

"Jonathan, shh," I hissed.

"Is that him?" Holland asked. "Oh, my gosh, it is. You found him. I'm so happy for you."

A mix of emotions rushed up my throat. I wished I could share with her, but I didn't want to let her in. I couldn't. "Sorry, Holland, I'm hanging up."

"Chase, no, wait." Someone was whispering to her in the background. Zorn?

A boat in the harbor blasted its horn.

"Good-bye, Holland. Call me when you get settled." I ended the call and stared at my father.

Blast him for bursting into song. Curse him for being shut down.

"What did you do, Jonathan? That night, at Geoffrey's room?"

He didn't answer.

Did he still have the notebook in question? If not, had he stowed it somewhere? If he had retained it and I found it, maybe I could prove my innocence to Philips while proving Karl Zorn and Uma Noble's guilt, and we could both get out of this alive.

CHAPTER 41

A short while later I was below deck fetching a couple of V-8s from the refrigerator when I felt the boat rock. The hairs at the back of my neck bristled. We had visitors. Only Reggie, Manuel, Nita, and perhaps Kimo knew where I'd gone. Wouldn't one of them have yelled *hello*? Had Zorn figured out Reggie's coded phone message? Had his lackey strong-armed Reggie into giving me up? Jonathan was sitting up there all by himself. Exposed. I set down the juice cans and quickly searched the kitchenette for Kimo's Smith & Wesson. Kimo usually stowed his gun in a cabinet to the right of the fridge, but it wasn't there.

Stealing to the ladder, I edged up two steps and peered out. Holland. She stood on the deck, still dressed in the clothes she had worn last night. Officer Hugh Vance, out of uniform, stood beside her. The muzzle of his Beretta PX4 flared in the sunlight. Jonathan sat on the cushion, gazing forward as if unaware of the visitors.

Irritation at my own stupidity swelled inside me. Holland had followed me for years. She had to have known that Kimo and I regularly played poker with a group of guys on the *Calypso*. She must have heard the horn blast from the motorboat and put two and two together. If only I'd hung up earlier or stopped myself from answering her call.

Something glinted. From a slightly different angle, I spied one addition to Holland's wardrobe: handcuffs, the old metal kind, not zip-ties. She hadn't betrayed me, after all. Vance was using her as bait.

"Where is he?" Vance whispered. He nudged Holland.

"I don't know." She coughed hard then tucked her chin into her shoulder and muted a second cough. "I don't feel so good."

"I could care." Vance raised his hand as if he might hit her with the Beretta.

I muscled up the ladder and emerged, hands held high. "Don't," I said to Vance. "I'm here. Holland, are you okay?" She looked pale. Even from a distance, I could feel the fear oozing out of her.

"I'm coming down with something," she said and coughed again. "The flu, I think."

Vance pushed Holland ahead.

"I'm sorry, Chase," she said.

"You shouldn't be so predictable, Day." Vance shoved Holland. "Sit on the bench. Day, sit next to her."

"I need to use the head," Holland said. "I'm going to heave."

"Tough."

"Cut her a break, man," I said.

"You stay out of it."

Holland licked her lips. "I was going to leave town, Chase, like you suggested, but—"

"We showed up," Vance cut in, "and convinced her otherwise."

"We?" I looked from Holland to Vance.

"Uma and me."

The click of high heels preceded her. Uma Noble appeared at the top of the ramp. She was a striking older woman. Blonde hair, taut body, luscious mouth, big eyes. Like a lady, she slipped one slim leg over the edge of the boat, the toe of her shoe first. Instinctively, I offered a hand. She dismissed it and fixed the collar of her Chanel suit.

"Chase," Holland said. "Meet Uma Noble."

"Call me Uma." Her voice had a sultry yet superior quality, like a femme fatale in a classic movie. I despised her instantly.

"Where's Yuji Tanaka?" I demanded. "Where's the man who killed my mother?"

"He's working for Zorn now," Holland said. "When Uma fired him, he switched allegiances."

"Traitor," Uma said.

"Duplicity sucks," I countered.

Uma lifted her chin. "I want you to know your mother's death wasn't my fault."

"Bull. Your bodyguard—"

"He insisted we bring the gun." Uma rolled her upper lip between her teeth. "He said she would dun me for more money, but that wasn't the case. Sybil actually changed her mind. She didn't want to give up your father. That made me so mad. I grabbed the gun from Yuji to threaten her."

"What are you saying?"

"She ran at me. I had to protect myself."

"*You* killed her?"

"We struggled. The gun went off."

"Why you—" I lunged toward her.

"Stop, Day!" Vance moved his gun to Holland's head.

I settled back on my heels. What had made my mother change her mind? Seeing my father in this feeble state? Realizing she still loved him? I didn't care. She did the right thing. Call it a moment of conscience. That was all that mattered now.

Uma moved to Jonathan and lowered herself onto the cushion beside him. "Luther. Is it really you?"

"Luther is dead."

"And buried," I added.

"Dead and buried," Jonathan echoed.

Uma glowered at me. "What's wrong with him?"

"He's not himself," I said, the irony of the statement making my head hurt.

Uma tapped his knee. "Luther, don't you recognize me?"

Jonathan looked up. His eyes registered recognition. "Evil woman." He growled like a cur.

Uma's eyes widened and her lips parted. She sucked in a sharp, frightened breath. "Where's the blue book, Luther?"

Jonathan didn't respond.

Uma raised her chin. "The blue book," she said louder, as if to reestablish her authority. "It's worth a lot of money. I want it."

"What's in it, Uma?" I said. "Something to do with nuclear power?"

"Don't be ridiculous."

"My father keeps saying the word *nuclear*."

"He doesn't know what he's talking about."

Or she didn't. What did Zorn tell them was in the blue book? That was how it had to have started. He went to the frat party and boasted about what his roommate had invented. He invited them to watch him steal it.

Holland coughed, big gagging rasps. "Vance, I really need the head."

"Uh-uh," Vance said. "We're on a timeline here. First, we tie up your lover."

"I told you. He's not my—"

"Do I look like I care?"

"I'm going to heave."

"You've been on the boat all of two minutes."

"What don't you understand about I've got the flu, you imbecile?" Holland coughed against her shoulder again. "Unlock my cuffs."

Vance hitched a thumb. "Puke over the side. That's what oceans are for."

Uma said, "Hugh, let her go below. We don't want people staring."

What was she talking about? The marina was empty. Weekends, not weekday mornings, were when sailors came out in droves.

"Unlock my cuffs," Holland demanded. "I'll fall down the frigging ladder otherwise."

"Do it, Hugh." Uma pulled a Smith & Wesson LaserMax from her tote. "Go with her. I've got Luther and his son in hand."

Vance said, "Where did you get that?"

"It was my husband's." Uma aimed the gun at me. I'd handled a double-action revolver; the LaserMax was small, but it was reliable and would work well in self-defense, even against a man of my size. "Go, Hugh."

Reluctantly, Vance unlocked Holland's cuffs and shoved them at Uma. "Hold these."

She gripped them like brass knuckles and asked my father again about the notebook. He remained silent.

"No funny business," Vance said to Holland, "or I will shoot."

As Holland descended the ladder, she glanced over her shoulder at me and winked. Was she really sick, or was she trying to divide and conquer? With Vance and her below, did she expect me to disarm Uma? I flashed on the scene at the trailer with my mother bleeding out. If Uma fired wildly, a stray bullet could hit my father.

I heard the door to the head close. Then I heard Holland heave. She banged something—maybe the sink counter—four times, as if she were suffering terrible cramping.

I peered into the cabin; Vance stood by the head door, examining his nails.

Holland pounded the counter again. *Three. Two.*

Was she counting down?

I peeked at Uma, who was trying to keep an eye on me while still questioning my father.

One. The door to the head flew open.

CHAPTER 42

Vance reeled back. He lost hold of the Beretta. Holland dove for it.

At the same time, I lunged at Uma, grabbed her gun arm, and wrenched upward. She flailed at me with the handcuffs. Metal whacked my cheek, my shoulder. Each blow stung, but I didn't let go.

Holland raced up the ladder, Vance's gun in her right hand. With her left, she gripped the handrail that flanked the exit. Then suddenly she slipped. Vance must have seized her by the ankles. She released the Beretta. It clattered below deck. Vance roared, and Holland careened downward. Her fingernails clawed the ladder for traction, but it was no use.

I couldn't help. I had to control Uma, who was stronger than she appeared. I grabbed the handcuffs. Yanked. Uma popped off a shot. Upward. The noise echoed. My father moaned. I cut a look in his direction. He wasn't shot. He was rising to his feet.

"Jonathan, sit down," I ordered.

The temporary distraction gave Uma leverage. She pulled the handcuffs free and whipped me across the face. The pain caromed to my brain. My grasp on her gun arm weakened. She twisted free and aimed the muzzle at Jonathan.

"Don't move, young man, or I'll shoot dear old dad." Uma drew her lips back over her teeth like a tigress.

"No, you won't," I said. "You need him."

"I don't need you." She swung the revolver around and aimed at my face.

"I'm sorry, Chase." Holland lurched forward and landed on her knees.

Vance appeared behind Holland. He planted his boot against her spine and shoved his Beretta into the nape of her neck. "Don't try anything heroic, Day."

Stinging disappointment zipped through me. The plan had failed. I tried to convince myself it was only a setback. Holland and I could still outsmart these two. But how?

Uma said, "Tell me what's wrong with your father."

"Dementia is my guess, maybe early-onset Alzheimer's," I said. I wasn't an expert; I didn't know the difference between the two. A friend of my grandmother's had Alzheimer's, but I hadn't spent a lot of time taking notes on the finer points of her behavior. "He doesn't remember things in whole chunks." I wasn't sure he would ever piece together when he brought me into existence. The realization pierced me to the core.

"Do you know where the notebook is?" Uma asked.

"No."

"You're lying."

"If I knew where it was, do you think I'd be on this boat? I'd have it in hand, and I'd be spilling my guts to the police."

Vance said, "You don't trust the police."

"I do now."

Uma turned to Jonathan. "The blue book, Luther. I need it. You took it." She spoke softly as if addressing a dimwitted child. "You were with me that night, Luther. At the frat party. Sybil was there. We went to Karl's dorm room. You remember Karl, don't you?"

Jonathan's eyes narrowed.

"I can see you do." Uma pointed two fingers from her eyes to Jonathan's eyes. "We were having fun that night. We were all high. We were laughing. Karl was telling us about his goofy roommate. He said Geoffrey had been inventing weird stuff for years. Remember? Karl opened the safe and he pulled out three blue books."

"Three?" I said. "Why were there three?"

She ignored me and kept focused on my father. "Karl handed us each one and said, 'These are the keys to the world. This is going to be so'—"

"Nuclear," my father intoned.

"*Far out,*" Uma said, lacing the words with Valley Girl-like sassiness.

If the blue books didn't contain a nuclear invention, what else could they contain that was worth killing for? Or was that night, as Uma intimated, a prank gone wrong? And now two forces—one powerful, one desperate—were trying to get rid of the only person who, if he were clear-headed, could expose the whole incident. No, that wasn't exactly true. Uma wasn't trying to kill my father. Yet. She wanted the blue book my father stole. Why? To use as a bargaining chip? To protect herself from Zorn? When my father ran, did Zorn coerce Uma and my mother to hand over the other two books? Did he need the third to make a set?

Uma continued. "You took the third booklet, Luther. What did you do with it?"

Jonathan didn't respond.

"Karl is mean and spiteful, Luther. You don't want to meet up with him. He and I agreed after that night to part ways. We would never see each other again. I kept that promise. I rebuilt my life. I have a daughter, Luther. But now because of you—" She slapped him and, then, as if regretting the action, stroked my father's face.

How I wanted to rip the revolver out of her hands. Shoot her. Knock Vance three ways from Sunday. But I couldn't. Not without risking both my father and Holland's lives.

"Why didn't you stay gone, Luther?" Uma said. "Do you remember when we met? That night, Karl was trying to get into my pants. He always was. When I flirted with you, it made him jealous. He bragged that he had something to show me. If only you and Sybil hadn't come along. It was all just in fun."

"Fun that went horribly wrong," I said. "You killed Geoffrey Gaynor."

"Not me. Karl. It was an accident."

"Another accident?"

"Fine. Karl pulled the trigger. On purpose."

"You did nothing to stop him."

"You don't know Karl. He's a very powerful man."

"He wasn't then. He was a student, just like you."

"He came from nothing. His father abused him. Hit him. Told him he was worthless."

It's always the father's fault.

"Karl was none of those things. He believed in himself. He was smart, clever." She refocused on my father. Her voice held a bitter edge. "Karl wants the notebook you ran off with, but then you screwed him and he's angry. He will kill you and your son and anyone else you love."

"Has he threatened your daughter?" I asked.

"Yes."

"Did he kill your husband?"

"No. My dearly beloved did that all by himself, the coward, right after he ran through our life savings in less than a year."

So she needed money and believed Zorn would pay her to hand over my father.

Uma gripped the front of Jonathan's shirt. "Show me where you've hidden the blue book, and no one will get hurt. Do it fast, Luther. I have an engagement that I can't miss."

"Your daughter's wedding is tonight," I said. "At Frost Amphitheater."

"How do you know that?"

"There are no secrets thanks to the Internet. Does she know what her mother is? Does she know you're a murderer?"

"Shut up." Uma trained her revolver on me. I could see her considering whether shooting me was worth the delay. It wasn't. She re-aimed the gun on my father. "On your feet."

He folded his arms across his chest. "No legs."

I grinned. Maybe Jonathan, aka Luther, was more aware than I gave him credit for.

Vance said, "Babe, let's move this along."

"Babe?" Holland sniped. "Are you two an item?"

I snickered. "Honestly, Vance, are you going to leave your wife for this piece of—"

Uma slapped my cheek.

"Don't rise to the bait, babe," Vance said. "You know I'm leaving her. I love you. Now pull yourself together. Let's get moving."

A moment passed, and then Uma, like the polished wedding planner she was, swiped a hair off her face, licked her glossy lips, and grinned. "You know what? I've had enough. Hugh, get rid of these two."

"Kill them?"

"Do you have a problem with that? You were going to do away with Day at the hostel. If you love me like you say…"

Vance shifted feet. "How about I let them rot instead? I've got just the place. A relic like Day belongs in a crypt."

"A crypt?"

"Yeah. The mausoleum on Weyford campus."

Vance threw me a nasty look. Apparently my flip comment at the precinct, when I said Dean Hyde belonged in a crypt, had inspired this bright idea. It was Christmas break; the Kwanzaa celebration was over; the place would be deserted. A guard might pass by every other day. Other than that—

Uma clapped the handcuffs on my father and sat beside him. She slipped her hand through his elbow, placed the nose of her revolver against his waist, and smiled in a sultry way. The image was just this side of bizarre. "We were having such a good time that night, weren't we, Luther? You had the hots for me."

"Luther is dead," Jonathan muttered.

"That's right," I said. "Luther died that night because he saw you and Zorn kill an innocent kid and he checked out."

"I didn't shoot him," Uma yelled.

"That's enough, Day," Vance said. "Let's move out."

CHAPTER 43

Uma's cell phone rang. "Hugh, hold on."

While she fetched her phone from her pocket, Vance placed the nose of his Beretta at the base of Holland's head and said to me, "Stand still. Keep quiet."

I obeyed. I couldn't figure out how to jump Vance and not endanger Holland or my father.

Uma answered, "Noble Wedding—" She grinned and pressed the speaker icon on her phone so we could hear. "Karl, darling. How are you?"

"Cut the crap, Uma," Zorn shouted. "I know what you're up to."

"Why, Karl, whatever could you mean?" Uma sounded like she was flirting. Was that how she had acted years ago? Was that why the night in the dorm room got out of hand? She goaded him on, and he flaunted his power.

"You're looking for Luther," Zorn said, "but you'll never find him because, get this, Luther has changed his name."

"How did you discover that, Karl? Did Yuji Tanaka—the traitor—tell you?"

"Tanaka's an asset, Uma. You should have paid him what he was worth."

"May he die a slow death."

Zorn chortled. "Tanaka wasn't the one who put it together. My kid figured it out."

Apparently, Tommy didn't tell his father that he had made that connection by kidnapping me. Heaven forbid he admit he lost me. How much of a disappointment was Tommy to his father? His ineptitude had to eat at Zorn, who was obviously a perfectionist. Did he go light on the kid because of his own history of parental abuse?

Uma smiled at Jonathan. "Karl, look no further. I've got Luther." She shoved the phone toward my father's mouth. "Say hello, Luther."

He didn't.

Vance yelled, "He's here, Zorn. Trust me."

"Who's that?" Zorn demanded.

"Yuji's replacement," Uma answered. "Officer Hugh Vance. He persuaded your Miss Tate to be of service to us. Say hello, Holland."

She pressed her lips together.

"Holland, have they hurt you?" Zorn sounded genuinely concerned.

What was up with that? He had destroyed her father and threatened to kill her mother. Or had he? Was all of it a lie? Had Holland played me? Was Zorn in love with her and she in love with him?

Vance prodded Holland to speak. She opened her mouth then closed it. She shot me a look. What was she trying to tell me? I felt like I was stuck in a bad game of monkey in the middle.

"Let's negotiate, Karl." Uma looked excited. Her skin was flushed.

"Tell Luther I'm going to cut his son's heart out unless he turns over that notebook."

Uma laughed. "Which son would that be? I have Chase Day with me."

"Jack, Jr."

A pang gripped my insides. By blurting Jack's name in front of Tommy, I had put him in danger. *Me*. My fault.

"Jack!" I yelled. Jack didn't respond. "If you've hurt him, Zorn—"

Vance whacked my ear with his gun. Pain shot through me.

Uma said, "I'll get the blue book, Karl, and then you'll make it worth my while."

"What do you mean?"

"Thanks to Miss Tate, I happen to know you followed Chase Day for years. Thanks to Sybil, I know you paid her hush money. This isn't about killing Luther to keep the past buried. Whatever is in that third blue book is something you've craved all these years. What's in it? The key to world peace? No, that's not your style. The recipe for world domination? Yes, definitely sexier."

"Nuclear," Jonathan mumbled.

Uma whispered, "Yes, *nuclear*. Definitely far out." Full voice she said, "Here's what I'm going to do, Karl. We're taking Miss Tate and Mr. Day to the mausoleum on the Weyford University campus."

"I want Miss Tate intact."

"Aw, Karl, women have always been your weakness." Uma sniggered. "You know what? I'm feeling magnanimous. Go to the crypt. Capture them or kill them, I don't care. In the meantime, I'll get Luther to tell me where the notebook is, and we'll get down to bargaining."

"You're nuts."

"Karl, darling. Do you know why you never killed me? Because as long as Luther was alive, I wasn't the only one who knew about that night. You worried that Luther would surface and tell all if you offed me. He was always sweet on me. Now that I've found him, I have the upper hand." Uma ran a fingertip along my father's cheek. "Here's the deal, Karl. Twenty million in good faith and a salary of five million, with yearly bonuses commensurate with my performance."

"Your perf—"

"When you gather the cash, call me, and I'll give you a location. Bring a written contract, Karl. I know you have lawyers who can whip that together for you in no time. *Ciao*."

CHAPTER 44

"You two," Vance said to Holland and me, "march." He nudged me then Holland with the nose of the Beretta. "Don't try anything stupid."

I glanced at my father. He wasn't looking at me; he was studying the handcuffs around his wrists. I trusted Uma wouldn't hurt him, not until she found what she wanted. But after that? How long did I have until he spilled a hint, a clue, of where he had stored the blue book? Maybe he hadn't stored it at all. Maybe he had disposed of it the night he joined the Navy. I raised a hand to catch my father's attention. If Holland and I didn't escape and this was the last time I would see him, I wanted to remember his face.

Vance whacked my arm with his gun. "What did I say? Move."

"Chase," Holland warned.

I fell in line. Vance steered Holland and me to a blue Econoline van. The rear compartment smelled of marijuana, sweat, and rope. Newspaper littered the floor. Ants skittered in and out of an empty soda can. "Get in." Vance ordered Holland to tie me and gag me with newspaper; he warned that he would be checking the knots.

Before she began, I said, "Zorn and you."

"What are you asking?"

"He wants you."

Her eyes brimmed with tears. "Not like you think. He wants to punish me. He's all about control." While she stuffed newspaper into my mouth, she whispered, "Not that it matters, but I never stopped loving you."

It mattered. Despite the fact that she had tailed me for seventeen years. Despite the fact that she had lied to me to win my confidence. She was my first love and my past, and I had believed, from the moment I reconnected with her at the hospital, that she was my future. I couldn't erase the deep-seated feelings. Love was screwy that way.

When she finished her job, Vance grabbed her and wrestled her to the ground. He bound her with ropes. "Nice and tight," he muttered. After stuffing newspaper into her mouth, he took great pleasure in slapping her face. Real big man. Then he checked my knots. Satisfied with Holland's handiwork, he kicked me hard enough to send me rolling into the wall of the van.

"See you on the other end," he quipped and climbed out of the rear of the van.

The door slammed, and Holland inched toward me. She curled into me, her back to my front.

I wished I could tell her I was sorry for doubting her. I wished I could say out loud that I loved her, for what it was worth. I had never said those words to anyone. Not even to Tina the attorney. I nudged her with my knees. She wriggled to leave her be. I bumped her again. "Taillight," I mumbled, though the word sounded more like, "Taw-wah." I kicked with my feet and hoped she would do the same.

She got the message. She slithered until she was in place and then kicked at the left taillight. I aimed at the right, but neither of us could bust out a light. Holland grew quiet. Her shoulders heaved.

For the next few minutes, I worked to loosen the ropes around my wrists. My skin grew raw from the effort. I gave up. Instead, though I knew it would be fruitless, I shimmied toward the side of the van and jammed with my heels. Over and over. If the van were at a standstill, the noise would be intense, but it was in motion; the sound to a passing driver would be nothing more than dull thuds.

After a lengthy drive, the van pulled to a stop. Tires screeched. Seconds later, Vance opened one of the rear doors. The hinge groaned. Vance entered the van, scooped Holland up, and left. He slammed the door hard. I kicked the walls of the van repeatedly, to no avail.

A couple of minutes passed, and then the rear door squeaked open again. Vance smiled, his lips pulled back over his teeth in an evil grin. "Your turn, fella." He jabbed me in the jaw. Once. Twice. Stars caromed inside my head. "Atta boy."

Vance lifted me like a sack of potatoes, slammed the van's door, and lugged me to the rear of the mausoleum.

I had visited the place before. The front door, fitted with a keyed bolt lock, was meant for family only. The rear metal door, which was used by service people—even a tomb needed dusting—had a keyed sliding bolt. Somehow Vance must have picked the lock. He slid back the bolt and opened the door. Metal scraped the threshold. Vance moved inside and flung me onto the marble floor. My head struck a corner of the crypt that stood in the center of the room. Pain exploded behind my eyes, but I didn't pass out.

Holland lay still beside the crypt.

"A history buff like you should appreciate this place, Day," Vance said. "It was a stroke of brilliance to bring you here, don't you think? I don't have to put a bullet in you. If Zorn wants to kill you, let him. If he leaves you locked inside, in the long run, you'll die of starvation or thirst. When the cleaning crew finds you three to six months from now, depending on the schedule"—Vance chuckled—"they'll think you accidentally locked yourself in."

Accidentally bound with rope and mouth stuffed with a gag? Even an idiot could figure out the truth.

Vance added, "By then, no one will be looking for me, and even if they are, I'll be long gone. I've always fancied Mexico." He kicked me in the thigh. "Fully experience your last moments on earth, pal. Deep breaths. I hear it's good for the lungs." He closed the door and drew the bolt. The click of the padlock followed.

My insides tensed. The place was dark except for dull light filtering through the narrow stained glass depiction of Weyford's father in safari dress. I scooted across the marble until I was close to Holland. I cradled her as best I could. I nudged the back of her head with my chin and mumbled,

"Let's get out of here." It didn't sound any better than my earlier gagged mutterings, but it would have to do. She roused.

Next I flopped onto my belly and turned until I had backed up to her. She picked up on what I was doing and reached for me with her fingertips.

"Uh-uh," I said. "You first."

Understanding, she went still. I picked at the short end of the rope and shoved. It wouldn't budge. I tugged on the loop. "Come on."

"Wha—?"

The loop loosened, ever so slightly.

As I continued to work the knot, I thought about my father. It was my fault Uma had him in custody. If only I had left him at the asylum. Maybe Uma wouldn't have found him. Was his memory issue a permanent situation or drug-induced? How frustrated was Uma by his non-answers right about now? I hoped plenty.

CHAPTER 45

I heard a sound outside the mausoleum's main entrance. Someone was picking the lock. Had luck gone my way? Was a student or guard trying to enter? I shimmied to the crypt door and thrust my heels against the metal while howling like a trapped animal.

In less than a minute, the door to the mausoleum swung open.

Sunlight outlined the visitors. Three of them. I couldn't distinguish faces. The square-faced one to the left looked familiar. He moved first. As light caught him, I realized it was the Asian, Yuji Tanaka. Broken nose, permanent scowl. He looked beefier than I remembered, maybe because he wasn't charging at me like a rhino on steroids. He aimed a Glock 19C at my head and grinned.

I screamed through my gag. Loud. Steady. Was anybody within range of the mausoleum? Anybody at all?

Zorn moved into the light. He hadn't changed much since our single encounter. His eyes were as sharp as a bird of prey's. He looked ropier, tanner. His Armani suit fit him to a tee. He was taller than I remembered, but my perspective from the ground up was hampered. "Shut him up."

Tanaka clipped my cheek with his weapon. Blazing pain shot through my skull. Blood seeped around my mouth. I must have bitten the inside of my cheek. I tried not to gag while the wad of newspaper absorbed the blood.

"Move," Tanaka said to the middle of the trio, which turned out to be Jack Jr. I had hoped Zorn was lying about capturing him. Jack's face was a mass of purple bruises. His mouth was stuffed with red cloth. His hands were tied behind his back; his feet, unencumbered. Tanaka shoved Jack forward, closed the mausoleum door with a clang, and sideswiped me again for good measure.

Holland moaned. I rolled onto my side and blinked at her to let her know I was okay.

Tanaka pushed Jack forward. "On your knees."

Jack stumbled. He garbled something unintelligible. Talking through gags wasn't a well-defined art.

Zorn said, "Once again, Mr. Day, you're too late to save the ones you love."

The jibe sucker-punched me. He was right. I had failed to save either my mother or my father, and now I had Holland and Jack's blood on my hands.

"A man of few words." Zorn grinned. "My kind of guy." He circled me. "You're a tough nut. I shouldn't be surprised after following you your entire life. Your mother was the same. Resourceful, defiant. Accepting my hush money for so many years and then, out of the blue, staging her death in a fire. Brilliant, actually. I had her ashes brought to me. I ran my fingers through them. I felt her bones. I believed."

I thought back to what my grandmother had told me after learning my mother had been murdered. She said my mother had faked her death to give me a chance. It was the one selfless thing she'd ever done. What was amazing was that Mom, despite her drawbacks, had been able to dupe Zorn.

"Your mother was sly. Very sly." He removed the gag from my mouth and held it between two fingers as if my saliva might poison him. "Tell me something, Mr. Day."

"If you're up for a fight," I said, "you've come to the right place."

Zorn brayed like a donkey. "Tough talk for a man in your situation. Where is your father? Where is Uma taking him?"

Jack inhaled sharply. He scrambled to a sitting position and eyed me with outright hate. I didn't blame him. If I had left things alone… But how could I have? My mother called. Pleaded. Died.

I said, "I don't know where he is."

Jack's gaze didn't ease up. He was in unfamiliar surroundings and wondering if he would survive.

"On his way to a wedding, perhaps?" Zorn eyed Tanaka, who nodded. Of course Uma's former bodyguard would know where she was headed. He probably had her calendar seared in his brain. Would she take my father to Frost Amphitheater? Was Vance supposed to meet up with her? Vance. How I wished I could shove my fist down his throat.

Zorn moved to Holland. He crouched and caressed the tips of her hair. Holland curled into herself, drawing her knees into her chest. "Dear Holland. You disobeyed me yet again. What do you think your punishment should be this time?" He yanked on her hair. She squealed. So much for pretending he cared about her. "Eagleton is on his way to pay your mother a visit." Eagleton, the Australian thug who beat her up, hounded my grandmother, and left Kimo for dead. "Would you like to watch her die?"

Holland mewled, probably remembering what Zorn's man had done to her.

"I thought about having him hold off," Zorn went on, "but I think the timing is right, don't you? It's the perfect price for your betrayal. I know how much you love her, despite her feeble moral character." He released her and pushed her head to the ground, then rose to his feet. "Tanaka, pick her up and put her in the car."

"Don't," I said.

"Your objection has no merit. After watching her mother die, I have a special"—Zorn paused, as if selecting just the right word—"*plan* for Holland. It will involve sharp knives and dark spaces."

Tanaka scooped Holland into his arms.

Holland mumbled something.

Zorn reached for her gag. "One scream, and I'll kill your friends, right here, right now. Blink to let me know you understand." She obeyed. He removed the gag. "You have something to say?"

"What's in the notebook?" she demanded.

"Darling, don't worry your pretty head."

"You killed your college roommate. If I'd known you were this obsessed—"

"You still would have done my bidding." Zorn grinned. "If you really must know, my roomie was the one who was obsessed. I merely recognized opportunity. You see, Geoffrey"—he paused and licked his lips—"had a pet project, which he called PEP. What kind of puerile title is that for a self-sustaining battery?"

I gawked. "He successfully created perpetual energy?"

"So he claimed. Scientists have failed repeatedly to create it. It's worth billions on the open market if it really works. Geoffrey kept it under lock and key. The month before he died—"

"Before you killed him—"

"He talked about it nonstop in his sleep. I knew what that discovery was worth, and I knew what the world would give me in return. A Nobel prize, to start with."

"You killed Gaynor for that?" I said.

"Don't be shortsighted. With wealth and fame comes power. Power to run for office. To run global corporations. To alter the future."

"My father took one of the three blue books," I said, "which means whatever you have is incomplete. I'm assuming your fixation on obtaining the book indicates you couldn't devise the rest on your own. Does it gall you to realize you aren't as bright as Geoffrey?"

"Shut. Up."

"How did you plan the murder? It wasn't spur of the moment. I imagine you dared Geoffrey to go out by himself. Celebrate. Live it up. Get drunk so he'd be easy to manipulate."

Zorn hissed air through his nose.

I was on the right track. "The question is how did you let Geoffrey know you'd returned? That had to be a matter of timing. You referred him to a particular bar, didn't you? You anonymously called him at the bar and said he was being robbed. Am I warm?"

Zorn grinned, his lips sealed together, his gaze cold.

"You knew Geoffrey would be armed."

"He never went anywhere without his Colt 45," Zorn blurted, unable to keep his victory a secret any longer.

"I assume you wore gloves."

"Driving gloves."

"Very vogue."

Zorn smugly tugged down the cuffs of his suit.

"Why bring witnesses?"

"I only intended to bring Uma. She insisted on including your mother and Luther."

"Even so, you could still carry out your plan. They were all loaded, right? Their impressions would have been impaired. You would kill Geoffrey and convince them you fought him in self-defense." I assessed him from head to toe. "How do you live with yourself, Zorn?"

"Rather well, thank you." He offered a jaded smile. "I own a mansion. I run a thriving business. And I have a beautiful family."

"Except for that slug you call a son."

Zorn ground his teeth together but let my insult pass. "All my life I took shortcuts, mainly because my father required sooner rather than later results."

"I hear he beat you."

"Not entirely without cause," Zorn said. "At the age of five, he called me an amoral SOB. I can't remember the exact circumstance, maybe because I kicked the dog, but the words and his dismissive tone affected me. When I was fourteen, he tried to have me committed after I broke into a bank vault just because I could. Mental institutions wouldn't take me. I was a bit edgy for them. Even after high school, I loved carrying out pranks. For some reason, I felt the need to continually prove to my father that my mind was superior to his. I went to college. I graduated with honors. I became a millionaire. He did none of that. And won't. He's dead now."

"At your hand?"

"Heart attack. He deserved worse. Do you know that whipping scars never fade?" Zorn sneered. "Where were we?"

"The third notebook."

"Ah, yes, PEP. Geoffrey's pet project. You guessed right. Without that third notebook, I can't seem to complete the formula. Believe me I've tried. Carbon-based grapheme is the up-and-coming thing, but does it work?

No, it does not. I've done numerous in-house tests with induction coils and oscillating magnets, but neither my people nor I can devise anything good enough to power something larger than a AA battery. A device to handle a semi-truck? Forget it. Geoffrey had it figured out." He tapped his head. "He claimed he had it all in his brain. He didn't realize I knew about those books."

"You memorized the combination to his safe."

"Where did you hear—"

"I spoke with Geoffrey's father."

"Simple man." Zorn clicked his tongue against his teeth. "Yes. I broke into the safe, disarmed the idiotic alert he'd installed, and the rest is history." He clapped his hands. "Okay. That's enough. I've told you plenty. You can die a contented man, knowing the truth." He addressed Tanaka. "After you put Miss Tate in the car, come back and shoot these two."

"No, wait," Holland said. "If you kill them, you won't have anything to bargain with."

"I won't need—"

"Yes, you will if Luther doesn't tell Uma where the notebook is. I saw him. Luther's tough. He'll be hard to crack."

Hadn't Jack revealed that his father was suffering some kind of mental illness? Maybe we had more time than I imagined.

After a moment, Zorn said, "You're right and what better place to leave Luther's boys than this place. Tanaka, rough them up a bit more. Pain is good for developing character. That's what my daddy used to say. He grinned at me. "You've been granted a reprieve, Mr. Day. If I were you, I'd pray."

Zorn forced the gags back into my and Holland's mouths and exited the crypt. Tanaka set Holland on the floor and warned her to stand still. What could she do? She was tied up. Then he grasped Jack by the elbow and hurled him into a wall. Jack crumpled to the ground. His head slammed the floor. He moaned.

Grinning, Tanaka came at me. He kicked me in the stomach three times and moved around to my back and wailed on my kidneys. I curled in on myself, but I wouldn't give him the satisfaction of a grunt.

"Loser," Tanaka muttered and then hoisted Holland over his shoulder and exited. Her efforts to pummel him with her knees were fruitless.

The door clanged shut. The engine of a car kicked over. Tires peeled across the gravel. Silence.

Seconds later, another sound caught my attention. Girls singing Christmas carols. Were students on the campus, after all? How close were they? Had they noticed Tanaka carrying a struggling woman out of the crypt? Had they seen a car drive away?

I howled, but the singing voices diminished. The girls were moving on.

CHAPTER 46

A minute later, Jack roused. Grunting while using his chin for balance, he thrust himself to his knees and then scrambled to his feet. I banged my heels on the marble floor of the crypt to attract his attention. I might not have been able to untie Holland in time, but I sure as heck was going to get my half-brother to untie me or vice versa.

"Remove the gag," I tried to say, but it sounded more like *rema-da-gah*. I bobbed my head to get the point across.

In Jack's eyes, I saw dawning recognition. He hurried to me, knelt on the floor, and backed up to my face. Using thumbs, he pulled out the wet newspaper.

I gulped in air. "Thanks. Now work on my rope."

He sidled behind me, but he didn't try to untie me. He butted my fingers.

"What do you want?" I asked.

He muttered a command much like mine when my mouth was gagged.

I understood. With stiff fingers, I grabbed hold of the cloth in his mouth and tugged. It came free.

Jack said, "How did you find my father?"

"How about a thank you?"

"How did you find my father?" he repeated.

"*Our* father."

"Answer me and untie me."

Sitting back to back, I worked on the ropes around his wrists while explaining, over my shoulder, about my ability to recreate and decipher the topographical map from his office and my subsequent raid on the hospital.

"Is he with the Noble woman?" Jack asked.

"Yes." The ropes were scratchy and tied tightly. "Where is the notebook that Zorn wants?"

"I don't know."

"Dear old Dad never mentioned it?"

"Don't call him that."

I kneaded a section of rope with my thumb and forefinger. It started to give. "What does he have, dementia or early-onset Alzheimer's?"

"The latter."

"I'm sorry. I know nothing about the disease."

"It sucks. Dad was always so sharp. A couple of years ago, he started having anger issues. Mom didn't understand. They divorced. Looking back, it was because he couldn't remember things. He couldn't do what he used to. The littlest stuff like, kid you not, screwing in a light bulb."

I wedged my thumb beneath a loop of rope. It budged more. "Why was he at Keystone Hospital?"

"He acquired an infection."

"That put him into a coma?"

"No. He was doped up but not out for the count."

"They couldn't treat an infection at the asylum?"

"Until now he's been living in my care, but I couldn't—" Jack faltered. "After the stint at Keystone, it was time to move him. I didn't think going back to my place was the best idea. I—" His voice caught. "Are you close to untying me?"

"Getting there." I wiggled the loop of rope. It loosened a bit more.

"How did my father get mixed up with these people?"

I explained my theory, from the past to the present, including the night of the murder and the disappearance of the blue book, up until Uma Noble and her toady Vance captured me. "From what I can tell, Luther Marcussen joined the Navy that night. He went off the grid by changing his name to Jonathan Battle, which was the name of a childhood friend, an orphan who died in a car crash. Luther assumed his identity. He must have liked the Bay Area. He moved back and stayed out of the limelight."

"How does this guy Vance fit into the picture? Do you think the cops are part of this?"

"I think Vance is acting alone, enticed by a big payoff from Uma Noble. My guess—he also expects to get lucky with her. I'm hoping Detective Philips is legit." I wanted to trust somebody. I massaged the rope some more and finally was able to release the binds around Jack's wrists. "There. Now untie me."

When he finished, I loosened the rope around my ankles, then stood and stretched. Every inch of me ached. I wasn't sure if Vance or Tanaka's assaults had made me bleed internally; I couldn't worry about it now. I wasn't spitting up blood. "By the way, I've got pictures of my mother with Zorn, Noble, and our father."

"Luther Marcussen."

"Yes. The photos prove they knew each other. I've also got Zorn's confession."

"Hearsay." Jack scrambled to his feet. "We can't prove a thing unless we get out of here. How are we going to do that? It's sealed tight."

I pulled my cell phone from my pocket.

"How do you still have that?" Jack said.

"Vance was in a hurry. He's a few bullets short of a full clip. Tanaka was so intent on kicking me, he neglected to strip-search me. " I tried to dial out but couldn't get a signal. I stuffed the phone back in my pocket and hurried to the mausoleum door. "Do you realize how ironic it is that we are stuck in a crypt dedicated by a father to his son?" I pounded the door; the metal reverberated like a bomb exploding, but it didn't give. There were no cries of alarm outside. I moved to the stained glass window and peered through a frame. No one was walking in the area. "How about breaking the window?"

"Too narrow to crawl through," Jack said.

"When did you become an escape artist expert?"

"It can't be more than five inches wide. Even sucking in my gut"—Jack had a flat belly—"I won't fit through that opening, and I'm leaner than you. We could break it and scream."

"I doubt it would do any good. No one's out there." I studied the walls and floors. "This is an above-ground entombment."

"Good observation." Jack's mouth quirked up, but his eyes held no humor.

"I know a little about tombs. I'm an historian."

"You study dead people."

"Don't mock me. Actually, I'm an expert on war." I pointed upward. "Look there. See the stainless steel clamps and dowel pins? They hold the blocks of cement in place."

"You think we can unpin them?"

"Not on a bet. But it tells me that this crypt has been updated, which means it's ventilated to eliminate moisture and vapors. See that vent overhead?"

Jack tilted his head. "The one out of reach?"

"It looks to be about twelve inches by twelve inches. We should be able to fit through it."

"It's twelve feet up. In case you hadn't noticed, we don't have a ladder."

"I can reach it if I climb on your shoulders. I'll dislodge it and I'll crawl through the system to the outside and unbolt the door."

"I'll crack under your weight."

I scowled.

"I'm lighter than you," Jack said. "Why don't I climb on your shoulders?"

"How do I know you'll open the door for me?"

Jack grinned then winced. He massaged his bruised jaw. "I guess you'll have to trust me."

"I don't know you well enough to trust you."

"Well, it's about time you get to know me. I'm trustworthy. I don't assault people on the street. And I don't let friends get swept into life-threatening dramas. When I get out, I'm coming back for you, and then you and I are going to find my father."

"*Our* father. Concede the point."

"I want a DNA test."

"Fine. Climb on." I started to create a stirrup with my hands, then remembered something. "Wait. You'll need this." I pulled the paperclip I snagged at Jack's office from my pocket; it still had a shred of the Lansing Mental Asylum flyer wedged beneath. I pried the paperclip open and handed it to Jack.

"What's that for?"

"To pick the lock outside."

"Do you think that will do it?"

"Vance and Zorn's goon were both able to unlock it. Neither had a key. You're the dot.com genius. Figure it out."

Jack put his foot into my hands. With a hop, he stepped up on my shoulders. Within seconds, he wedged open the vent. "I need another few inches if I'm going to climb through."

Grunting, I hoisted him like a cheerleader.

He wriggled inside the hole and disappeared into the duct. "FYI, I'm only slightly claustrophobic."

"Now you tell me."

Minutes passed. I didn't hear a vent fall to the ground outside. I didn't hear footsteps. But then I heard a click and a rattle. The bolt on the crypt slid back.

CHAPTER 47

I stepped out of the crypt. Sunshine stabbed my eyes. I hitched a thumb. "Follow me."

"Where are we going?"

"We need wheels."

The art museum at Weyford University is a major attraction. It remains open over the holidays. Cars would be parked in the lot. I jogged ahead, my knee and ankle hitching with pain, and pulled my cell phone from my pocket. I called Reggie and quickly explained the situation.

"I'll be right there," she said.

"No time to wait."

Kimo stole the phone from her. "Bro, you've got to contact the police or I will."

"I'll call Philips the minute we're on the road. If I don't reach him..." I told Kimo what I believed was going down between Zorn, Noble, and my father. If Kimo didn't hear from me in an hour, he was to go to the police and tell all. I hung up and handed the phone to Jack. "You're up. Call Detective Philips."

"Got a number?" He was breathing as heavily as I was.

"Redwood City PD. It'll be on the Internet."

I veered right into the museum parking lot and scanned the remote area where staff parked their cars. "This way." I beckoned with my hand.

"What are you planning to do?" Jack asked. "Steal a car?"

"Borrow."

"Using what keys?"

"I learned a few bad tricks when I was a teen." Holland wasn't the only one who knew how to hotwire a car. One, a gray Cutlass, had the old kind of locks. The knob on the rear right door was poking up, which meant the door was unlocked. I gripped Jack's shoulder. "Keep an eye out."

I slipped into the car, crawled over the front seat, and yanked the plastic-coated wires down beneath the console. I peeled back the plastic and notched the copper-tipped wires together. A spark arced between them. The car chugged to life. The gas tank held an eighth of a tank. Enough to go about twenty miles. I rolled down the driver's window. "Get in."

Jack slid into the car. "The seat belt's busted."

"We'll be busted if we don't get moving." I yanked the gearshift into reverse and pulled out of the parking spot slowly so as not to draw attention.

A minute later, I was tearing away from the campus. Adrenaline pumped through me. I felt good. Alive. I cut a look at Jack, who sat hunched forward in the passenger seat, glaring at the cell phone. "Gotten through to a real person yet?" I asked.

"I haven't been able to open the Internet. No signal."

"Give it a second. There's dense Internet activity around here." I wasn't sure Detective Philips would believe that Vance was a dirty cop and holding our father hostage, but I wasn't showing up at Frost Amphitheater with Jack and no other backup. Jack, the shadow I couldn't shake. Jack, the brother I never knew about. I had always wanted a brother, a family. To have one instantly was a shock. Granted, Jack wasn't accepting that I was family, but I had time to work on that. At least, I hoped I had time.

Jack, still glowering at the readout, snarled. "Dang."

"Keep trying."

"What does it look like I'm doing?"

"Don't snap at me."

"I'm not snapping."

"You—" I opened my mouth and jammed it shut. No need to carp. I focused on the road. "Does our father have any lucid moments? Other than recognizing Uma Noble, he's been babbling about ships and sailing. What's with that? Is the Navy all he remembers?"

"So it seems." Jack huffed. "Ah, finally." He stabbed the Internet icon. When a page emerged, he typed in a string of letters.

"Did you pick up sailing because of him?"

"How do you know I like to sail?"

"I went to your office, remember? You've got pictures of ships up the wazoo. You even painted one of the *Niantic*. What's up with that?"

Jack tapped in a telephone number and hit Send. "The *Niantic* was one of the first whaling ships to enter San Francisco Bay."

"I know that. There's a California Historical Landmark for it right next to the Transamerica Pyramid."

"Exactly. When I was a kid, Dad and I visited all the buildings in San Francisco dozens of times, including the Transamerica Pyramid. I wanted to be an architect like him. He thought seeing works of architectural brilliance—" He scowled at me. "Don't make that face."

"What face?"

"Like you're jealous."

"So what if you did things with him and I didn't?" I hissed, instantly wishing I could put a cap on it. Yes, I was jealous. I didn't have memories with my father; this guy did. He had memories with his mother, too. He'd gotten the whole shebang. The real deal. Family with a capital F. "Back to the *Niantic*, is that why he's obsessed with it?"

"I don't understand. He's not—" Jack whacked the dashboard. "Shoot! I lost the signal."

"Try again while telling me about the *Niantic*."

He tapped Send over and over. "Come to think of it, one time when we went to see the memorial, I think Dad was trying to find the courage to tell me who he really was. He was going on and on about how the *Niantic* brought fortune seekers to San Francisco during the Gold Rush. Maybe he—" Jack pointed at the phone. Someone was answering. "Yes, Detective Philips, please." After a moment, Jack continued. "Detective, hello. I'm Jack Battle. Yes, sir, the dot-com guy. I'm calling because I'm in a car with Chase Day. No, sir, he can't talk. He's driving. He's… Yeah, sure." Jack thrust the cell phone at me. "He demands to talk to you."

I seized the phone. "Detective."

"Mr. Day."

I gave him a quick briefing about the night my father's life turned upside down, then followed up with an account of my own search and rescue efforts. "I didn't tell you that I found my father until now because—"

"You didn't trust me."

"Because of Vance. When I came to the precinct and told you about the kid holding my dog at gunpoint—"

"The kid that didn't exist?"

"You and Officer Vance thought I was out of my gourd. With good reason. The kid didn't exist because his father had rescued him. Tommy's last name is Zorn. He's Karl Zorn's son."

"Karl Zorn of Zorn International?"

"The same, but back to Vance."

Philips blew out a stream of air. "Go on."

I swerved around an SUV filled with partying teens gesturing lewdly. "I know you have a history with Vance. He saved your life. But hopefully that won't color your opinion. Vance is working privately for Uma Noble." I told him about Vance's break-in at the hostel and the possibility that he took the fax with Tanaka's image. "He warned Uma Noble that she could be implicated."

"How do you—" Philips paused. "Never mind. You're probably right. I can see Vance needing a second paycheck. So you thought I was a dirty cop, too?"

"I didn't know what to think. All I knew was you were focusing on me as the main suspect in my mother's murder."

"I never said—"

"You didn't have to." I elaborated about Vance's joining forces with Uma Noble, the two of them taking my father hostage, and Vance hauling Holland Tate and me to the crypt and leaving us to die. "I believe Vance is on his way to the site where Noble's daughter is getting married—Frost Amphitheater."

"Why would he take your father there?"

"Because Noble won't let Vance interrogate him without her present. She's too wrapped up in the outcome. She might not grill my father while her daughter is getting married, but she'll want to know that he's close by. Now back to Zorn." The driver of a Jaguar tried to cut me off. I swore at him and slammed on the breaks.

"Day? What's going on?"

"Reckless driver. Anyway after Vance left, Karl Zorn and Yuji Tanaka—"

"We're hunting for him."

"Look no further. He's working for Zorn. Those two showed up at the crypt. They exchanged my half-brother, who you just talked to on the phone, for Miss Tate."

"And who is she again?"

"A bounty hunter in Zorn's employ and now their prisoner. Zorn is on his way to Frost Amphitheater to capture my father. Noble doesn't know that Zorn is on his way."

Philips whistled. "Where are you now?"

"Two to three miles away."

"When you get to the amphitheater, do not budge. Got me? You wait in the parking lot for me and my men."

"Yes, sir."

CHAPTER 48

I flipped the phone to Jack and proceeded past the Stanford Golf Course, past the first batch of high-end shops, then veered right. I took the back roads at fifteen over the speed limit. The amphitheater, fondly called the Grass Steps, was built as a tribute to Frost's son who died of polio. The stadium-style setting was situated on approximately twenty acres of land between the main Quad and the Stanford Football Stadium.

At the entrance to the parking lot, I pulled to a stop. The area was packed with cars, vans, and Winnebagos. Uma hadn't skimped on invitees. Guests in evening attire were climbing the rise into the open-air theater. Though it was an hour until dusk, torches lined the pathway.

"Where do you think Vance parked?" Jack asked.

"Not here but nearby. There are trails around the stadium. I'll bet he's hidden the van along one of them."

"And Zorn?"

"He'll show up. He's after Uma Noble. Vengeance is best when you do it yourself. He'll make Tanaka keep watch over Holland."

Jack shook his head. "I'll bet Zorn has her tied up, maybe sedated, so she's out of the way."

"Did he sedate you?"

"Yep. I was in a public parking lot. Out of the corner of my eye, I saw someone coming toward me, but it didn't register. Tanaka jabbed me with a hypodermic. Whatever he hit me with knocked me out for about two hours."

Headlights flashed in my rearview mirror. I drove into the lot and parked. A four-door sedan pulled in behind mine. Detective Philips exited the driver's side. Detective Bruno emerged from the passenger's side. A trio of police cars streamed in behind the sedan.

I introduced Jack to Philips and Bruno.

Jack held up his hands. "It's not my fault. I wanted no part of this. I—"

The night went still. Music that had been playing inside the amphitheater stopped. Then musicians started in on *West Wide Story's* "A Time for Us."

Philips said to Jack, "Mr. Battle, we'll talk about your involvement later." He faced me. "What kind of vehicle are my men looking for?"

"An Econoline van. Dark blue. Medium-sized. California license plate ending in nine-five-oh- or nine-six-oh-something."

"That makes it a commercial vehicle. Do you have a picture of the hostage?"

I handed him my mother's locket. "My father is thirty-seven years older now. Gray hair. Thin. He's wearing hospital pajamas and a zippered sweatshirt."

Jack scowled. "When were you going to tell me about the locket?"

"Sorry. We were working at cross purposes." I'd shown the picture to his mother. I had intended to show him at his office. From the moment we were tossed into the mausoleum and afterward, I had been too eager to find my father to remember.

Philips addressed his men. "We want the captors and hostage alive, got me?" His men already held printouts of Uma Noble, Officer Vance, and Karl Zorn. Philips passed around the locket. "No trigger fingers. No heroes." He faced me. "You, sit tight."

"I'm coming."

"No." Philips jabbed a finger. "What did you not understand about *sit tight*? Make a move, and I will arrest you for obstruction. You're a history professor."

"Formerly a Naval Officer."

"Then you understand the definition of obstruction, don't you?" Philips didn't wait for a response. He headed toward the entrance and disappeared from view.

Seconds later I saw movement near one of the Winnebagos. Two figures—Tanaka and Zorn by the shape of them. A woman with short red hair exited the trailer and descended the steps. I didn't recognize her. Was she part of the wedding party? Was Uma inside? Zorn and Tanaka approached her. They conversed. The woman pointed to a second Winnebago. Zorn and Tanaka strode toward it. My gut tightened. Did they intend to hurt Uma or her daughter to get to my father?

I said to Jack, "Stay here."

"Didn't you hear Philips—?"

"No, I didn't." I tapped my ear. "Temporarily deaf. Nasty side effect after that beating I took."

Without knocking, Zorn entered the second Winnebago. Tanaka remained outside.

I sprinted closer and stole to the far side of the Winnebago, wondering what my next move would be. What could I do to thwart them? Tanaka was armed. Zorn was probably armed, too.

Despite the brisk weather, a window was open.

A young woman was talking to Zorn. "My mother's not here." Her tone was clipped and purposeful. "I don't know where she's gone. She might be discussing floral arrangements with the florist. The last time I talked to her, she was headed inside the amphitheater."

The trailer rocked a bit. Was Zorn moving down the length of it, checking in the restroom and bedroom? Didn't he believe the girl? Why wasn't she protesting? The trailer steadied again.

"I'm sorry to have disturbed you, my dear," Zorn said. "You look lovely, by the way. You'll make a beautiful bride."

Zorn exited the Winnebago and barked, "This way," to Tanaka. Gravel crunched beneath their feet.

I waited a moment and then peered around the corner of the Winnebago. Zorn and Tanaka were jogging toward the pathway lit with torches. I turned, intent on going back to the parking lot to wait for Detective Philips, but I stopped when I heard whispering. Inside the trailer. Two female voices.

"Who was that, Mother?" Uma's daughter asked. Her voice was trembling.

"No one, darling."

"I didn't like the sound of him."

"He's not a nice man."

"And he smelled. Too much cologne. He searched for you. Why didn't he find you?"

"I hid in the shower."

And left her daughter to face Zorn by herself? What kind of parent was she?

The girl whimpered. "What's going on, Mother?"

"Nothing. Everything is fine. Let's put on your tiara."

I slipped around the corner, ready to return to Detective Philips and fill him in, but I paused when I realized Zorn had slammed the door, but it hadn't shut all the way. An inch of light glimmered from inside. I peered through the crack.

Uma Noble, clad in a silver suit, was fitting a crown with veil on her daughter's head. The daughter sat in a chair. Both faced a long, narrow mirror, their backs to me.

Though I was reluctant to involve the daughter, I couldn't pass up the moment. As Uma was anchoring the crown with hairpins, I stole into the trailer. No weapon. No plan. Before Uma had time to spin completely around—she must have felt the weight of my entrance—I grabbed her and wedged her against my chest. Strong. Resolute.

"You," she said.

"Me."

"Mother, what's happening?"

Uma kicked back with a heel. The point of her shoe scraped my pant leg.

I didn't loosen my grip. "Where's my father?"

"How did you find me?"

"Where is he?"

"Mother, who's here?" Her daughter rose unsteadily; her fingers groped the air. I recognized the blank stare. I had two blind students this semester.

I whispered, "Tell your daughter to freeze."

"Rachel, stay still." Uma's voice quavered. "Mommy's fine. A friend has come to visit."

"A different man," her daughter said. "A different voice."

"I'm a friend, Rachel." I clenched Uma more tightly. "I simply need some answers."

Uma swallowed hard. "Darling, this man and I need to talk. We're going outside for a minute. You stay here."

I tightened my hold. "Uh-uh. We're not going anywhere. Not yet." I didn't intend to expose myself to danger until I had more information.

"You're choking the breath out of me."

"Mother?" The young woman quavered.

"It's just a phrase, Rachel," I said. "I've got her in a warm hug."

"Please, I can't breathe."

"Mother?"

"Sit down, Rachel!" I rasped.

The young woman groped for a silk purse with a drawstring. "I'm calling the police." She fished inside and withdrew a cell phone.

"They're already here." I squeezed Uma harder and whispered, "Tell her to relax."

"Darling, put down your phone. Be a good girl."

Reluctantly, Rachel obeyed.

I said, "Tell me where my father is."

"I don't know."

"You wouldn't leave Vance fully in charge. He's a loose cannon. My father is nearby. Where is he?"

"I don't know."

I scanned the area for a walkie talkie, something that could help Uma communicate with Vance, but then realized Uma wouldn't talk to Vance in front of her daughter. Rachel knew nothing about the situation; that much was clear. I looked for Uma's cell phone and spotted it on the kitchenette counter. The face of the phone glowed. Someone had sent her a text.

Muscling her toward the phone, I said, "Pick it up. Show me the readout."

Uma lifted the phone. The message was from Vance: Come to van NOW!

The urgency jolted me. Vance had to have heard the music starting. He wouldn't interrupt the ceremony unless he had something to report. Had my father told him where the notebook was? Had Philips or Zorn found them?

"Where's the van?" I demanded.

"I don't know."

I tightened my grip. Uma gagged.

"Mother?"

"Quiet, Rachel! I won't tell you again." I whispered into Uma's ear, "Take me to the van or you won't hear your daughter say, 'I do.' Understand me?" I eyed Uma's tote, the one she had with her on the sailboat. "Grab your purse."

"Why?"

"I want your revolver."

"Mother, you have a gun?" Rachel gasped.

"He's joking, darling. I don't own a gun."

I kicked the hollow of Uma's ankle. "Move, or Rachel dies."

Uma must have believed me. She didn't resist.

I guided her to her tote. "Pick it up. Don't open it." When she had it in hand, I steered her out the door.

CHAPTER 49

Outside the Winnebago, I said to Uma, "No screaming for help. Otherwise—"

"You'll kill me and my daughter."

I knew I couldn't do either, but I had to keep the threat alive. I nodded. "Open the purse. Slowly. Pull out the revolver with your pinky."

Uma obeyed.

I grabbed the gun, knocked the purse to the ground, and anchored the crook of my left arm against Uma's windpipe. "The van," I said. "The Econoline van. Where is it?"

"On the path beyond the limos."

We moved as a team.

At a junction, I said, "Left or right?"

Uma hitched her chin left. "Past the camellias. There. See it?"

I did. An interior light was on. No cops in sight. No sign of Zorn or Tanaka.

A shadowy figure darted from behind a bush. One of Philips's men? The figure paused, turned his head. A glimmer of moonlight struck his face. *Jack.* Hadn't I told him to stay put?

Jack gaped at Uma then me. "What're you doing?"

I shoved Uma at Jack. "Restrain her."

He grabbed her, one arm firmly in place around her neck, the other around her waist. Uma didn't struggle.

To Uma, I said, "Remember what I told you."

She whimpered. "Rachel will die."

"I won't hurt her unless you screw up." I jogged to the van.

"Where are you going?" Jack said.

"Vance is holding our—" I stopped myself.

"Father."

"In that van. I'm going inside."

"Why don't I get Philips?"

"Vance sent a text. It sounded urgent. I think he might have gotten Luther…Jonathan to talk. If so, he wants the go-ahead from Uma to kill him." I faced Uma. "What's the code?"

"What code?"

"The code for Vance to open the rear doors."

"There is no code."

"Of course, there's a code. Vance is a cop. He may be an idiot, but he's not stupid. He's locked those doors. If I try to enter without the code, he'll kill me. If I die, your daughter dies, right, Jack?"

Jack nodded, albeit hesitantly.

Uma worried her lower lip with her teeth. "Knock once, pause, then knock twice. Fast."

"How can you be sure she's not lying?" Jack said.

"She loves her daughter too much." I continued to the van and knocked as instructed.

Vance opened the door. His face registered surprise. He glanced at the gun in my hand and at Jack holding Uma. Rage flooded his eyes. He kicked out. Connected with my wrist. Idiot that I was, I hadn't expected him to react so quickly. The gun flew out of my hand. I didn't go after the gun. Instead, I gripped Vance's ankles and pulled. Vance fell backward on coils of rope. The van heaved.

I dove inside and scrambled on top of Vance. I punched him in the jaw and the ear. He clawed my face. I whacked his arm to the side. Then I smacked his jaw a second time. Vance's head lolled to the side. I smelled smoke. Was something burning? I glanced at my father, who was tucked into the corner strapped to a chair. "Jonathan, are you okay?"

"Burning," Jonathan said, his voice trembling.

"What's burning?"

"Matches." He brushed his lap.

I understood. Vance had been lighting matches and dropping them in my father's lap. An old tactic, designed to instill fear. I grabbed hold of Vance's ear and twisted. "Have you been torturing my father?"

"He admitted he hid the notebook."

Using two hands, I banged Vance's head against the floor. Once. Twice. Unfortunately the rope softened the blows; the thrusts barely injured him.

"Is that all you've got, pal?" Vance wedged his beefy arms up through mine. He pressed apart. Grabbing hold of my shoulders, he flipped me over. The floor of the van sent a chill through my jacket. "You don't stand a chance. I was all-state wrestling."

"US Navy," I retorted. I had hated wrestling in high school. Guys sweating and kneeling above me. Give me lacrosse or basketball any day. I shoved the heel of my hand into Vance's jaw then karate chopped his larynx.

Vance keeled to the side. I shoved him over and climbed on top of him again. I punched his ear and his nose. Vance shot his arms up and gripped me in a bear hug. He squeezed like a boa constrictor. The breath wheezed out of me.

A shot split the air. Followed by another.

Vance flinched. I jutted out with my elbows and broke Vance's hold. Stiffening my arms, I created distance between us, and then jammed my fingertips into his throat. Vance gasped for breath. I wriggled off him and leaped to my feet. He struggled to his knees. I kicked him hard enough to send him staggering out of the van. He landed, head first, on the ground.

Jack rushed to him and jammed Uma's revolver in his nose. "Don't move."

I appreciated Jack's no-nonsense tone. "Where's—" I looked beyond him.

Nearby, Uma lay on her back, eyes open, red goo dribbling from her mouth. She was clutching her bloody stomach. Her chest was rising in short bursts.

"She wrestled free," Jack said. "She grabbed the gun. I dove at her.

We struggled. I—"

"It's okay." I felt a peculiar satisfaction that the woman who had murdered my mother was suffering in the same way.

"Dad," Jack said. "Where's Dad?"

I leaped back into the van. My father's head drooped forward; his chin rested on his chest. The chair he was tied to had been anchored against the back of the driver's seat. I untied the ropes and gripped him by the shoulders. "Jonathan, are you all right?" There were singe marks in his pajamas and on the zippered sweatshirt, and the hem of his pajamas were singed from lit matches that must have tumbled down his legs, but I didn't see any burns.

My father looked up. His eyes were moist. Hands free, he reached for my face. "Johnny B. Goode."

"No, sir. I'm Chase." I understood that the similarities between Jack and me might confuse him, not to mention I'd initially called myself Johnny B. Goode to win his trust.

"You want the blue book," he said.

I sank onto my haunches. Was the old man lucid? For how long? "Yes, I do."

"You need it."

"I need the truth."

He stared into space as he said, "'All truths are easy to understand once they are discovered; the point is to discover them.'"

I tilted my head. "You're quoting Galileo Galilei."

"Correct. He said, 'The earth orbits around the sun.'"

I reached for my father's hand. "Sir, I hope we can spend some time together, even if you don't remember me."

"But I do. You saved me."

I felt like I had been sucker punched, my need for confirmation so deep-seated that I felt as raw as an open wound. How I wished my father recognized me, but he didn't. Not now. Maybe never. I clutched his hands. They felt damp with fear. "Jack is outside." I yelled out the van. "Jack, come in here and take over."

I heard the smack of footsteps. A man yelled, "Stand down." Was it Philips?

A shot rang out. Bullet hit flesh. A man cried out in pain.

"Jack?" I yelled. No answer. "Philips?"

A second shot pierced the night, followed by the same wet smack. A grunt. Then a third. A body hit the ground.

"Jack!" I lunged toward the rear door.

Jack lay next to Uma; his right shoulder was bleeding. Vance had been shot in the gut. Blood stained his shirt.

Tanaka lay on the ground, too, a bullet wound to the back of his head. In my haste to help my father, I had forgotten to keep an eye out for him and Zorn. Where was—

"You!" Zorn charged the van aiming a SIG Sauer. He had meant to shoot me and nailed his own man. He fired again.

I lunged right. A bullet whizzed past me and slammed into the wall of the van. I hoisted a coil of rope and hurled it at Zorn. It hit him in the knees; the weight sent him reeling. I jumped out of the van and knocked Zorn to the ground. He whacked me with the butt of his semi-automatic. Not hard enough. I gripped his forearm. We struggled for control of the gun.

"Out of my way, Day," he bellowed. "I want that notebook. Move."

"No."

I fought to gain control of his gun. Zorn pulled the trigger. The barrel was pointed upward. A bullet shot into the air.

From inside the van, my father shouted, "Evil!"

Out of the corner of my eye, I saw him lurch toward the edge. He steadied himself by gripping the upper rim of the door. Then he leaped out.

Zorn's eyes widened; his face contorted; the muscles in his neck drew taut. He roared and heaved me out of the way. He lunged at my father.

My father gripped Zorn's arms.

The SIG Sauer fired. Once. Twice. The two men collapsed to the ground, Zorn on top of my father. Neither moved.

CHAPTER 50

"No!" I hurried to them and pulled Zorn off. Each man was hit. Blood oozed from a wound in Jonathan's gut. Zorn was bleeding more profusely. His eyes were open but unblinking.

At the same time, Philips and four of his men charged toward me, guns drawn.

I raised my hands. "Don't shoot. There are six people down."

"Are you kidding me?" Philips said.

"Call 911. My father has been shot. So have Zorn, Noble, Vance, Tanaka, and my brother Jack. Tanaka's dead. I'm not sure about the others. I'll explain further, but please call 911. My father is dying, and my brother has taken one to the shoulder."

Philips said to a colleague, "Do it." He gestured to another to check the wounded. Through a walkie-talkie, he said, "Bruno, come in. Over."

Bruno's voice crackled through the system. "Bruno. Over."

"East side of the amphitheater. Southernmost trail. Kidnappers apprehended. Over."

"On our way. Over."

Philips turned to me. "Drop your hands and explain."

"In a sec." I addressed my father. "Why did you do that?"

My father blinked. His mouth moved but no words came out.

"Jack!" I shouted.

Jack stirred. He crawled to us and clutched Jonathan's hand. Jonathan said something. Jack bent near. Jonathan said something else and then went still. Jack pressed his fingers against Jonathan's throat, searching for a pulse. After a moment, he began to keen.

"Is he—" I swallowed hard.

Jack bobbed his head as sobs wracked his body. He set his forehead against Jonathan's and muttered, "Dad…Dad."

I sucked in air. My breathing grew short. To come so far and never get to know my father. To rip him from Jack's life. Tears filled my eyes. I didn't fight them.

Minutes passed. I wasn't sure how many. When I regained control, I rose to my feet and gave Philips a rundown: I saw Zorn and Tanaka near the Winnebago; that's why I disobeyed his order and went to find Uma Noble. I explained how my threat to injure Noble and her daughter had persuaded Noble to lead me to Vance. I replayed the fight, Uma's attack on my half-brother, and Tanaka's and Zorn's arrival.

Jack joined us. His face was caked with dried tears and splattered blood. He offered up Uma's Smith & Wesson, butt first. "Detective, he's telling the truth. I was outside the van."

"I understand why he disobeyed my order," Philips said. "Why did you?"

"No good answer, sir. I'm sorry."

Philips grunted. "Tell me your side of this."

Jack shifted feet. "While Chase and Officer Vance fought in the truck, Ms. Noble wrestled free from me and went for the gun on the ground. *Her* gun. I tried to stop her. To keep her from, you know..." He drew in a quick breath and released it. "We struggled. The gun went off. We struggled some more. It fired again."

Was Jack lying? Was he putting on the shaky, stilted delivery? Had he killed Uma outright? His eyes looked steady—gunslinger cool, even. Would Philips see through the lie? Would Uma tell a different account if she survived?

A siren pierced the air. The blare grew louder. Bruno, on foot with other policemen, raced up.

Philips said to Jack and me, "Don't go anywhere, you two. I'll want to question you at the precinct."

"Before you do," I said, "there's one more person to locate." I held out hope I would find Holland alive.

Holland was alive. Barely. Two of Philips's men found her tied up in the trunk of Zorn's Mercedes, which was parked on a side street. She hadn't been drugged, but she was dehydrated and wired with fear. EMTs were called to the scene.

After the EMTs set her on a stretcher and checked her vitals, Philips allowed me to go to her. I clutched her hand as though it was my lifeline. I had lost my mother and my father and realized that I couldn't bear it I'd lost Holland, too.

I leaned down and kissed her swollen cheek. "Zorn's dead." He died moments after my father.

"They told me."

"Then you know about the others."

"Yes."

Vance died. Uma was in recovery, her fate was to be determined.

"Chase"—Holland licked her lips—"what about us?"

"What about us?"

She squeezed my hand. She meant it to hurt.

I winced *for show*. Then I kissed her forehead. "We'll have time to heal."

CHAPTER 51

Hours passed at the precinct before Philips finished interrogating Jack and me, but ultimately he released us on our own recognizance. He believed Zorn had stolen Geoffrey Gaynor's blue books. He also believed Zorn had built his empire upon other ideas he'd stolen from Geoffrey Gaynor. I felt sorry for Zorn's wife; I doubted she was complicit. I was glad to hear that Zorn's kid Tommy, however, was under investigation for terrorizing me and my dog and for, in general, being an idiot.

On our way out of the precinct, Jack said, "We've got to talk."

"About?"

"Dad."

"Day!" Detective Philips bellowed. He stood in the doorway and beckoned with a sharp gesture. "Get back in my office."

I tensed. Was I going to be arrested for obstruction after all? I jammed my hands into my pockets and trudged into Philips's office. Jack traipsed after me.

"The last time you were at the precinct, I forgot to give you your mother's effects," Philips said. "She ran out of the hospital without being checked out." He handed over a yellow padded envelope. "Interesting woman, your mother."

"What do you mean?"

"Have a look."

I opened the envelope and dumped the contents on Philips's desk. My mom had kept a few more photographs—one of me at Lake Tahoe, another at a lacrosse game, another at graduation. My grandmother must have been supplying my mother with updates. Surely I would have seen her if she had been in attendance at these places.

Other items included a ring, earrings, a wallet with four singles in it, and a bank passbook.

"Open it," Philips ordered.

The leather passbook was old and cracked. It had my name written down as the owner of the passbook. All deposits had the word *Zorn* beside them. The date written beside the initial deposit was my first birthday. Zorn hinted that he had paid my mother hush money to keep quiet about the murder. Every month for five years she had deposited one hundred dollars. The deposits stopped the day she *died* in the fire. I eyed the total deposit: nearly six years' worth of deposits plus interest. It wasn't much, but it represented a wealth of love.

On Jack's and my second exit from the precinct, halfway to the Ford Escort that Reggie had brought over for me—she offered to return the car I'd hot-wired to the museum's parking lot—I said, "What were you going to tell me about our father?"

"Get in and drive."

I climbed into the vehicle and switched on the ignition. Jack got into the passenger seat. I yanked the car into reverse, whipped into forward, and pulled out of the precinct parking lot. Night had fallen. Headlights strobed the windshield. "Talk."

"Dad had a lucid moment before he died."

I drew in a quick breath of air. "Lucid, as in he remembered something?"

"He said, 'Johnny B., look beneath the eye of the needle. Treasures ye shall find.'"

"That's not lucid. That's lunacy."

"No. He was giving me a clue. I'm sure of it. Then he winked and repeated, 'The eye of the needle.'"

I whacked the seat. "That's it!"

"What's it?"

"Oh, man, how did I miss it?"

"Miss what?"

"The Transamerica Pyramid."

"What about it? I told you Dad used to take me there."

"Right. You bonded. Yada yada. Listen up. The Transamerica Pyramid is often called the Needle in the Sky because of the spire on top."

"So?"

"When I first found Luther"—I stopped myself—"Jonathan, he babbled about the eye of a needle. I asked if he meant it in biblical terms. He rephrased and started talking about a needle in a haystack. When I asked him about the missing blue book, he said, 'Buried. Gone.' Don't you see? He was trying to tell me where he hid the notebook. He buried it.

"The Transamerica Pyramid is on the site where the *Niantic* went aground." I sped toward the freeway, cutting fast around slow-moving cars. "I told you, there's a plaque dedicated to the *Niantic* there." I used my right hand to explain the rest of what was cycling through my mind. "That night, Luther ran off because he was frightened that the police wouldn't believe a young man with his track record hadn't committed murder. Maybe, as he left the Berkeley campus, he saw the Transamerica Pyramid across the bay soaring into the sky"—I pointed out the front windshield—"and he headed toward it as if it were a beacon.

"When he got there, he spotted the plaque honoring the *Niantic*, realized he was holding what Zorn considered a *treasure* in his hands, and he had an *aha* moment. He couldn't be caught with it, but he could bury it and know it would be there, when and if he needed it as evidence." I hitched my thumb. "Then he ran off to join the Navy."

Jack swiveled in his seat. "How could he have stored a book of any kind beneath the plaque?"

"I don't know, but I think that's what he did. He said to you, 'Look beneath the eye of the needle.' *Beneath*. We're going there. We've got to find out."

Jack gripped my arm. "He was a good man, Chase."

"Yes, he was. He kept the book a secret because he thought, in his frightened state, that it contained an equation that might lead to nuclear evil."

"He wasn't addled when he came back from his stint in the service. He could have told the police about Zorn at any time," Jack said.

"Yes, but when he returned from duty, he decided to let the past remain buried. In his interpretation of evil, he meant to save the world and to protect you and your mother in the process."

"We've got to call Detective Philips."

I flipped my half-brother my cell phone.

❖

Within the hour, Philips and a team of San Francisco policemen joined Jack and me at the Transamerica Pyramid. A city engineer was employed to remove the *Niantic* plaque. A set of klieg lights provided illumination. A crowd started to gather.

Jack and I stood just inside the perimeter established by the police. Minutes passed. And more minutes. My heart pounded in anticipation of what we would find.

The engineer said, "Something seems to have been stuck in place with cement."

"That's not typical, is it?" Philips asked.

"No, sir."

Jack said, "My dad told me he did occasional construction work as a kid. Maybe he stopped off at a hobby store on the way?"

I whispered, "Or perhaps he swiped something from a local contractor on his way into the city. Does it matter?"

Finally, the engineer removed the plaque. He reached into the hollow beneath and pulled out what looked like an oilskin bag, the kind used by cowboys to keep gear dry. He handed it to Philips, who opened it and withdrew the contents: a blue notebook. On the cover, written in Geoffrey Gaynor's scrawl, was the title: *P.E.P. III.*

CHAPTER 52

A couple of hours later, following yet another debriefing by Philips, I entered the hospital room and caught sight of Holland. She had looked bad at the crime scene. Now her face was tinged blue and swollen. Tubes radiated out of her like something in *The Matrix.* Kimo, Reggie, and Manuel stood on the opposite side of the bed.

Kimo said, "Better late than never, bro." He gave me a quick nod; Holland was going to be okay.

I tamped down worry and drew close. "Hey."

Holland turned her head ever so slightly and smiled.

I kissed her forehead and took her hand in mine, careful not to disturb the tube inserted into it. "The detectives contacted Texas Troopers. They've located your mother."

Holland blinked her relief.

"Your mother is safe," I continued. "She caught Zorn's man Eagleton snooping around her diner and hit him upside the head with a fry pan. I guess she's as tough as you."

Holland rasped, "Good genes."

"She's on her way to the Bay Area."

The delight in Holland's eyes made me smile.

"More good news," I said. "The police recovered the other notebooks. Zorn was holding them in a home safe. His family—his business—will suffer, but after a lengthy legal process, Geoffrey Gaynor's parents will be the benefactors of anything that proves to have been Geoffrey's discovery. Scientists—very excited scientists—from around the nation have already been alerted. They're on board to review the material. Imagine what will happen if they're successful?" I felt like a political rally leader. "Clean air. No more dependence on fossil fuels. Maybe a global warming shift."

Everyone in the room hooted.

"Bro," Kimo said. "Speaking of a global warming shift, Dean Hyde contacted me."

I grinned. "Man, you know how to bring down a crowd. Okay, so what's the plan? Is he going to fire me?"

"May I finish?" Kimo said. "It seems a few students went in to talk to the dean on your behalf. They're passionately devoted to you."

"Let me guess," Reggie said. "Pretty young co-eds?"

Holland hummed a chuckle.

Kimo laughed. "Hyde said he would cut you some slack for now, but you're on probation next semester."

Congratulations circled the room.

Reggie said, "Where's Jack? I want to meet him."

"You will. At the funeral. Right now he's with his mom and making plans."

Two days later, I stood beside the gravesides of my father and mother. Yes, he was my father. Detective Philips had pulled strings and rushed a DNA test, which confirmed that Jack and I were half-brothers.

Barbie, now knowing the whole story, accepted that my mother should be buried in California, not Mexico, beside Luther, aka Jonathan. Jack's mother agreed.

Kimo, Reggie, and Manuel had come to the service. Holland had wanted to, but the doctor wouldn't release her.

When the pastor who presided over the ceremony finished, I glanced at Jack and his mother Gert, who stood holding hands on the opposite side of the dual plot. As the last shovel of soil covered the caskets, Jack looked up and smiled. Before the ceremony, he said he believed our father was at peace.

I hoped it was true.

AUTHOR'S BIO

Agatha Award-winning and nationally bestselling author **DARYL WOOD GERBER** ventures into the world of suspense again with her second novel, ***DAY OF SECRETS***. Her first suspense, ***GIRL ON THE RUN***, earned rave reviews. Daryl writes the bestselling ***Cookbook Nook Mysteries*** and will soon debut the new ***French Bistro Mysteries.*** As **AVERY AAMES**, she pens the bestselling ***Cheese Shop Mysteries***. Fun tidbit: as an actress, Daryl appeared in "Murder, She Wrote." In addition, she has jumped out of a perfectly good airplane, rappelled down mountains, and hitchhiked around Ireland by herself. She absolutely adores the San Francisco Bay Area, where ***DAY OF SECRETS*** is set, she loves to cook, and she has a frisky Goldendoodle named Sparky who keeps her in line! Visit Daryl at www.darylwoodgerber.com.

CPSIA information can be obtained
at www.ICGtesting.com
Printed in the USA
LVHW04s2041270718
585150LV00002B/449/P

9 780997 361124